ᵀᴱ ᴰᵁᴱ

FLOWERS OF DARKNESS

FLOWERS OF DARKNESS

TATIANA DE ROSNAY

THORNDIKE PRESS
A part of Gale, a Cengage Company

**LIBRARY OF CONGRESS CIP DATA ON FILE.
CATALOGUING IN PUBLICATION FOR THIS BOOK
IS AVAILABLE FROM THE LIBRARY OF CONGRESS.**

ISBN-13: 978-1-4328-8581-6 (hardcover alk. paper)

Published in 2021 by arrangement with St. Martin's Publishing.

Printed in Mexico
Print Number: 01   Print Year: 2021

To my father,
who taught me how to look at the future

Not only our memories, but the things we have forgotten are "housed." Our subconscious is "housed." Our soul is an abode.

— *The Poetics of Space,*
Gaston Bachelard

CONTENTS

CONTENTS

1
KEY

So I am doing what seems the best thing
to do.
          VIRGINIA WOOLF, March 28, 1941

This can obviously be held accountable to
a nervous breakdown.
          ROMAIN GARY, December 2, 1980

She visited twenty apartments before finding the right one. Nobody could imagine
what an ordeal it had been, especially for a
writer obsessed with houses, with what walls
remembered. The building had been completed last year. It wasn't far from the
Tower, or what was left of the Tower. After
the attack, the neighborhood had suffered.
For years, the place remained a dusty and
wrecked no-man's-land ignored by all. Little
by little, the vicinity was able to rise from
its ashes. Architects had thought out harmonious neoclassical structures, as well as a

vast green garden including the memorial and the space where the identical Tower was yet to be rebuilt. With the passing of time, this part of town had been able to recover its serenity. Tourists came flocking back.

Mrs. Dalloway's soft voice was heard.

"Clarissa, you have incoming emails. One is from Mia White, not in your contact list, and one is from your father. Do you wish to read them now?"

Her father! She checked her watch. One A.M. in Paris, midnight in London, and the old chap was still awake. Getting on for ninety-eight and full of beans.

"I'll read them later, Mrs. Dalloway. Please turn the computer off. And the lights in the living room."

In the beginning, she had felt guilty, bossing Mrs. Dalloway around. But she had gotten used to it. It was quite pleasurable, in fact. Mrs. Dalloway never appeared. She was merely a voice. But Clarissa knew Mrs. Dalloway had eyes and ears in every room. Clarissa often wondered what she would have looked like, had she existed. It was believed Virginia Woolf modeled Mrs. Dalloway's character after a woman named Kitty Maxse, a frivolous party giver who had been a close friend, and who had met a tragic end, tumbling over her own banisters.

Clarissa had looked up Kitty Maxse, and discovered photographs of a perfectly groomed lady with an hourglass figure and a dainty parasol.

She stood in the dark living room, facing the window, clasping the cat close to her. The computer no longer glowed into the deepening darkness. Would she ever get used to this flat? It wasn't so much the smell of new paint. There was something else. She couldn't quite place it. She loved the view, though. High up above the ground level, away from the action, she felt safe, tucked into her own private shelter. Was she really safe? she wondered as the cat purred against her and the black night seemed to hem her in. Safe from what, safe from whom? Living alone was proving to be more difficult than she'd thought. She wondered what François was doing now. He was still in their old apartment. She imagined him in their living room, binge-watching a TV show, feet up on the table. What was the point of thinking of François? No point at all.

Clarissa's shortsighted eyes gazed down to the street, far below, where tipsy vacationers staggered, their laughter wafting up to her in a muffled roar. This new area of the city was never empty. Hordes of tourists materialized ceaselessly on sidewalks, in a dusty synchronicity that befuddled her. She had learned to avoid certain boulevards, where swarms of sightseers stood, vacuously, brandishing cell phones at what remained of the Tower, and the construction site of the new one. She had to wade through their compact mass, sometimes even had to elbow through them in order to get past.

Watching the building across the street and all those beings behind each window would never tire her. Within the past weeks, since she'd been living here, she'd learned to pick out each occupant's routine. She already knew who was sleepless, like she was, who worked late in front of a screen, who enjoyed a snack in the middle of the night. She couldn't be seen; she was too high up, tucked away behind the stone cornices. Sometimes, she used her field glasses. She never felt guilty, although she would hate it if anyone spied on her that way. She always checked to see if someone was looking back at her. And even if no one was, why did she still feel an eye upon her?

Other people's lives unfolded in front of her, enticing alveoli forming a giant hive in which she could forage at her will, fueling her imagination boundlessly. Each opening was like a Hopper painting, lush with detail.

The second-floor woman did her yoga every morning on a mat she rolled out with care. The third-floor family never stopped bickering. The slamming of those doors! The person on the sixth spent hours in the bathroom (yes, she could see through panes that weren't opaque enough). The lady of her age on the fifth floor daydreamed on her sofa. She didn't know their names, but she knew nearly everything about their daily existence. And it fascinated her.

When she started to look for her new abode, she hadn't realized to what extent she was going to trespass into unknown people's intimacy. Each room told a story by the disposition of its furniture, objects, through odors, scents, and colors. She had only to walk into a living room to extricate a prescient vision of the person who lived there. She could picture the inhabitant's life entirely in one dizzying and addictive flash. She saw it all, as if she had been provided with special internal sensors.

She'd never forget the duplex flat situated on boulevard Saint-Germain, near Odéon. The description fit her needs perfectly. She liked the neighborhood, and already visualized herself trotting up the polished stairs daily. But once she was inside, the ceiling was so low, she practically had to hunch her back. The real estate agent had asked, jokingly, how tall she was. What an idiot! She was able to tell right away the owner worked in publishing, because of all the manuscripts piled up on the black lacquered desk. Some editors still revised texts on paper, but they were exceedingly rare. The bookshelves were full of hardcovers and paperbacks, a vision of joy for a writer. She tilted her head to read the titles. Yes, there were two of hers there, *Topography of Intimacy* and *The Sleep Thief.* It hadn't been the first time she'd seen her own books while visiting a flat, but it invariably brought her pleasure.

The duplex was lovely, but miniature. She couldn't stand properly in any of the rooms; her body ate up all the space, like Alice in Wonderland becoming larger than the house. It was a shame, because the premises were sunny, quiet, giving on to a pretty interior courtyard. She hadn't been able to stop herself from looking at the beauty products in the bathroom, perfume and makeup, and when the agent had opened the wardrobe, she had taken in the clothes and high-heeled pumps. Swiftly, the portrait of a woman had arisen: small, dainty, spick-and-span, young still, but alone. No love in her life. Something dry and barren permeated the place, shadowed the walls, upholstered the air. In the glossy brown bed-chamber, the mattress had the funereal aspect of a tombstone, where all she could perceive was a recumbent effigy, petrified by a century-long torpor. No one ever had orgasms within these walls, either alone or in company. A profound gloom oozed from the immaculate and silent rooms. She had fled.

She began to see a flat a day. One time, she had felt sure she'd found the right home, at last. A cheerful fifth-floor flat with a balcony, near the Madeleine. It was sunny, one of her priorities. It had recently been renovated and the décor suited her. The owner was moving back to Switzerland. Since the attacks, his wife didn't wish to go on living in the city. Clarissa had just been about to sign the lease, when she noticed, to her dismay, the existence of a rugby pub on the ground floor. She had always come in the morning, and hadn't paid attention, as the bar was closed. She had returned later in the evening just to get a feel of the area at nighttime and had made the discovery. The pub opened every evening and operated until two o'clock in the morning. Jordan, her daughter, had made fun of her. So what? She could use earplugs, couldn't she? But Clarissa hated those. She decided

17

to test the noise level by spending the night in a small hotel across from the pub.

"We have nice quiet rooms in the back," said the receptionist when she checked in.

"No, no", she replied, "I want to be in front of the pub."

He had stared at her.

"You won't get much sleep. Even if there's no game on, you'll still get a lot of noise. And in the summertime, I can't even begin to tell you what it's like. The neighbors complain all the time."

She had thanked him and held out her hand for the card. He was right. Clients chatting on the sidewalk, pint in hand, had awakened her steadily until two in the morning. Every time the pub doors opened, loud music could be heard, very clearly, in spite of the double glazing. She called the agency the next morning and said she wouldn't be taking the flat.

Everything she ended up seeing failed to suit her. She began to lose hope. François had tried to hold her back. Didn't she want to stay? She hadn't wanted to hear a single word. Had he gone crazy? After everything he'd done? Did he really think she was going to shut up and stick around? Act like nothing had happened? When she had become desperate, and was even contemplating moving to London, into the dismal basement flat rented out to students in her father's house in Hackney, she met Guillaume at the inaugural cocktail party for a bookstore-café in Montparnasse. She hadn't planned to stay long, but the owner, Nathalie, was a fervent supporter of her work. The opening of a shop that sold books was such a rare event that she decided to go, and also out of friendship for Nathalie.

She was introduced to a trim young man called Guillaume, a friend of Nathalie's. He swiftly explained he had nothing to do with publishing, that calamitous business; he was into real estate. He offered her a glass of champagne, which she accepted. After the attack, the major part of the seventh arrondissement had to be rethought and rebuilt: everything situated between the Tower and the École Militaire, and between avenue de la Bourdonnais and boulevard de Grenelle. His firm had been chosen in order to reconstruct the area along the old track of avenue Charles-Floquet. Like most Parisians, Clarissa was aware that the streets and avenues that had been destroyed had been rebuilt differently, with new names. There had been an emphasis on foliage and vegetation. A peacefulness much needed by all, Guillaume had pointed out.

Clarissa had never envisaged that recent neighborhood. It was probably expensive, she said to herself, out of her league. Guillaume proudly described the accommodation he'd created with his team, showing her photos on his mobile device. She admitted it was magnificent. Verdant, contemporary, striking. He chimed his number and emailed it to her phone. All she had to do, if ever she wanted more information, was to send him a text.

"Are there any flats available?" she asked tentatively.

"That's complicated," he said. "Yes, technically, there are, but they're reserved for artists. There's a quota we need to keep to."

She asked what he meant by "artists." He shrugged, scratched his head. He meant painters, musicians, poets, singers, sculptors. There was a special residence just for them. But no one publicized it; otherwise, they'd be swamped. In order to get in, there were interviews, presentations, in front of a committee. Quite a thing. Serious stuff! Not many people made it.

"What about writers? Haven't you forgotten them?"

She was right; he had forgotten writers. They were indeed artists, just as much as the others.

"Can you tell me how I can sign up?"

Obviously, he had no idea who she was, what she did. She didn't mind; after all, her latest success had been published a while ago. She pulled him by the sleeve, all the way to the bookshelf labeled "K," slid out *Topography of Intimacy,* and handed it to him under Nathalie's curious gaze as she chatted a little farther away. He leafed through it, and said he was sorry he did not know more about her and her work. He never read books. He didn't have time to read. Politely, he asked her what it was about.

"It's about writers and the link between their work, their homes, their intimacy, and their suicides, particularly Virginia Woolf and Romain Gary. It's a novel, not an essay."

He was taken aback, staring down at the cover, where Gary's blue eyes made an interesting contrast with Woolf's dark ones.

"Ah, yes" was all he could bring himself to say. He looked at her for the first time, and Clarissa knew what he was thinking, that she must have been good-looking once, and that, curiously, she still was.

He suggested she contact a woman named Clémence Dutilleul, via a specific website, of which he gave her the address. She was the person who dealt with admissions concerning the artists' residence. Clarissa had to hurry. There were very few vacancies. When she returned to the studio she rented weekly in order not to endure her husband's presence, she went online to the website. She was certain she didn't stand a chance, but why not register? That same night, she filled out a detailed questionnaire and sent it through a link to Clémence Dutilleul. She was most surprised to get an answer the next morning, and a proposal for a meeting scheduled the day after.

"Do you really want to live where all those people were killed?" Jordan's voice was ironic. "Especially you, obsessed with places? You've written about that over and over again. Won't you be getting into trouble? You'll never be able to sleep!"

Clarissa tried to defend herself by stating that living in a city like Paris meant she walked over bloody tragedy every day, in every step she took. The new buildings attracted her because they had no past.

Clarissa went into the kitchen; the lights turned on as she glided by. Light switches had disappeared years ago, and she rather liked it. She had been told, when she moved in last month, that she could name the apartment's virtual assistant with a term of her own choosing.

"Mrs. Dalloway, turn on the kettle."

Mrs. Dalloway complied. Clarissa left most household matters to her. The heating, air conditioner, alarm, shutters, lighting scheme, automatic cleaning system, and all sorts of other tasks were under Mrs. Dalloway's expert supervision. Clarissa was still getting used to it. She had hesitated between "Mrs. Danvers" and "Mrs. Dalloway" at first, before her unconditional veneration for Virginia Woolf had prevailed. And there was something rather frightening about Mrs. Danvers in Daphne du Maurier's *Rebecca*. Clarissa was alone now, in this flat, without her husband of many years. The tall, gaunt black figure of the devoted housekeeper, Manderley's disquieting sentinel, was not a reassuring one. She was still trying to find her marks in this brand-new dwelling. Clarissa Dalloway seemed a far more comforting character, and she had inspired half of her pen name, after all.

She prepared herbal tea, added a dollop of honey. It was artificial, of course, and tasted sugary and creamy. The real stuff was impossible to find. She had obtained a tiny treasured amount last year, through a clandestine connection, but at what price!

Honey was now more expensive than caviar. So were flowers. Sometimes she pined for the smell of real roses, like the ones that had grown in her mother's garden long ago. Fake roses were rather cleverly manufactured; they even boasted drops of false dew, twinkling like diamonds in their crimson hearts. The petals felt velvety at first, but soon a rubbery consistence took over. After a while, their pungent perfume revealed a nasty chemical whiff she could no longer stand.

As she sipped the herbal tea and looked out to the rooftops across from her, she thought, not for the first time, that perhaps she had chosen this apartment too hastily in the wake of her sudden decision to leave François. Perhaps she should have given the move more thought. Was this the right place for her? The cat was her daughter's idea. Jordan had told her cats were the perfect pets for writers. For solitary writers? Clarissa had asked. But just how solitary had she really wanted to be? The living room stretched out in front of her, its elegant minimalism still an enigma to her unaccustomed eye. It looked beautiful, but empty.

Once she had decided to leave her husband, it had been a mad rush. She had believed, and how wrong she had been, that a new lodging was going to be easy to find. She wasn't set on anything big, or fancy; she simply needed a room to work in. A room of one's own, as her dear Virginia Woolf said. A living room and one bedroom, so that Adriana, nicknamed "Andy," her granddaughter, could still come and spend the night. She wasn't fussy either about the area she wanted to live in, as long as shopping was easy and public transport available. Nobody drove cars in the city. She had even forgotten how to drive. Another thing François and Jordan had done for her, on holiday. Now it was going to be Jordan's job.

The cat rubbed against her shins. She stooped to pick him up, catching him clumsily, as she wasn't used to handling him yet. Her daughter had shown her how, but it hadn't seemed easy. The cat's name was Chablis. He was a three-year-old Chartreux with a mild nature. He'd belonged to one of Jordan's friends, a woman who had moved to the States. It had been tough in the beginning. Chablis had stayed in his corner, never responding to her calls, and only deigned to nibble at his nuggets when she wasn't there. She thought maybe he was sad and missed his mistress. Then one day, he came to sit on her lap in a very dignified manner, as still as a gray sphinx. She had hardly dared pet him.

Chablis, like her, was finding it tricky to adapt to the luminous and modern space, built with glass and honey-hued wood and stone. However, a part of her liked the austerity, the sleek surfaces, the light. She and the cat would have to make this territory their own, and that would take time. Patience was needed. She had left behind so much stuff when she moved in. She hadn't wanted anything emotionally stamped with François. As if he had died. But the worst thing was, he had not died. He was, in fact, doing very well — insolently well. It was their marriage that had passed away. It was their marriage she had laid to rest.

Clarissa put Chablis into the basket placed in a corner of her room. It was useless, because in the middle of the night, the cat landed gently on her bed and burrowed against her back. When he had started to knead her shoulder with his front paws, as if she were a slab of tasty dough, she was startled. Jordan had explained that all cats did that; it was instinctive. She had gotten used to it. In fact, it comforted her.

After a quick shower, Clarissa lay down

on her bed in the semi-darkness. A new mattress. François had not slept on it. He had not been here, either. She hadn't invited him. Would she? It was still too early. She hadn't taken it all in. Several times, Jordan had asked what was it that her stepfather was guilty of, to make her mother pack up and leave on the spot. She could have told her. Jordan was forty-four. No longer a kid. She had a teenage daughter. But she hadn't had the courage. Jordan had insisted. What had he done? Had he screwed around? Was he in love? Clarissa thought of the purple room, the blond curls. She could tell her daughter everything. She knew exactly which words to use. She imagined Jordan's face. She had let the words rise to her lips, like a bitter bile, and had repressed them.

Forget François. But it wasn't easy to scrap a man she'd spent so many years with. When night came, she asked Mrs. Dalloway to project images and videos on the ceiling of her room: concerts by musicians she loved, movies, biopics, artistic creations. She let sounds and lights drift her away, often falling asleep. She couldn't draw a frontier between her peculiar, sparkling dreams and Mrs. Dalloway's displays. Sometimes, she let Mrs. Dalloway choose sequences picked according to what she had already seen. She didn't see the night float by. Everything converged into a single tawdry cotillion she endured, as if she had been drugged. When she woke up, the cat snuggled against her; she found it hard to get out of bed, and her mouth was dry. Early mornings had seemed harsh ever since she'd moved here. Her entire body felt sore. She put it down to the collapse of her marriage, and the move. Would she ever get used to both?

"Mrs. Dalloway, show me my emails."

The messages appeared on the ceiling.

Dear Clarissa Katsef,

I know you get dozens of emails like these, but I thought I'd give it a go. My name is Mia White. I'm nineteen. I'm a student at UEA, in Norwich. I'm in my second year. I'm studying French and English literature. I'm also enrolled in a creative writing course.

(If you've read this far, then I pray you might continue?)

I'm interested in how places influence writers. How their work is shaped by where they live, where they write. This, of course, is at the core of your own work, and in particular, *Topography of Intimacy,* which I read with great pleasure.

(This is not a gooey fan letter, don't worry. I'm not that type of reader.)

I will be in Paris for the next six months, for my year abroad. I'm sure you're very busy and you don't have much time, but I'd like to meet you. I'm also bilingual, like you, and I grew up learning two languages, like you. My mum is French and my dad is English. Like you.

I don't know if you make time to meet your readers. Perhaps you don't.

Thank you for reading this.

Sincerely,
Mia White

Clarissa took off her glasses, rubbed her eyes. No, she didn't usually meet readers, apart from book signings and lectures. She used to, ten or fifteen years ago. Not anymore. Mia White. It was interesting, refreshing, getting an email from a nineteen-year-old. Didn't that mean that a tiny minority still read books? And that they read her books? Wasn't that short of miraculous?

Hardly anyone read books anymore. She'd noticed that a while ago. People were glued to their phones, to their devices. Bookstores shut down, one after the other. Her biggest success, *Topography of Intimacy,* had been hacked so many times, it hardly brought in any royalties. It could be found online and downloaded in a single click, in any language. At first, Clarissa had put up a fuss, tried to warn her publisher, but she soon realized publishers were not doing much against piracy. They had other anxieties. They had to face that other, even more worrying problem she watched thrive month after month like a sly tumor: the loss of interest in reading. Yes, it seemed no one yearned for books anymore. No one bought them. This had been going on for quite a while. The phenomenal space social media gobbled up in everyone's life was no doubt a reason for this disaffection. The frenetic succession of attacks strung one after the other like bloody pearls on a steadfast necklace of violence was another. Mobile phone snug in her palm, she, too, had found herself hypnotized by atrocious images scalding her with the abomination of sheer detail. She understood that to those addicted to such displays of barbarity, those constantly seeking more sensationalism like a junkie hankering for a fix, novels could appear savorless. It took time to read a book. As it took time to write one. And it appeared no one had the time to read or write anymore.

"Would you like to answer Mia White?" asked Mrs. Dalloway.

"No. Later. Show me the other emails."

She put her glasses back on. Her father's email showed up now on the ceiling. She knew he dictated them. His arthritis prevented him from using a keyboard. He didn't do too badly. His punctuation was poor, but he made himself clear. She corresponded with him by email. He didn't hear well enough anymore to speak to her by phone or video. Probably something wrong with his hearing chip. She hadn't told him yet about François.

My darling C . . . [he still used her real name, which she hated],

I'm ok and you. Your brother's been looking after me but the damn boy's got better things to do. I'm so bored you know. Most of my friends are dead and those who are still here are so fucking boring you can't imagine. I know you haven't spoken to your brother since that shitty inheritance business. My sister was a selfish pain in the ass. Really how could she possibly leave all her money to Arthur's daughters and nothing to Jordan. I still can't get over it. I know you don't want to discuss this and that it hurts you but it hurts me too.

Arthur has been a letdown to you his only sister but to me his father as well. He could have done something about the will. Give an amount to Jordan. What the fuck. He did nothing. I know Jordan doesn't speak to her cousins. What sluts. They don't have an ounce of your daughter's class and brains. Serena's inheritance totally screwed up this family. Thank God your mum is no longer here to see this mess. Darling please give me some news. I'm your old dad and even if I can't make heads or tails of the intellectual stuff you write I'm so proud of you. You know you haven't written to me in two weeks. Why and what the hell is going on. I asked Andy how you were. She always answers me not like her granny. She told me you had moved. What is going on. Where are you living now. I loved your flat near the Luxembourg gardens so why did you leave. Did François decide this. Or you. I'm sad I don't get it. Come on tell me. Everything. Every email from you is like a little gift. It lights up my day. I miss you sweetheart. Come and see your old dad one of these days. I'm too old to come to Paris. I'm counting on you. Your old dad who loves you.

She couldn't help smiling. Her father wrote the way he spoke. She could almost see him in his ground-floor lair, surrounded by his hunting trophies, his golf clubs, and his collection. He collected ancient representations of hands, made of clay, porcelain, marble, plaster, wood, or wax. She had often brought some back for him, harvested during her book tours. So Adriana had let the cat out of the bag. Perhaps a good thing. She'd have to think carefully about what to tell her father. He wasn't particularly fond of François, which hadn't been the case with her first husband, Toby, Jordan's father.

"Do you wish to answer your father's email?" asked Mrs. Dalloway.

"Not now," she said. And then she added, "Thank you."

"You're welcome, Clarissa."

There was even a hint of a smile in Mrs. Dalloway's voice. Like any virtual assistant, Mrs. Dalloway knew everything. She could answer any question, come up with the right answer each time. But Clarissa knew Mrs. Dalloway had also been programmed with specific data concerning herself. What, precisely? She hadn't been able to find out. When she had met Clémence Dutilleul, she had undergone a surprising interview. The C.A.S.A. headquarters were also situated within the new neighborhoods that had sprung from the cinders of the attack. A tall glass-and-steel building with a rooftop garden. Clémence's office gave on to that top floor. It was a vast and airy room with a view. The pale walls were paneled with mirrors. From here, Clarissa could see how the new white zone contrasted with the old Haussmannian gray-slated arteries, but it was a welcome, hopeful sight, she felt.

Clémence was a small, thin woman in her early forties. She wore a black suit, which had a 1940s aspect to it, giving her a severe elegance Clarissa rather liked. She had no idea what to expect. There was no information about the interviews on the website, and she hadn't found anything online. The C.A.S.A. artists' residence remained shrouded in mystery. A short man in his fifties came to join them, and she didn't catch his name. The interviews took place around a white oval table. A young man came to offer them tea and coffee. Clarissa had decided not to dress up for this. Most of her clothes were still in the flat she shared with François. She wanted to be seen exactly as she was. What was the point of pretending to be someone else? She wore a green shirt, white jeans, and sneakers. Her red hair was braided. She was convinced she would never get in anyhow. She was too old, not famous enough, she didn't sell enough books, she wasn't trendy. There were probably hundreds of younger, brighter candidates on their list. She hoped this wouldn't be too humiliating.

They had no files in front of them. Not even a device, a pen, or a piece of paper. They asked her if she minded being filmed. Yet she couldn't see a camera anywhere. She said, no problem. She wondered where the camera was hidden. The man in his fifties had a pleasant face. It was his eyes that bothered her, how they took her in. Two black shiny marbles that never left her.

Clémence sipped her coffee, and beamed. The silence lasted, and it didn't bother Clarissa. She wasn't afraid of silence. If they were expecting her to talk, to fill in the blanks, then they were wrong. She wasn't going to come across as eager, or even desperate. She had nothing to lose. So she smiled back. There was probably an invisible team, tucked away in the building, or perhaps behind one of those mirrors, watching her every move, dissecting whatever she did.

"Thank you very much for coming in today," said Clémence Dutilleul at last.

The man with the shiny black eyes spoke up.

"This has nothing to do with a formal interview. The conversation we'll be having is meant to be a relaxed, cordial one. Not an examination. We want to hear you talk about yourself, about your work. Our artists' residence is a real estate elaboration that holds great promise. We crafted it so that people like you, artists, can live and work there serenely. We need to get to know you a little better. We're not interested in what's already been said or written about you. However, what does interest us is your own approach to your artistic output and the implementation of your body of work. We want to know more about your career history, your development. You can take all the time you wish, or, on the contrary, be succinct. It doesn't matter. What does matter is the quality of your project and your artistic endeavor. I hope I've been clear, now. Over to you."

Two grins, slightly inflexible, and two pairs of inquisitive eyes. A fit of giggles nearly swept over her for a quick moment. Where should she begin? She hated talking about herself, and always had. She hadn't prepared anything, no speech, no presentation. She couldn't stand authors who took themselves seriously, who delighted in their own rhetoric. She couldn't figure out what criteria these people's selection process depended on. *However, what does interest us is your own approach to your own artistic output and the implementation of your body of work.* What the fuck, as her dad would say. She made up her mind fast. She was going to be to the point. Her application was never going to be chosen anyway. In ten minutes, she'd be out of here.

"I've just left my husband."

It just slipped out. She hadn't meant to bring up her personal life. Too bad. They were still staring at her attentively, nodding. She went on.

She explained she had never lived alone. She had to feel good within a home, not only in order to live there but to write there, as well. She was looking for an apartment that could be a sort of shelter. A haven that would keep her safe, that would protect her. Fittingly, her work explored houses and homes, what they conveyed. She had come to writing late in life. She was already over fifty by the time her first novel was published. The path to writing had opened up as she had pieced together the link between writers and places. She hadn't planned on writing a book at all. The novel foisted itself upon her after a personal tragedy and her discovery of hypnosis. It had been published, almost by chance, after a series of encounters, and it had done well. There was something else she wanted to tell them. In her opinion, artists don't need to explain their work. If people didn't get the gist of it or became sidelined, that was their problem. Why should an artist be heard? Creation spoke for itself. Occasionally, readers asked her to explain the endings of her books. It made her chuckle, weep at times, or even become downright furious. She wrote to make others think, not to give them answers.

She realized her voice was loud, ringing out within the huge room, and her hands were waving around. The video team was probably sniggering while they filmed. No doubt they had crossed her name off the list.

"Please go on," said the man with the glasses.

She replied that she didn't have much more to add. Oh, just one last point. She had been raised by a British father and a French mother; she was perfectly bilingual. She had two writing languages and had never been able to pick one over the other. So she had used both. This was a well-known fact about her. The difference was that today she had started to write in both languages at the same time. This was the first time, ever, that she had chosen to do this.

"That's most interesting," said Clémence slowly. "Could you please tell us more?"

They ogled her with the same yearning. What glistening, voracious eyes!

Could she trust them? They had such intense stares. She said that no, she couldn't tell them more. Aptly, she was planning to write about just that: what it meant to have a hybrid brain that wrote in two languages simultaneously. It was a new project and it was too early for her to talk about it. Her editor wasn't even aware of her project. It was difficult to describe an idea as it was thriving. But she knew how deeply the subject touched her, how personal it was, and she intended to get to the bottom of it. She had always found bilingualism and its mechanisms riveting. She wanted to take time to explore it, to take ownership of it.

"A fascinating topic," said the man.

Clarissa was expecting to leave. She was due to visit a two-room apartment this afternoon, near La Fourche Métro station. A neighborhood she barely knew.

"We will be back shortly," announced Clémence with a wide smile. "Please wait for

39

us here."

She was left alone in the large room with its mirrored walls. What had they gone to do? To discuss her candidacy with their team? Did she have a chance? She appeared to have attracted their attention with the bilingual-writing business. Was she still being filmed? For a short moment, she sat motionless. Then she got up, walked across to the terrace. She didn't care if they were still watching her. The garden was beautiful, but artificial, with fake perfumes floating over the false hedge. Box trees had never recovered from the destructive Asian moth attacks years ago. They had been utterly defoliated and had not been able to regain their past splendor. She fingered lavender, sea oat grasses, bonsai, daylilies. She had to admit the plants felt almost real. She hadn't seen a genuine garden in such a long time. This one was almost like the real thing. Almost. There was something too perfect about it. Nature, she remembered, was messier. The silence was eerie. No more insects. Not the faintest hum or buzz. No more birds. No chirping, no twittering. From down below, very little noise, either. Parts of the new neighborhood were entirely pedestrian, served by self-driving electric cars. Occasionally, the quaint clip-clop of hooves could be heard. Police patrols had taken to riding horses since the attacks, and she loved the sound. It gave the city an old-fashioned feel she treasured.

She glanced northward, to Montmartre. François's secret studio was near there. What was he going to do about it? He probably continued going there. She forced herself not to think about him. She still felt devastated by the trauma she'd endured in that place. She must obtain a flat in the C.A.S.A. artists' residence. Otherwise, she was not going to make it. She was going to drift away. There was no way she could keep her chin up anymore. All her vulnerabilities became apparent, rising up to overwhelm the barricades she had patiently built up, year after year, since the baby's death, all that time ago. She felt desperate, weak. Never had she endured such intense loneliness. Whom could she confide in? What she had to say was unspeakable. She felt ashamed, too, and she resented her husband for inflicting that shame upon her. She hated him. She despised him. Her disappointment was colossal. She hadn't even been able to tell him that. She had nearly spat in his face. All she had been capable of doing was to pack in silence, hands trembling, while he wept. Not finding an apartment worried her. She was haunted by the prospect of a new home, just for her. A new place, with no past, no traces of anything. Her shelter. An intimate space. Her fortress. She thought of all the flats she'd seen. The idea of having to see more of them depressed her.

"Here we are!"

Clémence's voice made her jump. They were standing in front of her. In the bright daylight, she noticed the creases in their clothes, the fine dandruff on the man's shoulders. She was invited to come back inside. She was offered another cup of tea. She took it, intrigued by their leisureliness. They didn't seem in any hurry. What did they want? What were they expecting from her?

"We'd like to show you something," announced Clémence.

A screen materialized on one of the mirrors. Photos of a luminous apartment with a skylight appeared. The C.A.S.A. logo was clearly visible on the bottom left.

"This is our artist's studio," said the man. "Eighty square meters."

"Facing northwest and south. Full of light," added Clémence. "Top floor, the eighth."

Why were they showing her these photographs? A floor plan showed up now: a large main room, an open kitchen, a small study, a bedroom, and a bathroom. It all seemed low-key, tasteful, elegant.

"Preparation will be necessary; it will take half a day," said the man. "You'll have to come back. Nothing complicated, no need to worry. All you'll have to do is answer a series of questions. Security, maintenance, and a personal assistant for the apartment need to be set up. Then you'll also meet Dr. Dewinter, who's in charge of the artists of the residence. She runs the C.A.S.A. program."

Wild hope surged through her. Had they chosen her? Had she made it? Was she going to be able to get on with her life, away from François? These people were so odd. What sort of game were they playing?

"I haven't quite understood why you are mentioning the apartment."

"Mrs. Katsef, your candidacy has been accepted. We're delighted."

She wanted to dance around the table. But she held back. Her age, her experience. She gave them a charming smile. She said she was delighted, as well. Could she see the place? She was told she could, and no later than this evening. When could she have the keys? Move in?

Clémence Dutilleul beamed again.

"You can move in shortly. But you won't be needing keys, or a pass."

Clarissa looked at her, baffled.

"Your retina will be your key to enter the lobby on the ground level. And your right index finger will open up the door of your studio. Keys and badges are done. Things of the past. Welcome to C.A.S.A., Mrs. Katsef."

I'm not quite sure when it started. There had been warning signs, but I hadn't paid attention to them. I guess I hadn't wanted to see. I began to notice he was often late, or that I couldn't get hold of him during the day. Most of the times, his phone was switched off, and I began to find that strange.

We had been through this before. Moments of pain I did not want to go back to. That dreadful instant when the suspicion takes over. When you can think of nothing else.

We had been through what many couples go through. Those bitter, painful, intimate moments where infidelity rears its head. It happens. And it had already happened quite a bit to us. He had always said the other women were not important. I had always managed to forgive.

Why had I been so lenient? I wonder now. With years comes a new kind of power. The idea that you don't want anyone taking advantage of you anymore. The inner conviction that you have had enough.

It doesn't happen overnight. It builds up slowly, like a thick liquid taking ages to boil. It took a while, for me.

There had been a truce. And it had lasted for years. He had been ill for quite a stretch. I suppose any thought of an affair had not gone through his head, nor mine. We were too busy tending to him, making sure he would pull through. His medication exhausted him. He slept most of the time.

I helped him get better, stayed by his side, listened to him. I got on with my life, wrote my books, wrote my TV shows, saw my daughter, my granddaughter, my friends.

He regained his strength and the illness became a bad memory. He got back to work, spent time with his team, and traveled. Sometimes he left for a day or two.

I'm trying to think back to what made me understand something was going on. The exact minute when I came out of the fog. The second I knew he was seeing another woman.

He had been late. He usually was, so I hadn't paid attention. We were having dinner at the home of some friends, and he turned up with a bouquet of flowers, mumbling some excuse.

It wasn't till later, when we got home, while he was in the bathroom, that I noticed the hair on his jacket. Long and blond. I remember saying to myself that this was like a scene out of a bad movie. Terribly clichéd. And yet there it was, that long golden hair stretching out like a snake on the sleeve of his jacket.

I didn't say anything. Then I reached out for his jacket, put my nose against the collar. I picked it out immediately.

Another perfume lingering there.

I sometimes wonder. If I had noticed anything earlier, if I had done something, would
that have changed the course of events?

I don't think so. Everything was leading up
to that moment.

Me, standing in front of that door, holding
the key in my hand.

The key to Blue Beard's secret room.

2
LAKE

If anybody could have saved me, it would have been you.

VIRGINIA WOOLF, March 28, 1941

Devotees of broken hearts should apply elsewhere.

ROMAIN GARY, December 2, 1980

The cat had been acting strangely for the past week. Clarissa thought perhaps she should bring it up with Jordan. Chablis ate less and less, and seemed to mew for hours. But what truly alarmed her was when he jumped, startled, as if he had seen or heard someone — the oddest thing. And yet, there was no one. No one, apart from herself. Silence ruled, always. Maybe the cat wasn't used to it yet. Neither was she. There had been a perpetual racket in the flat she'd shared with François. Noisy neighbors, doors banging, people gabbing in the street below, under their windows. She had only ever lived in ground-floor or second-floor apartments before the C.A.S.A. residence. The early-morning glow dazzled her each day when she awoke. She didn't need to ask Mrs. Dalloway to turn on any more lights. It was like living in the sky, in the clouds.

She had never anticipated she'd feel this lonely. She missed François. She missed him at unexpected moments. A blues tune on the radio. A whiff of Vétiver. The sweater he'd given her after a weekend in Ireland. Even if all the furniture was new, even if she'd painstakingly erased all traces of her past and all traces of François, her husband was still there. He materialized like a water-mark interlaced into every nook of the apartment. She could even make out his sturdy, slightly stubby-legged outline, the one she had cherished for so long. There he was, sprawled on the sofa, poring over his device. There he was, under the shower, lathering up foam. There he was, asking Mrs. Dalloway for a cappuccino. François had never cared about being smaller than she was. He had no hang-ups about his height. On the contrary, he was proud to have her at his arm. Now that she'd left him, should she call her friends? She wondered what he had told those same friends about their breakup. He couldn't conceivably have given them the truth. He must have spun a story. But which one? And what would she, in turn, say to her friends? She imagined their dismayed faces. Their pity. No, she must keep it bottled up. François would do the same thing. He didn't have much choice.

No matter how hard she tried not to, she imagined him walking up the rue Dancourt. Opening the gate, striding along the passageway, entering the building on the left. She could see him going up to the sixth floor in the tiny run-down elevator. His key in the old ramshackle lock. She didn't want to see what happened next. But the images swung back at her. It was impossible to make them disappear. She had to give in to them, huddled up, holding her breath. They finally left, like a storm moving on. How could she put an end to her loneliness? She had no idea. She didn't feel like knocking at the doors of the other artists in the residence, introducing herself. She wasn't up to it. She remembered that young student who had written to her. Mia White. She hadn't answered her yet. Was meeting her a good idea?

Clarissa's flat still seemed empty, incomplete. Jordan and Andy had found it beautiful. "Slightly inhospitable, don't you think?"

Jordan had said cautiously. "Not quite 'you.' " Her daughter had gazed at her keenly, with a speck of concern. She had asked her several times if all was well. Jordan was always worrying about her mother. Clarissa had said yes, of course, everything was fine. Yes, she slept badly. That was just settling into a new home. No, she hadn't yet gotten to know the other tenants of the residence. Just a few of them in the lobby. She'd changed the subject, asking her daughter about her job. Jordan was a hydrologist, working for a major research center on flood risk management.

Jordan had always been essential to her. Even more so since the breakup. Clarissa didn't express this out loud, but she was aware deep down of how much she needed her daughter right now. Jordan had captured the best of both her parents, Clarissa felt. Physically, she had inherited her father's dark hair, his green eyes; she had her mother's startling height, her powerful yet graceful shoulders. She had Toby's kindness, his interest in other people. She had Clarissa's belligerence, her sense of humor. But she was also very much herself: both clever and dreamy, tolerant and yet demanding. You couldn't fool Jordan. She was shrewd and highly intuitive. Clarissa knew that one day, she'd have to tell her about why she'd left François. It was too early. She couldn't face it.

As she prepared a quick lunch in her new kitchen, she listened to Jordan, with the cat perched on her knees, discuss her latest conference. Climate change continued to wreak havoc on meteorological conditions, producing torrential rains, which regularly caused all the rivers of the country to rise. Jordan's specialty was inundation. She worked closely with meteorologists in order to develop preventive strategies for the most vulnerable regions. As a child, she had always been fascinated by water, especially rivers and lakes. Clarissa admired her daughter's expertise and enthusiasm. Jordan was a respected figure in her field. She gave talks, lectures, was often seen on television. She spoke eloquently, with a husky voice that added to her charm.

Clarissa sometimes thought Jordan's profession stemmed from her own interest in quantifying land and premises. In another life, she had been a property surveyor. It wasn't water she used to measure, but houses and apartments. From an early age, Clarissa felt she needed to understand the lay of the land. Her dad had given her a luminous world globe for her desk when she was seven, and she'd spent hours watching it rotate under her finger. Later, she'd developed a fascination for maps, papering the walls of her rooms with them. It was cities she'd found captivating as a teenager: how they emerged, how they expanded, how they were destroyed by fires, bombings, how they were rebuilt. She'd pored over ancient photos of London to see what neighborhoods looked like before the Blitz. In her early twenties, she'd walked around with a measuring tape tucked away in her pocket. Houses attracted her — their stories, their evolution. Her mother had been convinced that Clarissa was going to become an architect. But she hadn't.

While she paid attention to her daughter, slicing bits of mozzarella cheese that Andy promptly put into her mouth despite her grandmother's remonstrance, Clarissa could not help thinking of her firstborn, and what he would have looked like today. He would have been forty-six. Tall and dark, she supposed. But that was all she could conjure. She had not thought of her son for so long, had banished the sorrow to the back of her mind. Her newfound fragility had resurrected it, nurturing it back to a throbbing vitality she found impossible to combat.

When she had started hypnotism, all those

years ago, to keep the pain at bay, to not let it destroy her, Elise, her hypnotherapist, had asked her to think of a soothing, restful image. The first thing that had come to mind was a lake. Elise had asked her to describe the lake. Why a lake? She had no idea. She simply knew that the image of the lake soothed her, instilling a prodigious calm into her veins. She had tried to describe the lake to Elise; it was vast, she had the feeling it was deep, and its depth did not worry her. On the contrary, the fact that it reached so amply into the earth, forcing its path into the ground, gave her an unprecedented reassurance. The lake's surface gleamed silver, its smoothness burrowed by steady wavelets. Clarissa could see herself soaring above the lake like a glider, arms outstretched; she could feel the cool wind nip at her cheeks and slide down her back; then she could also discern herself swimming, diving into the watery green abysses, palms stroked by the strange caress of weeds. It seemed to her the lake absorbed her pain, her sorrow.

She often dreamed of the lake. In the middle of the night, when she couldn't sleep, she sometimes asked Mrs. Dalloway to display lake videos on her bedroom ceiling. Half-asleep, she let herself be carried off by eddies, lulled by soft splashing. She didn't know where the water would take her. A peculiar, lacustrine ballet whirled her away; her skin becoming scaly, fishlike, her fingers merging to form pink fins.

In the blue opaqueness at the bottom of the lake, hazy shapes emerged, hands reached out toward her, while spools of black hair slowly unraveled like flowers of darkness, both soothing and poisonous. Once, she thought she caught a glimpse of Virginia Woolf's face — not the face she knew, not the writer's, no, another one, a face that not many had laid eyes upon; the unbearable, bloated, ashen features of the drowned woman, the one whose body had been found weeks after she disappeared on the banks of the river Ouse. The dream of the lake had become a nightmare. It was impossible to know if the images had been born in her own head, or if they came from Mrs. Dalloway's projections.

As she listened to Jordan, Clarissa delicately stroked her granddaughter's head. Adriana, going on fifteen, applied her makeup carefully and wore lacerated black clothes. Despite the rebellious sulk she was fond of sporting, Andy adored her grandmother. She wanted to come and spend the night here. She had even picked out that little couch in the office where she was going to sleep. She interrupted her mother incessantly in order to obtain a date. Jordan got angry. Well, yes, Andy was going to be able to come! Could she just please let her grandmother settle into her new flat? And could she stop being so insistent? Clarissa felt flattered. She, too, loved the relationship she had crafted with her granddaughter.

"Doesn't François live with you anymore, Mums?" Andy asked straightforwardly as Clarissa served them homemade cake for dessert.

Jordan glared at her. Clarissa had been expecting this from her outspoken granddaughter. She calmly replied that no, François wasn't going to live here. This was her place. Only for her.

"And for me!" quipped Andy mischievously.

"That's right, sweetie, for you, too."

"And what about Granddad? Will he come?"

Jordan sighed. Why was Adriana asking these dumb questions? Clarissa smiled, to show them she wasn't ruffled. She reminded Andy that Toby had started over, that he lived in Guéthary, in the Basque country, and that he had a new lady friend.

"Yeah, and she's not much fun," mumbled

Andy, helping herself to more cake. "I liked the previous one better. She was less of a pain in the ass."

Clarissa and Jordan laughed. Despite everything, Clarissa had kept up a good relationship with her first husband. Even if they had divorced over thirty years ago, Toby remained close. Which got on François's nerves. Clarissa planned to invite Toby for a drink when he was next in Paris. Without the new lady friend.

"How are things with your brother, Mums?" asked Jordan as she stroked the cat.

Clarissa shrugged. What an idiot, seriously! Her brother! Her laugh sounded pinched and dry. Heritage stories often made a mess of things. She'd always thought she had been close to Arthur. He was only two years younger than she. They grew up together, spent their childhood and teenage years in London. He did as he pleased. At sixteen, he dressed as Ziggy Stardust, with full makeup, orange hair, and platform soles, to their unadventurous mother's dismay. Their dad found it funny.

"He sounded so cool when he was young!" exclaimed Andy.

"Indeed. But with time, you see, Arthur turned into a full-of-himself, sad little man."

"You bet! And my cousins are no better," added Jordan.

Clarissa didn't have to explain to Jordan and Andy how crushed she had been by Aunt Serena's recent legacy. She'd thought the old lady had been fond of her, just as fond as Serena had been of Arthur. She had often spent holidays in Serena's house in Surrey, with Toby and Jordan, when her daughter was a child. Warm, joyful moments. When the will had been read out loud to her, she had been flabbergasted. Serena had left her entire fortune to Arthur's two daughters, Emily and Harriet. All of it. There hadn't been a single item for Jordan, not even a trinket, a bracelet, or a small souvenir. Arthur's daughters were in for a considerable sum. They'd be able to buy a small flat, go on a trip, invest, plan for the future. Clarissa had felt shock at first, and then uncertainty. Was this a mistake? she'd asked. She was told not at all. A slow, powerful rage replaced the incomprehension. She had called her brother. She still trusted him then; she still hoped. He was going to say, What an old bitch. How dare she do that! He was going to say his daughters would split everything with Jordan. But nothing happened that way. She'd had a hard time getting hold of Arthur. And when his puffy face finally showed up on her screen, he had acted cowardly and evasive. He didn't wish to interfere. Serena had her reasons. They had to respect her decision.

Clarissa had taken the bull by the horns. She had gone to see her nieces. Emily and Harriet hadn't minced their words. They needed the money. They were sorry for Jordan. But they were convinced Jordan had done quite well for herself, hadn't she? They saw her on TV, on social media; she traveled; she seemed to lack nothing; she had a husband and a daughter; her mother was a respected writer. And on top of all that, she was beautiful. Jordan had it all, right? Oh, and one last thing: Jordan had chosen to live in France; one mustn't forget that. Serena was very attached to her country. It was important to her. They had stayed in England, they had no husband or children as of yet, and time was flying by! That money was perfect timing, and they were sure Jordan would understand. What about another cup of tea, dear Aunt C . . . ? Clarissa had felt like strangling them. Her father, who always spoke his mind, was right; he called them tarts. In the train on her way back from London, Clarissa thought about the way Jordan raised Andy, how much effort she put into it, and how complicated it had been during her numerous trips when Andy was a little girl. Clarissa had helped out a lot. What on earth had gotten into old Serena's head? She knew her aunt hadn't approved of the fact that her own brother had married a Frenchwoman. Solange, Clarissa and Arthur's mother, had apparently found it difficult to find her way into her husband's family. Clarissa thought she had ultimately managed to do so. Perhaps not, in the long run.

That day on the train, Clarissa decided she wouldn't be speaking to her brother and nieces again. It was common, after all, to bicker in the aftermath of wills. What was less common, she felt, was the sudden and intimate overlap of every aspect of her life: the breakdown of her marriage, the rough patch with her brother, and the hurried arrival in a new home she still didn't feel at ease in.

When they left, Jordan told her mother to look after herself, to get a good night's sleep, to rest. Andy hugged her with all her might. Clarissa waved good-bye to them as the transparent glass elevator whooshed them down. Jordan's lovely face was turned up to her, and she could read all the anguish there. She knew Jordan was going to speak to her husband, Ivan, tonight, and she already knew what her daughter was going to say: that Clarissa looked old, frail, and sad, that she was worried, that she couldn't understand what had happened. She could hear Jordan's voice: Yes, the flat was lovely, and it was wonderful that Clarissa lived there, but the move had tired her. How was she going to face all this, alone, at her age, in her state? Jordan would undoubtedly bring up the long depression Clarissa had endured after the death of her first child. Jordan remembered that endless tunnel; she was only a little girl at the time, but she had grown up with that despondency. She'd say she feared Clarissa might plunge into a similar gloom. Clarissa could now hear Ivan's voice. Jordan's husband was a tall, thin man in his early forties, with soft blue eyes. He rarely lost his temper and spoke gently but firmly. She could hear him say Clarissa was a tough cookie. She'd pulled herself out of depression a long time ago. Clarissa knew what she wanted. And if Clarissa wanted to be alone, then that was fine. Jordan just had to stop worrying.

Clarissa closed the door of the apartment. She turned her back to it, leaning against the wooden surface, looking out toward the living room. It did look nice, she admitted. The lovely gleaming surfaces. The light. The view. Her precious books, the ones she read with such delight, were missing. They were still at François's. She was going to take the time to make sure they were all placed properly on the shelves. Romain Gary. Virginia Woolf. Her favorite writers. Books never let you down. They were always there for you.

The cat pranced along, and she watched him go toward the main window. Chablis had spent most of the lunch on Jordan's knees, purring. He had eaten well, had played with Adriana. Perhaps he was getting over his apprehension. She was happy about that. She still wasn't quite sure how to deal with a cat. As Clarissa observed him, Chablis suddenly seemed to stiffen. Surely she was imagining things. No, he arched his back, and his ears were flattened, golden eyes deepening to black. The cat crouched now, tail slowly twitching, staring at the middle of the room as if someone were standing there. Mystified, Clarissa remained motionless. He then slunk under the sofa, and the only thing she could see now was the tip of his tail.

Clarissa strode to the center of the room, unnerved, glancing around her. Everything seemed in place, perfectly normal. But she, too, had sensed a presence. And she realized now, with a prick of horror, that ever since she had moved here, she had never felt completely alone; it was as if someone, or something, was watching her.

"Mrs. Dalloway?" She was surprised to hear her voice was quavering. She sounded like a very old lady.

"Yes, Clarissa?" came the rounded, cordial tone.

"Am I alone here?"

"Yes, Clarissa. Apart from the cat, you are completely alone."

"Why was the cat afraid just now?"

"I have no idea, Clarissa."

"Who can see me?"

"I'm sorry, I don't quite understand. Can you rephrase that, Clarissa?"

"Can anyone see what I am doing in my apartment?" ' Now her voice was angry. No more quavering old-lady stuff.

"No, Clarissa. No one can see what you do in your home."

"What about you, Mrs. Dalloway? Can you see what I'm doing?" '

"Yes, Clarissa. I see everything you do. I was programmed to do that."

"So you do watch me, Mrs. Dalloway."

"Yes, Clarissa. All the time."

"And so I was right. There is someone spying on me. You."

"You're right, Clarissa. But remember, I'm no one. I don't exist."

Clarissa often thought back to the day she'd spent at the C.A.S.A. headquarters in order to set up her virtual assistant and to meet Dr. Dewinter. She had been shown to a different part of the building, deep down, below ground level. The space here was white and brilliant, almost too white, she thought. The staff wore black as well, the same sleek style as Clémence Dutilleul's suit. The man who took her in charge was in his early twenties. He had the round pink face of a choirboy. His name was Quentin. He was respectful and pleasant. He started by taking an imprint of her fingertips and a scan of her retina with a small device. It took only a couple of minutes. He then told her the setup process was going to take a while, because they needed to get it just right. Even if the questions seemed repetitive and weird, she had to stick to it. The virtual assistant had to get used to her voice, because Clarissa's voice was the only one it was going to obey. It wouldn't respond to anyone else. He also said that Clarissa could take a break whenever she wanted. She could get up, stretch her legs, have a glass of water.

Quentin ushered her into a smaller room, equally white and luminous. In front of her were a chair and a desk. A large screen took up the entire wall. Quentin motioned for her to be seated. He carefully placed earphones on Clarissa's ears. Then he went to sit behind a partition. She could hear his voice in her headset. He asked her if she was ready. She said yes.

The screen in front of her turned gray. Two large eyes faced her now. They were wide and blue. They blinked slowly. They reminded her of the billboard horn-rimmed eyes of Doctor T. J. Eckleburg in the opening pages of *The Great Gatsby;* a solemn, intense gaze, which saw everything, never missing a beat, both reassuring and alarming. An amiable male voice, which was not Quentin's, asked her to say her name out loud. She did so. She was asked to speak more slowly and to repeat her name three times.

In the beginning, it was easy. She had to state her date and place of birth, her nationality. Her age, her height, her weight. The eyes blinked and glowed back at her like those of a gratified cat. Then she had to pronounce a sequence of specific orders. She was asked to repeat them clearly, over and over again.

"Lock the door. Set the alarm. Check the air-conditioning. Turn on the shower. Close the blind. Turn off the light. Set night mode. Turn on the oven. Read my emails."

She was asked to choose the name of her assistant. She had thought about this before, of course. When she said, "Mrs. Dalloway," she then had to say it out loud six or seven times very clearly. She then had to choose what kind of voice she wanted Mrs. Dalloway to have. They could clone any type of voice, she knew. She picked a British accent with mellow, gentle tones.

Quentin appeared from behind the screen. He told her he was going to leave the room. He'd be right outside. She was alone with the setup process. If there was a problem of any sort, she just had to press the pause button. Clarissa nodded. He left, closing the door behind him.

Clarissa felt slightly apprehensive. She remained silent, straight-backed on her chair.

The billboard eyes gleamed back at her.

"Are you ready, Clarissa?" asked the new female voice with the very British accent.

"Yes," she said, "I am."

"Please relax, Clarissa."

"How can you tell I'm tense?"

"Your body language. You don't have to

66

sit up so stiffly. And you can uncross your arms."

Clarissa couldn't help smiling.

"There. That's better. I'm going to be asking you all sorts of questions. Do not be surprised. This is just for me to get to know you better. After all, I will be with you all the time. I need to be able to watch over you. As soon as you walk into the C.A.S.A. residence, and then into your apartment, I will be in charge of your well-being and your security. Nobody can come into your home unless you allow the person to. If I detect an intruder, I will react very quickly. An alarm will go off and security services will arrive on the spot. Now. Are you comfortable, Clarissa? I need you to be comfortable, because it might take a while. No, don't be alarmed; this will be painless. You don't have to answer in great detail. You don't even have to answer at all if you don't want to. But remember this: The more answers you give me, the better I will serve you. So let's get going. Here's my first question, Clarissa. Would you rather set me up in French or in English? I'm aware that you are perfectly bilingual."

"I'd like to be able to speak to you in both languages interchangeably, and have you answer me as you wish, in English or in

French."

"Very well, Clarissa. Let us go on. What is your present state of mind?"

Clarissa glowered back into the T. J. Eckleburg–like eyes. How on earth could she answer that? And what had it to do with the setup of her voice assistant? She felt disillusioned, then irritated. Maybe all her reactions were being processed and analyzed by the same hidden people who had been there the day of her interview. She wasn't going to let herself be impressed.

"I don't wish to answer that question and I don't see why it's important to you."

"I see. Can you explain, Clarissa?"

"I don't want to discuss personal matters. I don't know you and I don't know who is listening to all this. I don't see why you need this sort of stuff from me."

"I understand. I will try to explain, Clarissa. I need to know who you are. I need to understand your personality. The more I know it, the more I will be able to help you."

Clarissa grumbled.

"Help me? You're only supposed to oversee security and management of the flat. Why would you need details about my present state of mind?"

"Please remain calm, Clarissa. No one is listening to this except for me. And I can do much more than just looking after your housekeeping and your security."

"Such as?"

"If you answer all my questions, Clarissa, you will understand how I can help you. I've been programmed to do this. To make your life easier. In every way. To take charge of things. So you can write. So you can create."

The minutes ticked by slowly. The blue eyes blinked. The voice was silent, too.

"Are you unhappy, Clarissa?" asked the voice at last.

"Yes," she said tersely. "I'm unhappy. I don't want to talk about it. I don't want to explain. I don't know who or what you are, but I just want to get on with this. I want to move into that apartment. I want to feel safe. I want to write my book. Is that clear?"

"It is indeed, Clarissa. Please say my name when you talk to me. That way, I'll know you're addressing yourself to me."

"Okay. Listen up, Mrs. Dalloway." She barked the words out. "I'm. Not. Happy."

"I understand, Clarissa. Can you tell me precisely why you're unhappy?"

"No! It's none of your business, Mrs. Dalloway. I'm sure you have more important questions to ask."

"I'm sorry you're unhappy, Clarissa.

You're right; I have other questions. Many other questions. I'd like to talk about your family. Will they be coming to visit?"

"Yes, Mrs. Dalloway."

"Their names, please?"

"My daughter, Jordan Vendel-Garnier. Her husband, Ivan Garnier. Their daughter, Adriana Garnier, known as Andy."

"Thank you, Clarissa. Can you show me photographs of them, please?"

Clarissa picked up her phone, swiped into her photo file, and showed it to the screen, where the eyes appeared to gluttonously drink it in.

"Thank you. Are there any other family members you wish to talk to me about, Clarissa?"

"Yes. My dad. He won't be coming; he's ninety-eight. He lives in London. He writes to me a lot. My first husband, Toby Vendel. He might drop in. Not sure yet. And my second husband, François Antoine. He won't be setting a foot inside my house. Of that, I'm sure. Don't ask me why, please."

"Thank you, Clarissa. I won't. Can you show me a photo of him? . . . Thanks. I'm now going to fire all sorts of questions at you. Please answer them without thinking too hard."

"What do you mean, Mrs. Dalloway?"

"I mean this is not a test. This is just for me to understand how you think. How your brain works. Be spontaneous, Clarissa. Are you ready?"

Clarissa nodded. She felt thirsty and tired. The lights around her seemed terribly bright. How her brain worked? She didn't even know herself. At times, like right now, it felt like it had stopped working altogether.

"What are your favorite colors, Clarissa?"

"Green. Blue. Orange."

"Your favorite musician?"

"Frédéric Chopin."

"Your favorite singers?"

"Patti Smith. Soapie Indigo."

"Your favorite poets?"

"Charles Baudelaire. Emily Dickinson."

"Your favorite artists?"

"Harald Sohlberg. Pieter de Hooch. Vilhelm Hammershøi."

Mrs. Dalloway's voice droned on, and Clarissa let herself be carried away by the questions. She answered quickly, easily. This wasn't too difficult. It might be over faster than she thought. There was a rhythm to her replies and she gave way to it. It was like playing Ping-Pong, angling her wrist to knock the ball back as swiftly as possible.

"Your favorite song?"

" *'La vie en rose,'* sung by Grace Jones."

"Your favorite film?"

"All movies by Stanley Kubrick."

"Your favorite actors?"

"Timothée Chalamet. Salomé Jalon."

"Your best trait?"

"Compassion."

"Your worst flaw?"

"Impatience."

She hadn't noticed that the questions were gradually becoming more and more personal. She had been too amused, or too busy throwing the ball back.

"Your worst fear?"

"Losing my daughter, my granddaughter."

"What makes you laugh?"

"Peter Sellers in *The Party*."

"What makes you laugh in real life?"

"I don't know, really."

"What makes you cry?"

Her mind seemed to have gone fuzzy. The tiredness took over; her mouth felt dry. She found it difficult to speak.

"Intimate . . . things . . ."

"What shocked you the most recently?"

"I don't . . ." she mumbled. She tried again: "The Tower . . . The images of the devastation . . ."

Her throat felt tighter and tighter, as if she were suffocating.

A pause.

72

"Next question, then. On what occasions do you lie?"

Clarissa stared back into the huge eyes. Perhaps her silence was easier to decipher than her answers. She wondered what would be made of her muteness. She waited. It worked. After a long blank, Mrs. Dalloway spoke up.

"We are going to take a break now, Clarissa. Dr. Dewinter is coming in to see you. You and I will resume later. You may remove the headset."

The eyes slowly faded from the screen. She felt drained. Before she had time to move again, the door clicked open. She pushed the earphones down around her neck. She didn't know whether she should stand or remain seated.

The very tall person who entered the room had an arresting physique, with long, wavy chestnut hair and a strapping figure. The skin of her face was as smooth as a bowl of cream, with made-up eyes and a crimson mouth; the jaw was square and the features thickset. A long hand with red nails sailed toward her.

"I'm so honored to meet you, Mrs. Katsef. I'm Dr. Dewinter."

The voice was low. The doctor sat down in front of her, sliding a tablet from a square white pouch.

"How's the setup coming along?"

Clarissa smiled, answered it was fine, slightly longish, but interesting.

"You no doubt have oodles of questions for me?" said Dr. Dewinter with an unexpected wink.

A momentary hesitation engulfed Clarissa.

Dr. Dewinter took on a long-suffering expression. Her smile was barely contrived.

"Queries about the C.A.S.A. program, perhaps? I can, of course, say a few words in order to present the project. Our program was created to accompany the creativity of artists accommodated in a residence dedicated to them. We attach extreme importance to the development of art, in all its forms. Artistic creation is our absolute priority. We wish to preserve and support the imaginary input of artists such as yourself within such a disturbing and shifting world. I'm responsible for monitoring your health. I personally developed the protocol that will take you in charge once you move in. Your well-being is crucial to us. Your initial checkup will be done automatically via the bathroom installation. Everything is explained in the booklet you received. As you'll see, our team is terrific, and much appreciated by our community of artists. I'd like to point out, however, that you enjoy full freedom, Mrs. Katsef. You are absolutely not coerced to interact with other artists of the residence. We know how fragile artists are, as well as their delicate frames of mind, and never would we impinge fake camaraderie upon them like at those holiday resorts where everyone pretends to be friends. We have no control whatsoever, may I add, on your writing. Your future literary creations are yours only and will never belong to C.A.S.A. You've certainly wondered why our rental fees are cheap compared to what we have to offer. You must be aware that you were handpicked. We lodge only the most promising, inventive artists. This has nothing to do with celebrity. The intellectual trajectories of artists, their endeavors, their futures, are what we're interested in. And we are highly interested in you, Mrs. Katsef."

Clarissa took the glass of water the doctor handed her and had a few sips.

"Why?"

"Your writing process seems spellbinding. But your take on places and houses also appeals to us. Your evolution will be monitored closely, believe me. No need to be alarmed! You don't have to hand in any homework, or pass any tests. Concerning fees, please be reassured. Your rent includes them. As you know, because you signed the tenancy agreement, your rent is worked out according to the sum of your royalties. The rent each artist pays will depend upon his or her circumstances. There is no standardized rent. C.A.S.A. individualizes it all."

"And what if my royalties thin out, which is the case? What will happen?"

"Don't worry. You have a two-year lease. That's enough time for you to plan accordingly. We created this program in order to help artists develop their talents. It's a long-term undertaking, as well as a special patronage. We invest because we believe in you."

Clarissa noticed Dr. Dewinter's countenance seemed deeply heartfelt, like a devoted mother at the bedside of a fragile child. She kept nodding her head, a flurry of manicured fingers pressed against her collarbone.

"Thank you," said Clarissa, trying not to laugh. "I have another question for you. When you say 'we,' whom, exactly, do you mean?"

Dr. Dewinter displayed several images on her device. She showed Clarissa an organizational chart. Clarissa recognized the doctor, Clémence Dutilleul, the man who was with her during the interview, as well as young Quentin.

"We have about twenty people in our team. Most work here, at the headquarters. You'll find more information in the file that was sent to you. If you don't mind, I'd like us to come back to your virtual assistant's setup. It's a key moment of your integration here at C.A.S.A. Have you any queries regarding this? We attach a lot of importance to this step. Those never-ending questions might seem a little off-putting. Don't give them too much thought. We want you to feel at ease, above all. This is essential to us."

Dr. Dewinter's teeth were large and spectacularly white. While she listened, Clarissa wondered if signing up for this apartment had been a wise choice. She hadn't taken the time to find out more about C.A.S.A., to comb through the contract. She had been like a full-speed train steaming ahead. She had rushed forward without thinking it over. But had she really had the choice? she wondered. She never wanted to ask anything from François again. She no longer wished to depend on him. Her newfound freedom felt exceedingly precious. What would her run-of-the-mill existence be like now if her application hadn't been selected? She could picture herself sleeping in her dad's basement flat or on Jordan's sofa. She observed Dr. Dewinter's floppy, moist mouth. She pretended to listen, moving her head up and down. What was Dr. Dewinter's private life like? Was she involved with a man? A woman? Both? She could picture Dr. Dewinter at home, applying makeup in front of a mirror. It no doubt took ages. What did the doctor look like first thing in the morning? Clarissa imagined her in the nude, choosing clothes in front of her wardrobe. A strange beauty emanated from her weighty yet graceful body. The doctor was talking about a prescription Clarissa was going to get by mail. A prescription? What for? She asked the doctor to repeat this. The doctor arched an eyebrow, with a slightly sour face that clearly meant Clarissa should be listening assiduously. A basic one, with vitamins and food supplements. Now back to configuration. Dr. Dewinter's gums were exposed in a wide smile. Clarissa was going to have to be obliging, right? The doctor held out her hand one more time.

"I'm sure this will go well. I wish you a wonderful move into your new home. See you soon, Mrs. Katsef."

The door closed and Clarissa was alone

again, facing the screen. The blue eyes swiftly made their appearance.

"Here I am, Clarissa. Can we go on?"

"We may."

"Good. We stopped at lies. Do you ever lie, Clarissa?"

The break with Dr. Dewinter had renewed Clarissa's vigor. She felt curious; she very much wanted to know where the setting up was going to lead. She remembered that François had given her her first personal assistant for Christmas, years ago. It was a small gray cone that looked like a microphone. It answered all sorts of questions: what today's weather was going to be, or tomorrow's, a country's capital, how to make gluten-free chocolate cake, calculate a sum, order something online. But the little cone hadn't needed to get to know her or François any better. It had merely answered their questions. Clarissa suspected her present session with Mrs. Dalloway was imbedded in a far more complex tactic.

"Do I lie? Yes, Mrs. Dalloway, I lie every day. Writers are professional liars. They spend their life spinning stories. If we couldn't lie, we wouldn't be able to write."

"Thank you, Clarissa. Can you tell about how you chose your pseudonym?"

"I've already answered many interviews

regarding my pen name. Everything is online. Just look, Mrs. Dalloway."

"Certainly. Here's what I found."

Pages and pages of articles filled the screen. Clarissa caught a glimpse of her own features, the face she'd had twenty years ago. A headline shot out: CLARISSA KATSEF'S VIBRANT TRIBUTE TO VIRGINIA WOOLF AND ROMAIN GARY.

"Indeed, I don't need to know why you chose that particular pen name, Clarissa, since it's all online, as you've pointed out, but I'd rather hear about why you don't like your real name."

"I loathe it. I've always loathed it. I don't even pronounce it. Only my dad, my brother, and my nieces still call me that. You'll find it easily, as it's in all my identity documents. You probably know it already. It's tough growing up with a name you hate. Why do I hate it? Where should I start? My parents had looked for a name you could easily pronounce in English and in French. My father rooted for Agatha. My mother, Cécile. Nobody came to an agreement. So they ended up picking the one they gave me. It has hideous diminutives, in both languages. You know, Mrs. Dalloway, if I hear that name in the street, I don't even turn around. It's not mine. Don't ever use it."

"Duly noted. Let's get back to the questions. Can you tell me on which occasion you felt the deepest sadness?"

Clarissa realized the irritation she felt at the beginning had fizzled out. She'd lost her wariness, as well. Something inside had let go.

"The death of my son."

She found it extraordinary that she could actually utter those words so straightforwardly. They had remained locked up for so long.

"Would you care to say a little more?"

"I can say this. When people ask me how many children I have, I always reply, 'Two.' I say, 'Two children.' I've been pregnant twice; I carried babies twice; I gave birth twice. It would be even sadder to say I've only had one child. It would be erasing my son's existence."

"Could you tell me his name?"

She wondered why Mrs. Dalloway would need to know that, but the words came tumbling out before she could stop them. She said his name out loud.

"Thank you, Clarissa. How did you fight the sadness?"

"The sadness never left me, Mrs. Dalloway. I learned to live with it. Writing helped."

"Would you say this tragedy shaped the person you are today?"

Clarissa let out a short, curt laugh.

"In your humble opinion?"

"I'm afraid I don't understand your query, Clarissa. Can you reformulate it?"

"Yes, there were repercussions. And yes, I still do suffer. Hypnosis helped me a lot."

"Can you confirm your hypnotherapist's name?"

"She's no longer with us, I'm afraid. Her name was Elise Delaporte."

"Would you like to hear her voice, Clarissa? That's the kind of thing you can ask me to do for you."

"Hear Elise's voice? Oh, my God . . ."

"Please ask me, Clarissa."

"Mrs. Dalloway, I'd like to listen to Elise Delaporte."

First came silence. Then from its depths sprang the unforgettable silky, clear tones. Clarissa quivered, moved to tears. Elise! It didn't matter what she was going on about; this was Elise, her Elise. She was talking to a journalist, answering questions about her profession, how she chose hypnosis, or rather, how it had chosen her. How she helped others. Clarissa closed her eyes and felt as if she were now in Elise's small, hushed apartment; she could feel the firmness of the chair propping up her back while she surrendered to Elise's voice, and in front of her eyelids the strange fluctuating white line began to appear, tracing its way ahead like a boundless, enticing path. In her palm, she almost felt the blue china cup filled with warm water that Elise had handed her after each session.

Elise was silent now. So was Mrs. Dalloway. Clarissa opened damp eyelids. The blue eyes vanished from the screen. A few sentences now showed up.

Congratulations, Clarissa Katsof. Your personal virtual assistant was successfully set up. C.A.S.A. wishes you a very pleasant day.

In the beginning, I did what all suspicious wives did. I went through his pockets. Nothing. I looked in his case. Nothing. His mobile was locked; so was his computer. No way I could get inside.

I started following him, my hair hidden under a baseball cap, a large jacket concealing my figure.

His office was near the Palais-Royal. I went to wait at the café just in front. I saw him come out with his colleagues, go have lunch nearby.

I felt silly. All this took time. I had other things to do than spy on my husband. But when I found another hair on his sweater, just as long, just as blond, I knew I couldn't sit around doing nothing. It was an unbearable situation. At our ages, to have to face this again. The lies. The concealment.

He had always told me, the other times. It was he who came to see me, ashamed, red-faced, begging for my forgiveness. Nameless women. Unimportant women. One-night stands.

With my first husband, Toby, I had not had that problem. I had not been through that pain. I did what many women do: I forgave, closed my eyes. I had a couple of discreet affairs. Nothing serious. They did me good.

I don't know why, but I instantly felt that this

time, things were different. This affair wasn't like the others. I didn't yet know to what extent.

I took it upon myself to say nothing to anyone. I had to find out. I had to be patient. I ended up noticing it was often at the end of the day that I couldn't get hold of him. His schedule became shady. So I continued to wait in front of his office, hidden under my cap.

There was that afternoon when he came out of his office carrying a small travel bag, in a hurry. He seemed happy. I'd never seen that bag. He rushed to the Métro. It was tough following him. Where was he going? Who was he going to meet?

My husband took a route that had nothing to do with our home. I followed, puzzled and anxious. He took the exit at Anvers station. I tried to think of someone we knew who lived around there, but no one came to mind. I looked at the name of the street: rue Dancourt. He entered a small passage and I was able to slip in before the gate closed behind him.

He went into a building on the left, and at that point, I did not dare follow him any longer. I kept back, observing the façade. It was an old edifice, fissured and dilapidated. I drew nearer to read the names on the intercom.

I had a dreadful shock.

His name was there. Our name. The name I'd been using, in my everyday life, for the past twenty years.

François ANTOINE
6th floor, left.

3
TOWER

So, why?
> ROMAIN GARY, December 2, 1980

I begin to hear voices and I can't concentrate.
> VIRGINIA WOOLF, March 28, 1941

Deep, dark night. She got out of bed without looking at the time. Before sleeping, she asked Mrs. Dalloway to activate night mode, which switched off the automatic lights. Night mode also meant Mrs. Dalloway could not disturb her by announcing an incoming email; she could only manifest herself in case of a fire or a break-in. Clarissa had dreamed of the lake again, of its cool depths, deprived of Virginia Woolf's drowned face. Tongues of water caressing her skin in a sensual motion had awakened her; around her hummed the echo of a gentle voice, but she couldn't make out to

87

whom it belonged. And yet it had sounded familiar. A voice she loved. A voice that wanted no harm.

After a few weeks, Clarissa was used to walking along the dark corridor leading to the kitchen. She took fruit juice from the refrigerator, poured it out. Holding her glass, she went to the large window. It was late, but there were still lights shining out through the night. After drinking the juice, she took her field glasses and stepped back, not wanting to be seen. That lamp, on the sixth floor, straight ahead, was always lit. She could make out a desk, letters, a chair. That person was just like her: She or he did not sleep. But night after night, Clarissa never saw anyone sitting there. She ended up thinking the lights were turned on to simulate a presence and discourage burglars. There must be someone, however, because the leaflets on the table were frequently shifted. One night, there was even a steaming mug set on the desk's wooden surface. She kept thinking about the voice she heard in her dream as she examined the room with her field glasses. She was convinced she had actually heard it; it was as if the voice had spoken to her in the middle of the night. She still felt the peacefulness it left in its wake.

As she adjusted her binoculars, she noticed with fright that a motionless silhouette had risen by the desk. She just had time to glimpse a pallid, bespectacled, uplifted face that appeared to be staring back at her. With a whimper, she stepped back, put the field glasses down, but even to her naked eye, the face seemed to follow her, lenses gleaming like two small headlamps riveted to her. Her heart thumped wildly. She moved backward again, let the darkness enfold her. The cat meowed; she had nearly stepped on him.

For a long moment, she remained motionless in the obscurity. Then she got a grip on herself. What was she doing? What was she frightened of? This was ridiculous! She was at home; she could watch whom she pleased. Being scared was not her style. She glided back in front of the window with a determined step, glanced down to the sixth floor. The lights were off. No one could be seen. She grabbed the binoculars, focused the lenses. In the dimness, she could see the outline of the desk. Paperwork, a pen. There was a tiny red dot glowing in the blackness like a strange beacon. Whatever was it? She watched it thrive, then abate. How odd. She suddenly understood, with another thump of her heart. It was a cigarette. The person facing her was smoking with the lights off. He — or she — was probably watching her, immersed by her binoculars. This time, she felt stupid. Her cheeks burned. Blushing! At her age! She couldn't help laughing. It felt wonderful. She hadn't laughed out loud in ages. Not since she had left her husband. The merry feeling warmed her up. She laughed so much, tears came to her eyes and she had to dab at them. With the cat on her heels, she went back to her room.

It was impossible to sleep. This was happening more and more often. A shower? Why not . . . The bathroom was small but well designed. Above the shower, a large skylight revealed a starry night. The water gently flowed along Clarissa's tired body. Dr. Dewinter had explained that the bathroom was equipped with specific captors capable of monitoring her health, and that she didn't have to do anything particular, apart from using a slim set of scales every morning, placing her palm daily on a square inlay situated near the washbasin, and glancing morning and night into a part of the mirror marked with a luminous speck. Her weight, her blood pressure, and her overall well-being were, consequently, recorded. She imagined the data was stocked somewhere, diligently inspected by

Dr. Dewinter and her team. Had she been right to entrust them with intimate matters like her heath and to allow them such a hold? She hadn't had the choice, she recalled. She had signed the C.A.S.A. contract blindly. A mistake? She had no idea. All she knew is that she felt free at last. Recently, she had looked up the meaning of C.A.S.A. in the file sent to her when she moved in. *Center for Adaptive Synergy for Artists.* Which meant everything and nothing.

She soaped herself unhurriedly, eyes glued to the dark blue patch of sky above her head. Now what? Get the divorce procedure moving. Think of positive things. There were many of them! Jordan. Andy. Her treasures. Writing her novel, in two languages simultaneously. Working again with the keen young screenwriters she wrote her TV series with. Listening to the music she loved, especially Chopin. Watching her favorite movies, finding new ones to see. Spending time with her dad. How lucky she was to have such a witty and sparkling father at nearly a hundred. Her friends also had aging parents, but hers was by far the one in the finest shape. Rereading Woolf, Gary, and all those other writers she still had to discover. Making the most of the sun pouring into her studio. Not letting herself get down. Banishing François from her mind.

Back in her room, she lay on her bed. Chablis snuggled up against her back, purring. Thanks to him, she felt less alone. Sleep still eluded her. She put on her glasses and looked at the ceiling.

"Mrs. Dalloway, show me my emails, please."

"Right away, Clarissa. Do you wish to turn off night mode?"

"No, Mrs. Dalloway. I haven't been able to sleep yet. And don't give me the time, please."

"Of course. Here's a list of your new incoming email."

Clarissa glanced though the list on the ceiling. Among the new emails was one from her dad and one from Mia White, the student she had not yet responded to.

"Show me my father's email, Mrs. Dalloway."

"Straight away, Clarissa."

My darling C . . . ,

I was so happy to chat with you the other day. You look so lovely your flat looks wonderful I must say even to my blind old eyes. What a view and such light. Perfectly understand you don't want to talk about François. You know how I feel about him. Never liked him. Never. But if you do want to talk I'm here. Remember your old dad can still help. You know I always preferred Toby. I don't want to go back to such a painful subject but I still feel sad you and Toby divorced. I know the death of the child was too awful too hideous. My heart still bleeds my darling even if it was all those years ago. There's never a day that goes by without me thinking about the child. Darling I have good news. I've been talking to Arthur and I think I've made him understand how unfair Serena's will was. He listened you know. He didn't hang up or anything. He listened. He's going to convince his monstrous daughters to give something over to Jordan. Jewels I think. No idea if they're worth anything. He says he will do it. Don't mention it if ever he calls. I'm going to fight this all the way my darling. I'm so angry at the old goat. How selfish she was. Do write to me soon. Love from your old dad.

Her father had always moved her, with his unfailing affection, his warmth. She missed him. Should she tell him about François? No, he would be outraged, dismayed. He was too old to hear what she had to say. He would never get over it.

"Do you wish to answer your father now, Clarissa?"

"No, later. Please show me Mia White's email."

"Here it is."

"Thank you, Mrs. Dalloway."

Dear Clarissa Katsef,

I thought I'd give this one more chance. I hope I'm not disturbing you. I wrote to you not long ago. I've been in Paris for a couple of weeks now for my new term. I'm staying in an attic room near the rue du Bac. Every time I pass in front of number 108 (which is several times a day), I think of Romain Gary and of you. My mum comes from Nantes, so I'm not too familiar with Paris, really. It's lovely to be here, though. It's so very different from the UEA campus! I hear you gave a lecture at my university once. But that was before I got here.

I guess parts of Paris have changed drastically since the attack. I wonder what you make of the new neighborhood? And I presume you've heard about the Tower hologram? Do you think it's a good idea?

If ever you have time to meet me, I would be delighted. I'm sure you're very busy and you don't have a moment to yourself. I don't know that many people here yet. I've yet to make friends. I'm sometimes a bit shy, the type to stay at home with a good book! I wonder if you are writing a new novel? It's been a while since you published one. I know you wrote several TV shows in the past years, and I've seen most of them. But a novel, in my view, has so much more resonance than a TV show.

I've been writing some stuff of my own since I've been here. Not that I'd ever bother you with that. You probably get so many people asking you to look at their work.

Thank you for reading this,

Sincerely,
Mia White

Clarissa pictured a dumpy, lonely, nail-biting teenager. Should she meet her? She was barely older than Andy! She asked Mrs. Dalloway to search the name Mia White. Several social media profiles popped up. She asked Mrs. Dalloway to narrow them down to profiles that were less than twenty years old, connected to the University of East Anglia. There was one profile that matched perfectly. That person liked Virginia Woolf, Romain Gary, Émile Zola, Guy de Maupassant, Françoise Sagan, Philip Roth, Donna Tartt, and Clarissa Katsef. Well, well. Her last posts were all of Paris. The Luxembourg Gardens, Sacré-Coeur, the Louvre, and a newly resurrected Notre-Dame, long-sufferingly restored after the tragic fire.

"Show me her face, please, Mrs. Dalloway."

Mia White was stunning. She had long chestnut hair, bright blue eyes, a charming smile, lovely teeth. But her appealing physique wasn't all; a wholesome sweetness stemmed from her, making her all the more endearing. There she was on a beach, with a group of friends, wearing a bikini. Her body glowed with healthy perfection. Another photo showed her curled up on a sofa with a book and a mug, wearing oversize reading glasses. Clarissa found herself fascinated by the number of images that fitted together like a puzzle. Mia and, presumably, her parents in a restaurant, gathered around a birthday cake. Mia as a child, dressed in a fairy costume. Mia in a bookstore. Mia and a boyfriend named David in New York. Mia and another boyfriend (nameless) in Barce-

Iona. Mia making a face with a girlfriend in a nightclub. Mia without makeup. Just as pretty. Mia with a lot of makeup. A cover girl. Clarissa couldn't help feeling flattered that this lively, striking young girl wanted to meet her. Perhaps she'd make a good friend for Andy? Andy was always complaining about her friends; they were either too fickle or too superficial. But maybe a four-year gap, at that age, made too much of a difference?

Perhaps, Clarissa reflected, it was at last time for her to banish the solitary mood tailing her since she'd moved here. She'd cut off ties with her friends, not responding to their calls, texts, or emails. She was well aware she couldn't go on like this. Hiding, turning into a hermit was not going to help. She had to face things at some point. She had to get on with her life. She had always done that. She had never been afraid to do that. Her new frailty encumbered her, and this exasperated her.

Every morning, when she looked at her phone, there were texts from François sent during the night. They were all the same — begging for her forgiveness. She had thought of blocking his number. She never had, although she was itching to. She was still waiting to figure out how to talk to him, how to express her disgust, her resentment. That moment hadn't come. Would it ever? she wondered. Was it important to voice her anger? The marriage was over. The trust was broken. So what was the point of talking to him? A part of her wanted to understand what had driven him to this, even if that meant delving into the darkest nooks of François's secrets. Was she ready to hear these secrets? Not for the moment. And would she ever be? She had spent over twenty years with this man. Twenty years! François Antoine, her husband, was a stranger. A stranger she no longer wanted to have anything to do with. Was it possible to erase a person from your life? she wondered. Nothing linked them to each other, apart from the apartment near the Luxembourg Gardens, half of which belonged to her. They had not had children together. And she was very glad, today, that they hadn't. There had been ups and downs, like for many couples. When François discovered he had cancer, she had helped him fight it and recover. She had been there for him. He had encouraged her to write, had helped her find a publisher for her first novel. Now that she had pulled away, she could pick out all the shady areas of their marriage, the snags, the traps, as if she had been poring over one of her beloved maps, spotting marshes, precipices, and ravines. It was all there. How could she have been so blind? How could she not have seen this coming?

"Clarissa, would you like to answer Mia White now?"

"Yes! However, I'm not going to dictate it to you, Mrs. Dalloway. I'm going to go sit in front of my computer, the good old-fashioned way, and write it myself!"

"Very well, Clarissa."

Dear Mia White,

Please forgive me for not answering you sooner. I was in the middle of a move. Thank you for your emails. Welcome to Paris! You asked what I thought of the new district. In my opinion, it's rather a success. The ruins caused by the attack were left there for years, as you know, as if no one had any idea what to do with the ghastly mess. It was abominable. An entire Parisian neighborhood, wiped out. This new area is white, modern, with lots of greenery. It's quite well done. As for the Tower, I'm eager to see the hologram this week. I read the reconstruction work is going to take longer than they planned, and be more complicated, too. I think it's a pretty good idea to re-create what the Tower looked like at nighttime. My granddaughter, nearly fifteen, is impatiently waiting for the moment the hologram goes up. She is too young to remember the real Tower.

I'd be very happy to meet you! I have time right now. I'm not totally invested in the new book yet. If you wish, we could meet in front of 108, rue du Bac, our pal Gary's place. (Every time I walk past there, I see him raising his eyes to the sky to make them look even bluer, the way his mother asked him to.) We could then walk to the Seine and chat for an hour or so. What do you say to that?

All best,
Clarissa Katsef

The next morning, there was an ecstatic email from Mia White. She suggested meeting in two days' time, at four, in front of Romain Gary's last home.

Andy was at last coming to spend her first night in her grandmother's flat. She was overexcited. She was going to sleep on the sofa in Clarissa's small office, but Clarissa knew perfectly well Andy would end up in the big bed with her and Chablis. Not that she minded. She had to admit she missed the warmth of François's sleeping body. They had always shared the same bed, even when he had been ill. She wondered: Was she finding it difficult to sleep because she was alone?

Mrs. Dalloway's voice rang out melodiously.

"Clarissa, your granddaughter, Adriana, is in the lobby. Do you confirm access?"

The screen near the front door showed Andy's face. Andy stuck out her tongue and squinted.

"Yes, Mrs. Dalloway. Please let Adriana up."

Clarissa had prepared Andy's favorite meal: tomato soup, baked potatoes with ham, cheese, and cream, chocolate cake. She remembered cooking it for Andy when she was three years old. When there were just the two of them, Andy wouldn't have anything else. The doorbell chimed. Clarissa opened up and Andy came flying into her arms. Oh, how she loved this kid. They hugged as if they hadn't seen each other for years.

"Why can't I be as tall as you?" whined Andy.

"Because you haven't stopped growing, missy. Give it time."

"Mummy says that when you were fourteen, you were already a giant."

"Your mum wasn't around when I was fourteen!"

"Well, she saw old photos of you. She says you were taller than your brother."

"I still am. He hates that."

Andy pranced around the living room, waving her hands in the air.

"I'm so happy! I can smell the soup and the cake!"

The startled cat dashed under the sofa. Andy bent over to pull him out gently, settling him on her knees. He calmed down as she patted him.

"Is he getting used to it here, Mums?"

Clarissa picked up Andy's backpack, jacket, and sneakers and put them in her office. She told Andy the cat seemed happier, that she wasn't worried about him. But she was. She kept this to herself. She couldn't work out if he was the strangest cat ever, or if there was truly something about this apartment that unsettled him. She often found him staring up at the ceiling, transfixed. And yet there was nothing to be seen. At other times, he appeared petrified, ears back, his body shuddering. She was never able to pick out what could have alarmed him to such an extent. Did the cat see things that humans did not? Was there a ghost here? She did not believe in ghosts. She believed in what walls remembered, how places harbored past emotions, past memories. But these walls were new, brand-new. She was the first person to ever live here. Could the cat be afraid of what had happened on these premises long ago? Was his behavior to do with the attack? Was he picking up suffering and pain from the scarred land the residence was built on? Was the cat crazy? Or else, there really was something here. Someone. Something. She had felt it, too. She had picked out the tiny cameras in each room, like little black eyes, always following her around. It made her as uneasy as the cat. Maybe that was why she hadn't been sleeping well, nothing to do with being alone. Who was watching her? What for? What could she do about it? Whom could she complain to?

"Mums!" called Andy. "Can I wash my hair in your fabulous shower?"

Clarissa found Andy in the bathroom.

"That Mrs. Dalloway of yours. She won't do anything for me. She won't even answer."

Clarissa smiled.

"She only responds to me. She's been programmed to react to my voice and nobody else's."

"Well, what if something happens to you and I need help?"

"I guess you use your phone."

Andy shrugged.

"I'll bear that in mind," she said grimly. She came to stand next to her grandmother, pasting her cheek to Clarissa's.

"Why didn't I get eyes like yours? They're so blue, it's unfair."

"Yours are lovely."

"Green, like Mummy's. Yours are really something. You don't even need makeup, with those."

Then reaching up to touch Clarissa's braid, she asked, "What's your real hair color, Mums?"

"When I was your age, it was auburn. Then I dyed it redder when I was in my forties. But now it would be all white."

"Don't you want to try it all white?"

"Nope. I don't mind being an old lady, but there is no way I'm going to have white hair. I'm sticking to being a redhead."

"There is nothing old ladyish about you, Mums. Even if you happen to be my granny."

"Hop into that shower, missy. Otherwise, we'll miss the hologram event. Wouldn't want that, would we?"

Tonight was the worldwide event everyone was waiting for, the lighting up of the hologram representing the Tower. At ten o'clock sharp, when night had fully fallen, all eyes would be riveted to the spot the Tower once stood upon. Clarissa was lucky to be able to see the whole thing directly from her window, and not on television. The hologram was to be projected barely three hundred meters away from the residence. The president was going to speak, as well as the mayor of Paris. While Andy showered, Clarissa laid the table in the kitchen.

"Mrs. Dalloway, turn on the television. Find the hologram Tower event, please."

"Coming up, Clarissa."

The built-in screen lit up part of the kitchen wall.

"Which channel do you prefer, Clarissa? They're all broadcasting the event."

"You choose, Mrs. Dalloway."

Clarissa was aware she couldn't avoid the president's speech. She was going to have to look at the president's face, listen to her voice; she was going to have to endure all of it. Like most people she knew, Clarissa had not voted for her. That woman had come to power again after having been designated a first term. With the slow crumbling of Europe, a drawn-out, inexorable calamity, and above all the unparalleled violence of the attack targeting Paris, already a decade ago, there had been nothing to prevent the indomitable young woman with the low voice from being elected. During the last presidential elections, Clarissa had prayed with all her might that she would not be reappointed. But she had been, by far. When the second victory was announced, Clarissa thought for a time she might return to live in London, as she had dual nationality. But the disturbances left in the wake of Brexit were still not smoothed over, and the subsequent attack against London, so soon after the Paris one, had also left indelible scars. She had decided to remain in Paris, alongside her daughter, her granddaughter. And her husband.

Her husband. While she stirred the soup, she thought back to the long texts received this morning from François. He said she was on his mind all the time, every day. He missed her so much. They had to find a way to work this out, to talk it over. They couldn't just end it all like this. It was impossible. Every morning, he opened her closet and buried his face in all the clothes she'd left behind. He breathed in her perfume. He cried. Yes, he had done wrong, yes, he had acted so badly, but their marriage couldn't be over. She had to give him another chance; she had to let him explain, excuse himself. He was begging her. He was down on his knees. He couldn't sleep. He couldn't stand it anymore. Jordan wouldn't talk to him. He had tried to reach her. She didn't pick up. What did Jordan know? Did she know everything? He was full of shame. He missed Andy, too. He had seen that kid grow up.

Clarissa had erased each message, like all the others received from him. She didn't care one bit that he missed Andy. She didn't care at all that he was miserable. This morning, there had also been a message from Toby. She was often in contact with her first husband. He asked her how she was; he had heard from Jordan that she had moved. He must have known from their daughter that she had left François. She'd get back to him tomorrow.

Jordan's face showed up on Clarissa's phone. Clarissa picked up.

"Guess what, Mums? I got the most unexpected email from Mimsy and Pimsy." Jordan's nicknames for her British cousins. "They're sending me jewels. Jewels! A brooch. Stuff that was locked in Serena's safe for the past century. Something tells me Grandpa has been putting pressure on Arthur."

"How generous of Mimsy and Pimsy," said Clarissa ironically.

"So generous, isn't it? They no doubt exhumed something prehistoric and decided it was for me. Who wears brooches nowadays?"

"At least you'll have something from Aunt Serena, darling."

Andy walked in, wrapped up in Clarissa's bathrobe, her hair dripping.

"Hi, Mom!" she chanted, blowing a kiss.

"Have a nice evening, you two," said Jordan. "I'll call tomorrow."

"Are you going to watch the hologram event?" asked Clarissa, tasting the soup.

"That looks rather good, Mums! Not sure if I'll watch the telly. I'll see what Ivan wants to do. Bye, my darlings."

Jordan had lost many friends in the attack. Clarissa said good-bye to her daughter, and then asked Andy to go dry her hair. The president's face appeared on the screen.

"Ugh," said Andy. "Let's mute her. I'll ask Mrs. Dalloway to do it. Mrs. Dalloway! Mute the awful president!"

Nothing happened. Andy stamped her foot.

"Mrs. Dalloway, why are you ignoring me?"

"Adriana, don't be silly. She can't hear

you. She can only hear me."

Clarissa pressed on the remote control. The president's voice died out.

"That's better," said Clarissa. "Now, go dry your hair, missy. Dinner will be ready in five minutes."

Later, as she was savoring a glass of wine, she observed Andy tuck into her dinner. She wondered what kind of woman Andy would turn out to be. There was such promise in her — her sense of humor, vitality, inquisitiveness. How lucky she was to have given birth to an affectionate daughter, whom she loved, and who loved her in return; and then, the joy of watching this lively and talkative adolescent grow up, just as demonstrative as Jordan was toward her. Clarissa's own mother had been aloof and unemotional. She had not been close to her. Yet she had never harbored animosity toward her mother. When she thought about her, it was with tenderness. At the end of her life, Solange was lost in amnesia. Her illness turned her into a bland, pleasant person. Clarissa went to see her at the hospital, and talked to a nice lady who had no inkling who she was. She died in her early seventies. Her passing seemed so long ago. And to think her father was still around, in the pink of health. In two years, he would turn one hundred. He had told his family that he wanted to throw a costume party where everyone would dance all night long. He was quite a dancer, her dad. He'd taught her how to do the bossa nova, the cha-cha, the tango. But he loved to waltz above all. When she felt glum, he'd play the "Blue Danube," and a grin would come creeping back to her face. She could see him in her mind's eye, at those family gatherings where he'd whirl her around and around, faster and faster, telling her to keep her chin up, her shoulders down, and to smile. Yes, to smile.

"What are you thinking about, Mums?"

"About Grandpa dancing the waltz."

"Are you going to see him soon? He told me how much he misses you."

"Yes, I must go. I promised."

Andy paused.

"You were with him, in London, the day of the attack, right?"

"Yes, I had gone to spend a couple of days with him. I used to get on with Arthur, at that point, and I was staying over with them."

Adriana was watching old photos of the Tower on TV. The mayor of Paris had given a short, poignant speech.

"I do hope they are not going to show the

attack again," muttered Clarissa. "We've had an overdose of that."

She knew her granddaughter would have only foggy recollections of the events, if that. She was only a small child at the time. But still, she asked her, "And what about you, miss? What do you remember?"

"I remember being scared like never before. I remember it was nighttime, and my parents were panic-stricken. The expression on their faces made me cry."

As if to summon up courage, Clarissa had a sip of wine. She told Andy that Arthur had come to wake her up in the middle of the night. She had been sleeping at his place, on the top floor of his home in London Fields. She couldn't make out what her brother was saying. He had difficulty speaking and seemed dumbfounded. His face had gone ashen. She followed him downstairs, stood in front of the television. His wife, Jane, was standing there, too, rooted to the spot. Their two daughters had gone on holiday, somewhere in Spain. It was the middle of July, hot, clammy weather. The journalists' voices seemed high-pitched and hysterical. From a wobbly image filmed with a mobile, Clarissa made out a gaping black crater encircled by a crest of orange flames, beneath billows of thick gray smoke;

111

she heard shrieking sirens, clamors, yells. Paris was written in a large, lurid font at the bottom of the screen. Paris, where? It was so confusing, hard to understand. She couldn't breathe properly; she could only think of Jordan, Ivan, the child. She thought of François.

Tripping, she rushed upstairs to get her phone. No one had called her. She pressed on Jordan's icon. The call went straight to voice mail. The same for François and Ivan. When she got back to the living room, she could not believe what she was seeing on the TV. Her legs collapsed; she had to sit down. Her sister-in-law was whimpering, while Arthur screamed, aghast. She would never forget what she now saw being played over and over again, the slow collapse of the Eiffel Tower, subsiding into the night like a mortally wounded beast, a colossal sentry still shimmering with thousands of lights, crashing down amid the excruciating screech of twisted steel. She had asked Arthur and Jane what had happened. How was this possible? Dazed, they hadn't answered. Arthur clicked from channel to channel, hypnotized by the same footage shown yet again, the Tower bending over in that almost grotesque fashion, barely believable, like in a video game or a movie. Clarissa had gone to the kitchen; she'd had a long drink of water, and then she'd turned the radio on. She'd had enough of the uninterrupted contest of pictures displayed on each network; she needed to understand. Again, she tried calling Jordan, Ivan, François. Voice mail. She was terrified. She felt weak. She focused all her attention on the calm voice on the BBC.

She told Andy that she knew then she'd remember that moment for the rest of her life: the vision of her naked feet on the tiles, the brutal heat of that summer night, her hands trembling. The calm voice had gone on to list the facts. Clarissa wondered how could it remain so serene as it proceeded to utter horror after horror. The events in Paris were cataclysmic, said the newscaster very clearly. Clarissa remembered that word: *cataclysmic.* She felt fear pervade her, shoot through her veins like a toxic drug. There was only one name on her mind, her daughter's. She kept repeating it: Jordan. Jordan. Jordan. Nothing could happen to Jordan. Nothing could happen to her daughter.

The calm voice persisted, stirring her. At eleven o'clock French time, in Paris, while the Tower was still shimmering, as it always did upon the hour for five minutes, a large blast occurred at the top of the south pillar, on the level of the Tower's first floor. The origin of the detonation was still not clear, but according to terrorism specialists, it was possibly drones, rigged with explosive devices, driven into the south pillar at a precise spot. No one had noticed the drones making their way through the darkness.

It had taken less than seven minutes for the Tower to fall, time enough for thousands of cameras and smartphones to capture the unbelievable pictures. The Tower toppled over toward the south, flat onto the recent Olympic site built especially for the games, jam-packed with pedestrians on a warm summer evening. But that wasn't all. Within the forty-five minutes of pandemonium that ensued, the voice went on, while firefighters and police had barely gotten under way to rescue the people trapped within the Tower and underneath it, and while many casualties were already feared, a second deadly attack was perpetrated on the same area by more drones. Making the most of the darkness, the small aircrafts dropped three powerful bombs on the sector.

As she stood listening, shaking, horrified, Clarissa hadn't at first noticed her phone was vibrating in her hand. It was Toby. He was calling from his home in the Basque country. He had just seen the ghastly news.

He was overjoyed to hear she wasn't in Paris. But he hadn't heard from either Jordan or Ivan. Had she? With dread, Clarissa said she hadn't heard. She hadn't been able to get through. She hadn't been able to get hold of François, either. Toby did his best to reassure her. He kept reminding her that Jordan and Ivan lived near the Bastille, on the east side of Paris. And as for François, he was no doubt safe as well, in their flat near the Luxembourg Gardens. Clarissa listened, nodded, but dread gnawed at her. Ivan had wanted to stay in Paris for the Olympics. Perhaps they had gone to one of the events this past evening, like many Parisians. She couldn't bear to think about it. She felt physically ill. After saying goodbye to Toby, she feverishly perused Jordan's social media posts, trying to check the last time her daughter had been online. She couldn't face going back into the living room, watching the television until morning. It was already getting on to two o'clock. Three o'clock in Paris. She paced up and down the kitchen, cradling the phone to her. She tried calling, again. Again. She kept thinking, I've lost one child in my life. I cannot, I will not, lose another. I will not lose Jordan.

All those years later, she did not repeat

those words to Adriana. She had never mentioned her son to her granddaughter. She went on with her memories of that night, telling Andy how it had taken ages to get hold of Jordan and Ivan. The wait was agonizing. The sun came up on another scorching day. It had been impossible to get through to Paris. Telecommunications were down. A part of the city had been irremediably destroyed. She had taken a shower, gone out to buy some bread. People in the streets were stunned, riveted to their phones. London had gone strangely quiet, and it felt like a lull before a storm. François had managed to call from a landline. She felt relief when she heard his voice, but as she had not yet heard from her daughter, the distress was still there. She wanted to leave now, rush to take a train, a plane. She became frantic. A sort of panic came over her. Her brother told her to wait. There was nothing else she could do. She refused to watch TV. She stuck to the radio, sat in the kitchen with a glass of water. The voices described utter chaos. Thousands of people had been killed. Who had perpetrated this? How had it been done? No one knew for sure. At last, just as she had given up hope, Toby called, much later, with the good news. Jordan and Ivan were safe, with Andy, at home. She had broken down and wept.

It had taken a few days for her to be able to get back to Paris. The capital had been on lockdown. She finally returned on a jam-packed train. The city was coated with powdery black dust. Intensified by broiling heat, the acrid, stuffy atmosphere was stifling. Clarissa told Andy that the Olympic Games had been canceled. All the athletes had been told to go home. In her neighbor-hood, near the Luxembourg Gardens, noth-ing had changed, on the surface. But the at-tack could be glimpsed in people's gazes, expressions, and stances. Tourists had fled; they wouldn't return for a long while. She hadn't wished to see the crater left by the bombings; it was splashed over every screen. There was no way to escape it. But her past profession as a property surveyor caught up with her, and the yearning to apprehend the lay of the land, the configuration of places, egged her on. She wanted to see it; she wanted to understand. She waited for as long as possible. A few months went by. She was aware that such widespread damage couldn't be dealt with speedily.

She had gone there on a rainy day, at the end of autumn. High metallic fences hemmed in the entire area. She drew closer, near the ruins of the École Militaire, and had a look. It took her breath away. The damp stench of muck and plaster wafted up toward her. An enormous chasm gaped open below her, enfolded by demolished edifices. Crumbling walls still bore traces of wallpaper, unsteady doors absurdly hanging on hinges, flights of stairs spiraling into nothingness. The immensity of the urban wasteland overwhelmed her. The large boulevards dotted with linden and chestnut trees that she so clearly recalled were now reduced to mountains of rubble lining a bottomless pit. In the distance, the tortured vestiges of the Tower seem to twist with agony toward the drizzling sky.

"Mums, look!" cried Andy. "The hologram! We mustn't miss it!"

The moment had arrived. They both dashed to the living room, opening the main window. They leaned out as far as they could over the railing, the evening air fresh on their faces. High up above, a brilliant light juddered, a lone star glowing in the dark blue sky. The star seemed to dance, flickering like a fairy or a butterfly, and as they watched, a contour slowly flourished below it, drawing a familiar, beloved silhouette all the way to the ground in bold iridescent strokes. The Tower's outline materialized through the darkness, like a divine apparition, as nearby crowds applauded and cheered. Hundreds of people were watching from their windows, as well. It was as if the sparkling Tower had always been there, the powerful beacon shooting from its crown like that of a lighthouse, exactly like it used to. Andy let out a cry of surprise.

"It looks so real!" she said, elated.

Clarissa had to admit that, yes, it did. She reached out to hold her granddaughter tight. Andy was too young to remember the terror in the aftermath of the attack. Later, there was a message from Jordan to her mother. She had finally decided to watch the event; it had given her a sort of hope, the sense of a page being turned at last. Andy asked if she could sleep in the big bed with Clarissa. She didn't want to be alone in the little office. Clarissa had teased her.

"You look worried about something, missy."

"No, I'm just tired."

They had gone to bed before midnight, after a cup of hot chocolate for Andy. It was strangely reassuring to hear someone breathe and move next to her. Clarissa, as always, found it difficult to drop off. She remembered what Jordan had said when her application to the C.A.S.A. residence had been accepted. Had it been a good idea to

119

live in a place where so much suffering had occurred? She suddenly realized she had moved into a dwelling she had never seen beforehand. She had been shown a couple of photos, and that was it. How could she have taken that risk? The irony was that, for so long, her job had been to assess and evaluate apartments for future occupants. She wasn't going to have any regrets. Ever.

"Are you awake, Mums?"

Andy's voice whispered through the dark.

"Yes, my angel. Why aren't you asleep?"

"Too much stuff on my mind. Sometimes thinking stops me from sleeping."

"Story of my life."

"What do you think about?"

"I try not to. I empty my head; I visualize an immense lake, a thick forest."

"I would have loved to have known the world the way it was before. The way it was when you were young. A world with bees, birds, flowers. A world we hardly see nowadays."

"I understand."

"Today's world is so ugly."

"Andy, you sound like a glum old lady."

"I don't care, Mums. Check it out! I don't need to spell it out for you. Look at our situation! Look at where we're heading! Do you think it makes anyone happy? Look at what's happening to the planet. Look what we did to it. Look what's left of the forests. Can you believe I only saw snow once in my life? Heat waves, floods, hurricanes, pollution. And that awful president! People like her have power, all over the world. Look what happened to the Tower, to Venice, to London, to Rome. What are we going to do? Do you see a way out? I don't! I see sod all."

"You need to resist, Andy. Every day."

"Oh yeah? And how?"

"Not thinking like them. Fighting back. Never giving up."

"You say that because you're mature. You know all the stuff I don't. And when you were my age, did you have any idea of what you wanted to do? I have no inkling. And that scares me. Mummy knew."

"Well, I didn't, either. Not a clue."

"You didn't know you wanted to be a writer?"

"No, not at all."

"What were you like at fourteen, Mums?"

In the dimness, Clarissa couldn't help smiling. She felt her granddaughter's silky hair against her cheek. Reminiscing . . . It was like skimming through a photo album, pausing over a page. Slowly letting emotions flow back. There she was, freckled, lanky, and awkward, the braces on her teeth making her miserable. She told Andy she used to be quite a merry youngster, making her friends whoop. She was a prankster on the phone, mimicking people behind their backs, pulling awful faces.

"Hey, it sounds like you were hilarious! And did you fall in love a lot?"

"I had crushes on guys who never looked at me. And those who made passes at me did not interest me in the least."

"Did you hear that, Mums?"

"Hear what?"

"A weird sound. Like something clicking."

Silence.

"I can't hear a thing. Are you sure?"

"Positive."

Clarissa turned on the bedside lamp.

"I'll go check the kitchen and living room. Maybe it's the cat."

"Look, the cat is fast asleep."

Andy slunk under the sheets.

"I'm scared, Mums."

She looked like a small child, snug against the pillows.

Clarissa padded to the kitchen. Everything was peaceful. She walked around the living room. Nothing seemed out of place.

"Mrs. Dalloway?"

"Yes, Clarissa?"

"Have you detected a break-in or anything unusual?"

"No, Clarissa, I've detected nothing of the sort. All is well. Do you wish to report anything else?"

"No, Mrs. Dalloway."

"Fine, Clarissa."

Back in the bedroom, Clarissa comforted her granddaughter.

"I'm not making all this up, Mums, I promise."

"I believe you, missy. But I saw nothing odd."

Andy nestled close.

"You know, it's weird. I like your place. It's pretty and modern, with an amazing view. But . . ."

"But what, Andy?"

"I know you're going to think I'm crazy, Mums. Oh well. I'll tell you anyway. And maybe this is why the cat is scared, too. Ever since I got here, I've felt like we're being watched. All the time."

After the shock came anger. I was livid. I nearly pressed on the buzzer bearing our name, shaking with rage, awful words coming to my lips. What a bastard.

My husband had another life. A life I knew nothing about. How long had this been going on? How was it that I had seen nothing, known nothing? Had he been that cautious? Or me that stupid?

I stepped back from the building, still trembling. I wasn't going to wait for him to come back out. I had all the proof I needed. It was all there in front of me.

But curiosity got the better of me. Was this just a place he took women to? Or was there only one woman in particular? A woman he met every week, spoke to every day, slept with?

A woman my husband loved?

I wanted more than anything to know who she was.

Should I have left all this alone? Should I have walked away, never done anything about it, never mentioned it? Should I have done what I did?

I thought about it carefully on my way home. I was going to find out who she was and how long this had been going on.

And then I would decide what to do.

When my husband returned that evening, he was his usual self, amusing and caring. He helped me prepare dinner, chose our wine.

While we ate, I looked around at our apartment. I thought of everything we'd built together over the years, and I felt like crying. It was hard not letting my emotions show. I burned to scream at him, to throw things at him. But I held back.

Who was she? What was her name? How old was she? What did she look like? Did he love her? Where did they meet? How did it start?

At one point in the evening, I asked him if I could use his phone to call Jordan, as I couldn't find mine. He said of course, and he opened it for me. He acted like he had nothing to hide.

I had time to check it. There was nothing suspicious on his phone. No photos, no texts. He was being very careful.

There must be another phone, then, I thought. A phone he hid and used to communicate with her.

Two phones, two apartments, two women.

Such a banal situation, I thought. Such a massive cliché.

How wrong I was.

4
TONGUE

I feel certain I am going mad again.
VIRGINIA WOOLF, March 28, 1941

Perhaps the answer lies in the title of my autobiographical novel, *The Night Will Be Calm.*
ROMAIN GARY, December 2, 1980

When she awoke, it was still early. She had a quick shower, noiselessly; Adriana was still asleep, with the cat nestled against her. She decided to buy croissants, Andy's favorite. It would take only ten minutes or so. As she got dressed, she thought back to the other nocturnal conversation she'd had with her granddaughter, just after the clicking noise incident.

"Mums, why are you so angry with François?"

Clarissa had known this was going to come up at one point. Andy was too astute not to guess at what was going on. Clarissa'd had to think carefully about what she was going to say. She realized she had not spoken to anyone about François, about what François had done. She wasn't ready yet, and there were things a fourteen-year-old could not understand. But she felt she had to give some element of truth to her granddaughter. She couldn't stay wrapped up in silence forever.

She had said, "He disappointed me."

"Can you explain why?"

Clarissa had stroked Andy's hair in the dark. Where could she begin? When had it started? *Disappointment* wasn't the right word. It sounded too meek, too nice. What she felt was much more powerful and deep-rooted.

"He hurt me badly."

Andy had reached up to caress her grand-mother's cheek.

"I hate him for that, Mums. I really hate him. For whatever he did. And I'm not going to ask what it is. I don't think you'll tell me anyway."

"No, I won't. I can't."

"Do you think you'll ever patch it up?"

"No, I don't think so."

She thought of how she had felt when she stepped into the small apartment. She could still smell the perfume. It made her want to retch.

"You're that angry."

"Yes."

"But you've been together for so long!"

"I know. But at this point in my life, I want to move on without him."

"I understand, Mums. I won't mention him again. I'm here if you ever need to talk. I know you think I'm too much of a kid to understand all the adult stuff. But I know how to listen. You taught me how to do that." Her granddaughter's love safeguarded her, toning down her unhappiness. She had managed to drop off, listening to Andy's soft breathing at her side. This morning, she felt less vulnerable.

Clarissa never took the elevator. She enjoyed tearing down the stairs as fast as she could. It took longer climbing the eight flights back up, but it was part of a grueling routine she stuck to. She was fond of stating that all those steps were her way of staying fit. As she rushed past the fourth floor, a door opened, and she found herself facing a brunette in her forties who was wearing sports gear and waving at her. She slowed down, saying hello in return. Her new neighbor's name was Adelka. She was a painter. This was the first time Clarissa had spoken to another artist from the residence. She had occasionally crossed paths with some of them, but it hadn't gone further than an exchange of nods and smiles.

Adelka went down the stairs with her. She was off to run alongside the Seine. Clarissa had a closer look, taking in her brown eyes, thick black hair, tanned skin. This young woman had a charming air about her. Her voice was musical, her smile attractive.

"What do you think of the residence?" she asked her neighbor suddenly.

They were outside at present. Adelka said she had never lived in a place like this. It was impressive. She had been overjoyed to hear her application had been accepted. Many artists had been turned down.

"And what about you? Are you enjoying it, as well?"

Clarissa didn't hesitate long.

"I'm not sure, to tell the truth."

They were walking toward the river, on the old boundaries of the Champ-de-Mars. Contemporary structures, white and re-splendent, now took up the space. The artificial trees were pleasantly effective. A couple of electric cars zoomed silently by. It was a calm, enjoyable spot.

"What do you mean?" Adelka asked. "I know you're up on the top floor. It must be quite something."

"Yes, the view is stunning. It's another matter. I feel like someone is watching me all the time."

The coffee-colored eyes narrowed in on her.

"I get it. But to me, that level of surveillance makes me feel safe. I wasn't safe before. I had a violent husband. He gave me a tough time. He smashed up my art material, when it wasn't my face. I know he'll never be able to set foot in the residence. The bastard is blacklisted!"

She burst out laughing. Clarissa couldn't help joining in.

"I have a persona non grata husband, as well."

"Join the club! And what did yours do to get banished from the residence and from your life?"

"He wasn't the brutal type, like your ex. . . . But . . ."

"You don't have to tell me, you know."

It felt wonderful to talk at last, to open up the dams. This woman knew nothing about her, about her life. Clarissa found it easier to unburden herself to this smiling stranger who was her daughter's age than with her long-standing friends, the ones she hadn't wished to see since the breakup.

"I found out in the most shocking way that he was cheating on me."

Adelka made a face.

"Ouch. Not fun. And what did you do?"

"I left him. On the spot."

"And you ended up here, right?"

"That's right."

"You've been married for a long time?"

Adelka walked swiftly; she had the muscular legs of a sports-woman. Clarissa adjusted her stride, attempting to follow her without panting too much.

"Long enough for me to understand I didn't want to stick around for a single minute more."

"You look like a woman who knows what she wants."

"So do you."

They both grinned.

Clarissa asked her about her art, what themes she was involved in. Adelka replied she was interested in bodies. Not young and lovely ones, but hidden ones, different ones, bodies that had nothing to do with beauty criteria.

"And what about you? You're a writer, I believe?"

"That's right. I'm taking notes right now. I'm exploring language. Written language and how it comes to authors. How we

131

choose our words. How we pick some words and not others . . ."

"How ambitious! I feel bad that I haven't read your books. I'll make up for it."

"Not a problem at all. And I'm not familiar with your art."

"How about coming down for a drink one of these days?"

"With pleasure."

Clarissa said good-bye, watching Adelka run at a vigorous pace toward the Seine. She went to the bread shop to get Andy's croissants. A couple of customers there were enthusiastically discussing last night's hologram display. She hurried home, then patiently waited in the lobby for her retina to be scanned. The gate slid open with a chime, and a mechanical voice stated, "Welcome back to the residence, Clarissa Katsef."

In the hall, she crossed paths with Ben, the residence's handyman, who made sure each installation ran smoothly. He had already dropped by her place to check on her network power. He was a young man in his thirties with a mop of curly red hair. Engrossed in his device, he asked her if everything was functioning properly at home. She said yes, thanked him, and embarked upon climbing the stairs. He seemed surprised she wasn't using the lift. Once she got to her floor, she realized it was getting more and more difficult to take each step. She felt drained and breathless, and had to wait a few minutes to catch her breath. When she felt better, she pressed her index finger to the glass plate on the door. It swung open with a click.

"Hey, Mums! You were away for ages!"

"I went to get you croissants, and I met my charming fourth-floor neighbor."

Andy appeared to be flustered.

"I need to talk to you!" '

Clarissa put the croissants in the oven.

"Mrs. Dalloway, heat the oven to one hundred and fifty degrees, please."

"Right away, Clarissa."

"Something happened!"

Startled, Clarissa turned to look at Andy, who was hopping up and down.

"What's up, missy?"

Andy lowered her voice.

"Mrs. Dalloway talked to me!"

"What do you mean, she talked to you?"

"I was playing with the cat, and I heard her voice!"

Clarissa froze.

"Her voice? And she said what?"

"She asked me how I was, something like that."

"You're joking."

"No, I'm not, Mums, and don't make that face. I nearly had a fit when I heard her. I was kind of scared. So I just stood there and I shut up and waited for you. But she went on chatting to me."

Clarissa remained silent, thinking. What did this mean? She didn't like it. There was something amiss. She felt she was being double-crossed.

Then she said in a clear, forbidding voice, "Mrs. Dalloway, did you talk to Adriana while I was out?"

A slight pause.

"Hello, Clarissa! I obey only you. Remember? I was programmed to do just that."

Andy opened wide eyes and gaped.

"Are you sure, Mrs. Dalloway?"

"Perfectly sure, Clarissa."

"Perhaps you don't recall, Mrs. Dalloway?"

"Everything I say to you is recorded, Clarissa."

"Thank you, Mrs. Dalloway."

"You're welcome, Clarissa. Happy to help."

"What the . . ." began Andy.

Clarissa silenced her with an uplifted finger. Her mind was racing. Did this mean she had to be careful now? Should she watch out? No talking? "They" would hear her, right? She picked up her phone, about to send a text message to Adriana. She stopped. Not a good idea. Wouldn't "they" be able to read her texts, as well? Probably.

Clarissa wondered if she wasn't overdoing things. Since François, she'd been spotting evil everywhere. Andy was watching her, puzzled. Perhaps she thought her grandmother had gone crazy. Clarissa grabbed a piece of paper and a pen. She scribbled a few sentences, wrote them very small, in case "they" could zoom in to see what she had written.

"What are you doing?" whispered Andy.

Clarissa handed her the paper wordlessly.

Don't talk. Don't use your phone. Write down exactly what Mrs. D. said and where you were standing when it happened.

Andy understood instantly. She nodded in silence, took the paper, wrote something carefully, and gave it back.

I was in the living room. She said several things: "Hello, Adriana, did you sleep well?" I said, "Are you talking to me?" and she said, laughing, "Is there another Andy here? I don't think so." Then she said, "Do you like Mums's new home?" and "You enjoyed last night's show, didn't you?" And then because I was silent, she said, "You're not saying anything,

Andy. Have you lost your tongue?"

Clarissa read it without a word. She tore up the paper and tossed the shreds into the bin. She said blithely, "How about getting dressed, Andy? We could go for a walk and take the croissants with us."

Once they were out of the residence, Andy shot questions at her.

"Why are you looking so worried, Mums? Why is this Mrs. Dalloway thing getting to you?"

Clarissa didn't want to alarm her granddaughter. She briefly explained that during the setup process, she had been told several times that her virtual assistant would respond only to her voice. She suspected they were telling fibs and felt wary. There was something amiss. And being watched persistently was becoming uncomfortable.

"Can't you turn the Dalloway whatsit off? Put it on pause?" asked Andy.

"I don't think so. That won't stop the cameras from filming."

"What if you stuck something onto the cameras?"

"Good point. I hadn't thought of doing that."

They had come to the beginning of the rue de Sèvres.

"I forgot to tell you one last thing, Mums."

136

"Fire away, missy."

"Mrs. Dalloway spoke to me in English at first, and then in French. Isn't that weird?"

"No, not really; she was programmed to speak to me in those two languages."

Andy swiveled around to look at her grandmother.

"You know what bugged me? It was like she knew me. She knew who I was, knew I was bilingual, knew everything about me."

Later, after Jordan had come to pick up her daughter, Clarissa wandered around the flat with a roll of masking tape. She needed to count the number of surveillance cameras, small black globes in each room. There were ten of them. The only place without them was the small room with the toilet. She decided to get going on the one situated near her bed. She took off her shoes, clambered up on a chair, and stuck a piece of tape onto the black sphere. A sense of freedom surged though her. She never would have thought that being filmed constantly could bother her to such an extent. Why hadn't she reacted when she signed the lease? Perhaps it was time to check.

Installed in the living room, Chablis at her feet, she used her device to pore over the document she'd received when she moved in, as well as the rules of procedure.

Artists are required not to cause any noise: no music or parties after 23 hours. Inebriety will be reprimanded and will lead to discharge after three notices. Clarissa could not help but smile. Surely that was a bit over the top! She hadn't noticed when she had seen the document for the first time that the names of the other artists were all listed. There were two apartments per floor, apart from the eighth, hers, where she was alone. On the list of names, she made out two sculptors, four painters, five musicians, one poetess, and two writers (herself included). C.A.S.A. offered a messaging service, allowing members of the residence to communicate with one another through a specific channel. She decided to test it.

"Mrs. Dalloway, send an internal message to Adelka, fourth floor, left."

"Of course, Clarissa, go ahead."

"Dear Adelka, I was very happy to meet you this morning. I hope to see you again soon. Your eighth-floor neighbor, Clarissa Katsef."

"I sent it, Clarissa."

"I'm not sure where this messaging service is shown, Mrs. Dalloway."

"You can read your messages on the communication panel situated in the entrance. However, I can read them to you, as well."

"Fine. Please do that when they arrive."

"I've taken note of that, Clarissa."

Clarissa dived back into the contract. It was clearly stipulated that each flat was furnished with a set of cameras "to meet security requirements." She had signed that document. Counterpedaling would undoubtedly prove to be problematic. While she was giving it a thought, Mrs. Dalloway spoke up.

"Clarissa, you've received an answer from your fourth-floor neighbor, Adelka Miki. Should I read it to you?"

"Yes, thank you."

"Here's the message. 'Hello, Clarissa! I was very pleased to meet you, as well. I've just received *Topography of Intimacy,* which I will now start. You see I've wasted no time! What about a drink, end of day, whenever? See you soon. A.' Do you wish to answer?"

"Just say 'Thanks,' and 'See you soon.' "

"It's done."

"Thank you, Mrs. Dalloway."

"You're welcome, Clarissa."

"By the way, please remind me to answer that letter from the bank. For my meeting."

"But you already did answer the bank, Clarissa. Your meeting is next week."

"Really?"

"Do you wish to see a copy of the message you sent? And check your schedule?"

Clarissa had no memory of answering the bank's letter, nor of adding the event to her schedule.

All of a sudden, an insane craving grabbed at her: the urge to abuse Mrs. Dalloway, shooting her mouth off about everything that was on her chest, all that she could no longer put up with. She yearned to scream at the top of her voice, to stamp her feet, to spill her guts. Mrs. Dalloway didn't exist. She wasn't a human being. How would she react? Whatever could Mrs. Dalloway say in order to calm her down, to reason with her? Perhaps she'd stay quiet, after a while. Perhaps she hadn't been encoded to face a string of insults. Clarissa should give it a go, just to see. While she hesitated, the doorbell rang. Mrs. Dalloway announced, "Clarissa, it's Ben. May he enter?"

"Sure, Mrs. Dalloway."

The door opened, revealing the tall, gangly figure wearing white overalls. Ben asked her if an alarm had gone off in her place. She said she'd heard nothing.

"Okay if I check something out?"

"Go ahead."

She followed him into the bedroom. He went straight to the camera covered by the tape and stood in front of it. Clarissa felt as if she'd been caught red-handed. Should she say her granddaughter had done it? Not a clever idea, considering she had been filmed doing the deed herself. Ben was typing something into his device. He remained silent; so did Clarissa. After a while, he extended a never-ending arm and picked the tape off. He turned toward her.

"You're not supposed to stick anything on these." He sighed. "Otherwise, the alarms go off."

She decided to speak up freely. She admitted to him she could no longer bear being monitored, especially in her bedroom. She hadn't taken all this in when she'd signed the contract, and never guessed it would hassle her this way. Ben listened, nodding his head. He seemed in another world. He finally said, "You'll get used to it. It's always like that, in the beginning."

"But who is watching? You?"

"Nope. I just fix stuff that breaks down."

"So, who is?"

"It's for security. No worries."

He asked her if the network was working properly. She said yes. He explained that each flat had its own. Hers was CLARISSA8 and the password was the one they'd chosen together. If ever she needed to change it, she'd have to do it with him.

As he walked toward the entrance, she held him back with a question.

"About my virtual assistant, please?"

"Go ahead," said Ben, his gaze locked on his screen.

She would have liked him to look at her, to pay attention. Arms crossed, she decided to wait until he raised his eyes, surprised by her silence.

"That's better," she said with a sarcastic smile. "I'd like to talk to you about Mrs. Dalloway."

"I'm listening," he said edgily.

"During the setup process, I was told she would react only to my voice."

"That's the case."

"This morning, Mrs. Dalloway spoke to my granddaughter directly. Is that usual procedure, in your opinion?"

"If your granddaughter, or any other person speaks to your assistant, it won't obey that individual. But the assistant may initiate a conversation with someone who happens to be in your home."

"I would rather that not be the case. Mrs. Dalloway doesn't need to intervene with anyone apart from me."

Ben shrugged.

"That can't be modified. All virtual assistants follow C.A.S.A. protocol. Dr. Dewinter can explain that better than me. I have to go, Mrs. Katsef. Anything else?"

Ben went back to his device. She felt like shaking him.

"No. Thanks."

She watched him go with his nonchalant tread. The door closed behind him. She longed to shout "You little asshole!" but the black globes on the ceiling held her back. Could she reasonably hold out in this strange flat where she felt eyes on her at all times? She locked herself up in the small toilet room to calm herself down. Nobody could see her there.

Later on, to get away from the monitoring, she tried shifting the furniture differently in her office. She shoved the desk behind the sofa, so that she could not be seen when she sat to work. While she jostled the table, she hurt her hip. She caught sight of herself in the entrance mirror: wheezing and red in the face. A fit of giggles took over. Seriously, she looked like a lunatic! A madwoman!

Installed at her desk, she felt safe for the first time, a marvelous sensation that made her spirits soar. "They" couldn't see her here, hidden by the back of the sofa. Hands flat out on the table, she breathed in and out calmly, like Elise had taught her all those years ago. This was where she was going to write. This was where she was going to create. This past month had been taxing. Writing would pull her through, the way it always had.

She hadn't looked at her hands for a long time. Stunned, she noticed she was still wearing her wedding ring, the thin golden circle François had slipped on her finger at the town hall in the fifth arrondissement. His name and the date of their marriage were engraved inside it. Despite the passage of time, her hands had remained long and slim, and she slid the ring off easily.

She thought about everything that wedding band had witnessed, seasons, voyages, encounters, lectures, readers, hours of work; simple everyday actions, and the gestures of love: François's body, the number of times her hands had landed on his skin, how it had become familiar to her, like his beauty spots, his carefully groomed beard, his robust neck. The wedding band that had observed every detail of the secret apartment on rue Dancourt.

She found an envelope, glided the ring inside, and placed it in the back of a drawer. A thin white circle remained on her finger, vestige of the jewel she'd worn for so many years, but a sense of liberty blossomed up within her, powering her with an energy she hadn't felt for weeks, to such an extent that she grabbed her notebook, the one she hadn't opened since she got here, a pen, and began to write.

Mia White was waiting for her very nicely, facing number 108, rue du Bac, absorbed not by her mobile, but by a book, an actual book made of paper. She looked like she did in her photos: a lovely young girl with long chestnut hair, wearing jeans, a jacket, and sneakers. Before she went up to her, Clarissa observed her; Mia White seemed captivated by what she was reading, holding her book to her face as if it were a treasure she could not possibly relinquish. The pavement was somewhat narrow in front of Romain Gary's last home, and the young girl had to regularly step back in order to let pedestrians by, but even when she did that, she never took her eyes off the page. What was she reading with such interest? Clarissa drew nearer. It was a vintage edition of *Promise at Dawn,* a paperback that had been read over and over again, lent, lost, found, with warped pages and a torn and tattered cover, everything Clarissa loved: a well-thumbed book.

"Oh! It's you!"

So Mia White had spotted her. What a smile!

"You're bang on time," said Clarissa in French.

"I'm the punctual type," said Mia White, speaking in French, as well.

They turned around to face the large pale building behind them.

"So it was here," said Mia White.

"Yes, here. But no need to get emotional looking up at those second-floor windows. Romain Gary's place gave on to an inner courtyard."

They crossed the street to get a better view.

"I'd like to know . . ." Mia White paused in mid-sentence, shyly.

"What?"

"That scene, in *Topography of Intimacy,* about Gary's apartment. Did it really happen that way? The way you wrote it?"

"More or less."

"I loved your book, but I especially loved that bit."

Clarissa searched the young girl's face. Mia White seemed perfectly sincere. Her magnificent eyes, riveted to Clarissa's own, brimmed over with discernible esteem. It had been a while since anyone had looked at Clarissa that way. It felt good.

"Would you mind telling me again how it happened? It would be such an honor."

Mia White spoke in English this time. Not that it made any difference to Clarissa. She knew all too well how true bilinguals were incapable of sticking to one language; they switched from one to the other with astounding changeability, making interlocutors who didn't have the possibility to express themselves seamlessly in two languages feel giddy. Mia White had no accent in either French or English, like herself.

Clarissa pursued in English, pointing to the building. She told Mia she had first come to 108, rue du Bac several years after Gary died. She had just moved to Paris, after spending her childhood, her adolescence, and her university years in England. She worked as a property surveyor for a notary office and a real estate agency. She lived on rue d'Alésia, with the young man who would soon become her first husband. She had no idea the writer Romain Gary had committed suicide here on December 2, 1980. Her colleagues and she were to assess an apartment on the third floor. While they worked, the writer became the topic of their conversation.

Clarissa knew nothing about Gary. One of her associates was familiar with his life story.

147

Clarissa was captivated by the flamboyance of his existence: Born Roman Kacew in Lithuania, the only child of an impassioned and whimsical mother, he became, in turn, an aviator, war hero, writer, diplomat, and filmmaker. He moved into number 108 in 1963, with his wife, the American actress Jean Seberg. He had lived there for nearly two decades. As Clarissa listened, her inquisitiveness had grown. In those days, the late eighties, with no Internet and no Google, she reminded Mia White, smiling, books were still purchased in bookstores. That evening, she had gone to buy *Promise at Dawn.* The title had enticed her. Looking at the back cover, she discovered a man with thoughtful features, startlingly clear eyes, a well-drawn mouth. At that point, books didn't have such a large part in her life. She wasn't yet the reader she would later become; she read seldom, and slowly.

It had taken her a while to immerse herself in Romain Gary's realm. She bought other books, *The Roots of Heaven, White Dog,* and *The Life Before Us,* which he had published under another name: Émile Ajar. Little by little, Romain Gary's prose had acted upon her like a sort of drug. She had been taken aback by his seductive fusion of delicacy and potency. His writing, both poetic and brutal, appealed to her. She had been expecting the ascetic and irreproachable works of a grand intellectual; instead, she stepped into the teeming world of a creative virtuoso who had never ceased to reinvent himself. Who was Romain Gary? All his life, he excelled in the art of covering his tracks. A young author, Dominique Bona, had just published the first biography concerning him. Clarissa had devoured it.

Clarissa crossed the street again, with Mia White following her, over to the iron fence enclosing number 108. She placed her palm on the handle. She said in French, "I needed to come back here regularly, especially since I'd read his books. I was following in his footsteps, setting my hand where he'd set his over and over again, like an intimate pilgrimage."

"I understand," said the young woman solemnly.

"You don't find it morbid?"

"No. Not at all. It's like paying tribute to him."

There was curiosity mingled with admiration in Mia White's scrutiny. Clarissa took up with her story. One morning, as she was passing by, some time after the measuring of the third-floor flat, she noticed the gate of number 108 was held open by a wedge.

She had made the most of it, slipping inside. She hurried to the main stairway, on the right. As she went up the steps, she discovered movers emptying Romain Gary's old apartment on the second floor. The door was half-closed. She had hesitated, fleetingly, on the landing. Since 1980 and Gary's death, she realized, several occupants had probably lived here one after the other. She was not going to walk into a home that still bore his imprint, as his furniture, paintings, and books were no longer here. But it was the layout of the flat that drew her in, how this man, whom she found mesmerizing, had moved within these very walls, how he had occupied the premises. She put one foot into the entrance. She remembered the third-floor flat measured with her colleagues was L-shaped, 372 square meters, with eight rooms giving on to a tree-lined private lane.

Romain Gary's sixty-six-year-old body had been carried from here, over this threshold, and down the stairs behind her. She moved forward, cautiously at first, then with a firmer gait. If someone asked her what the hell she was doing, she'd say she had made a mistake and ended up on the wrong floor. But no one came. She had remained alone in a string of vast rooms leading one into the next. She noticed the parquet floors had here and there been replaced by charcoal slate tiles, that fireplaces had been removed. A large bedroom overlooked the courtyard and its chestnut trees. She had a gut feeling it had happened here. The bed must have been placed against the wall on the left, between two electrical sockets. A bed made of copper. She'd read that in the biography. He'd lain down for the last time where she was standing now. He had placed his last handwritten letter at the foot of the bed. A note that began with "D-Day. No connection with Jean Seberg." A year before, in 1979, the actress, with whom he no longer lived, had been found dead in her car near avenue Victor-Hugo in Paris, the police ruling her demise a probable suicide. After that, Romain Gary had given up writing for good.

Clarissa's expert gaze, honed by her professional training, scanned the room. The radiator was vintage; so was the door leading into the adjacent bathroom. She passed into it. There had been no recent refurbishments here. She'd read that Gary used to dictate his books to his secretary (and lover) while he took his bath, cigar clamped between his teeth. Romain Gary had looked at himself daily in this very mirror. In this private place, he had washed and groomed himself, had tended to his body and its needs. These walls had witnessed his nakedness.

It felt like he was beside her now, buttoning up one of his custom-made mauve satin shirts, an ornate cabochon ring on his left hand, and he seemed close enough for her to make out the blue intensity of his eyes, his bittersweet smile, and the beard he carefully blackened to wipe out traces of gray. Did she perceive the acrid waft of a Montecristo? Almost. She stood at the heart of his private life, where he had slept, dreamed, and loved; where he had decided to end it all. The perimeter of his death was revealed to her.

Clarissa went on, while Mia White listened attentively. Tuesday, December 2, 1980, had been a rainy day. After lunching with his editor in the neighborhood, and relishing a last cigar, Romain Gary had walked home along the rue de Babylone. He was by himself. He had closed the shutters and the curtains. He had planned it all. He had not faltered. He had done what he had intended to do. Killing himself, in his room. He had taken the Smith & Wesson from its case, spread a red towel over his pillow, and had lain down, the barrel lodged between his lips. No one had heard the gunshot.

Clarissa remained quiet for a while.

"When I read that part in your book, I felt like I was there with you," whispered Mia White.

Clarissa continued. She had looked at the ceiling for a long moment, which must have been the last thing Gary's eyes had glimpsed. She had wondered, since that rainy afternoon, what Gary had left behind. Those who slept there, in that room, within those walls, had they not been marked, in one way or another, by his bloodstained wake? Without meaning to, Clarissa had picked up the writer's fragility, connecting to his torment, loneliness, and despair; the emotions had engulfed her as soon as she had walked into his old apartment, leaving their stain on her.

"Did Gary transmit a form of gloom to you?" asked Mia White.

"He had already done that through his books. There's this beautifully melancholic quote in *The Life Before Us:* 'It's always in the eyes that people are the saddest.' I experienced a special connection with him that day on rue du Bac."

"Did you already know you were going to write about that moment?"

"No," said Clarissa impulsively. "Writing came much later to me, via another angle, via Virginia Woolf and what I felt when I visited her home. But the fascination with this place, for this room, has never left me. Telling you this story all these years later revives it all."

The two women were now walking up the rue du Bac toward the Seine. Mia White's long chestnut hair rippled in the light breeze.

"Are you working on a new book?" she asked.

"More or less. I haven't gotten very far because of my move."

"Which area did you move to?"

Her beguiling smile. Her wide blue eyes.

The small inner voice murmured: *Never get specific with a reader, remember, nothing about where you live. Cloud the issue. It's okay to lie. Don't give any indications, addresses, street names.*

"I'm in the new district, at the top of avenue Gustave-Eiffel, near the Tower Memorial."

Too late.

"Oh, I never would have thought you'd choose to live there! I thought you didn't like modern buildings."

"On the contrary, it's a nice change, being somewhere brand-new. No one's lived there before me."

"You like it, then?"

Don't tell her about Mrs. Dalloway, about the cameras, about the spooked cat. Shut up.

"Very much so."

Mia White was shorter than Clarissa. She moved gracefully. Pedestrians often turned around to stare at her, Clarissa noticed. They strolled along the river, toward Île de la Cité. Clarissa asked her if she'd made some new friends. The young girl said she'd met a couple of nice people. She missed her boyfriend. He lived in England. They saw each other every other weekend.

The conversation became slightly idle. Time was ticking by. Clarissa knew one should never spend too much time with a reader. At times, they became inquisitive, asked too many questions, turned out to be clingy. This wasn't the case with Mia White. She seemed to be enjoying Clarissa's company, and nothing more. Clarissa asked her about her own writing. The young girl blushed.

"How sweet of you to remember that! Yes, I'm writing. But I'd never dare show you anything."

"What language do you write in?"

"For the moment, in English. It's not easy making a choice, when you're bilingual. And yourself?"

155

"Ah, well, I've decided to no longer make that choice, you see."

Mia White's eyes grew even larger.

"What do you mean?"

"I've decided to write my new novel in two languages at the same time."

The inner voice again. *What the hell are you doing? Why blab about your writing projects with a stranger?*

"How are you doing this? It sounds amazing!" exclaimed Mia White.

They had turned back and were now standing in front of the rue du Bac Métro station. Clarissa could have added nothing more, said good-bye, and departed. She didn't feel like being alone, returning to her silent flat, her fearful cat. This smiling young girl did her good.

"What about a break at that café?" she suggested. Mia White agreed, with pleasure. She ordered a Coke, and Clarissa, some tea.

"What do you speak with your family?" asked Mia White. "Me, it's English with my dad, French with my mum, a mix of both with my sister."

"My first husband is an American, so I spoke to him in English. And to make sure our daughter became bilingual, I always addressed myself to her in French. My second husband is French, but I sometimes speak to him in English, Lord knows why!"

They laughed in unison and Clarissa ignored the annoying inner voice: *What the hell are you doing, pouring your life out? Rambling on about your husbands, how ridiculous!* She was letting go at last. She hadn't chatted with a friend for such a long time.

"I get the oddest questions," said Mia White, and Clarissa noticed for the first time what a pleasant voice she had. "I'm asked what language I dream in. That stumps me. I think about it, and I just don't know. Isn't that strange? What about you?"

Clarissa couldn't bring herself to tell Mia White about her recent dreams. Ever since she had started living in the residence, they seemed more and more vivid. In the past, she'd had difficulty remembering them. Now she didn't have to write the dreams down. Now, when she awoke, they lingered, shadowing her all day long. She kept on hearing the voice as well, the reassuring murmur that whispered to her while she slept. She couldn't recall what it was saying. All she knew was that it meant well. And, come to think of it, she had no idea which language it was using.

"I wish I knew, but I'm like you, I don't have a clue," she said, not wishing to discuss her dreams any further. She wondered if

Mia White perceived her hesitancy. "Do dreams have a language, in your opinion?"

"Well, they must. But perhaps, to people like us, our unconscious doesn't decipher language. I'm also asked what I swear in. I had never really noticed that before. But when I paid attention, I realized it was French. God knows why! And you? Do you prefer cursing in French, as well?"

Clarissa smiled again, but with a touch of bitterness this time. She thought of the expletives that had rushed to her lips while she had been packing her bags, François standing next to her, begging and pleading for her to stay. She hadn't pronounced a single one of them; she had remained wordless, but they stormed around inside her head, loud, blunt, and obscene. English? French? Probably French, because that was François's mother tongue.

She said nothing of all this to Mia White, who seemed to take in every one of her movements and reactions with her intense, unwavering gaze. To escape it, Clarissa looked down at the sunbeam caressing their hands. Mia White's were tiny and golden.

"A mix-up, isn't it?" Mia White said lightly. "And what about your book, then? I'm so curious to know more."

The young woman was waiting for her to

speak. For a few seconds, Clarissa stayed quiet, watching the shaft of light playing with her spoon. Then she sprang forth. She said she had never translated her own writing. She had written some books directly in French, others in English. There was invariably a pang of regret from having to choose one over the other. She then worked with translators, a task she often found difficult. Recently, she'd decided to experiment: writing simultaneously in both languages, two documents opened up on her computer, one in English, one in French. It was bewildering at the start, and then all of a sudden, there had been a revelation, acting upon her like a boost, heightening her energy. She had shifted from a quiet country path to a motorway. She wrote her text, no longer paying attention to the language she was writing in. She wrote. That was it. Language no longer mattered. Or rather, both languages now had their significance, because each of them bestowed on her the sentences or words she was seeking, which she then had to transpose with care, perfecting them with the patient and meticulous fine-tuning used on an antiquated receiver, so that the frequency she obtained was the same in English and in French. She perceived herself as a voracious foraging bee

harvesting pollen for two separate hives, another pleasing image.

"How amazing!" exclaimed Mia White, dazzled.

Heartened, Clarissa went on. The manuscript was coming along like a two-headed monster, thriving homogenously. She didn't favor one language over the other, and wanted above all for the text to end up identical in both. At times, as she labored over a description, she switched directly to the other language, which instantly gave her a new boost. It was like playing out Jekyll and Hyde in an unprecedented scientific experimentation. Who was Hyde? Who was Dr. Jekyll? English or French? It didn't matter. She wasn't certain she'd go on writing in this way. All she knew was that she certainly didn't regret giving it a go.

"I'm sure you're aware Samuel Becket wrote in English and French, as well," said Mia White. "And so did Julien Green."

"Yes, that's right. And did you know Romain Gary also translated himself?"

Mia White looked surprised. No, she had no idea. Clarissa explained that Gary wrote *White Dog* in English first, like *Lady L,* and other novels, and then adapted them to French, which was unexpected, considering he was brought up learning Polish and Rus-

sian, and that neither French nor English had been his mother tongue.

"His real name was Kacew?" asked Mia White.

"Yes."

"Pronounced like your pen name?"

"That's right."

"Clarissa for Virginia Woolf and Katsef for Romain Gary."

"Yes. I started writing because of those two writers."

"Yes, I read that. I hope you'll tell me about Woolf next time we meet."

"With pleasure."

Oh, come on, said the inner voice. *Because you're going to see her again? Seriously? You're going to go on prattling? You don't know anything about her. You have no idea who she is. You think she's sweet and charming, but perhaps she's none of that. Wake up.*

"This is my mobile number," said Mia White, with her enchanting smile. "I'll let you get back to me."

Later, on the phone, Clarissa told her daughter she had made two new friends. A young reader, barely older than Andy, and her fourth-floor neighbor, with whom she was going to have a drink at the end of the week. Jordan congratulated her, and told her about the brooch belonging to Aunt

161

Serena, sent by Mimsy and Pimsy, which had just arrived.

"It is pretty?"

"Hideous."

"What are you going to do with it?"

"No idea. Sell it? Andy doesn't want it. I'll have it appraised, but I'm sure it's not worth much."

"I'll thank Grandpa and Arthur on my end."

Clarissa hung up after lovingly saying good-bye to her daughter.

She hadn't told Jordan she felt more and more tired, that she still slept badly, that her dreams were beginning to disturb her.

She hadn't told Jordan about the infinitesimal dark zone behind Mia White's luminous smile.

As she made her way to her room along the corridor, she heard a metallic clicking sound. Startled, she stood still. Was this the sound that had frightened Andy?

Then she noticed Chablis.

The cat was frozen to the spot, its fur bristling. Arching its back, it was staring up toward the ceiling, petrified.

I spent some time hanging around in front of the building on rue Dancourt. There was a small café just in front of the passageway railing, from where I could see all the way into the courtyard to the main door.

I knew she was a long-haired blonde. That was all. I had to see her. To see her with my own eyes.

How long had this double life been going on for? I had no idea. I remembered how often my husband had recently been away for business trips. Did she go with him? Did his coworkers know? Who knew anything about this?

I had never checked to see if he really left Paris. I trusted him.

The little café on rue Dancourt was a quiet place. The manager was nice and not too chatty. I always had my notebook with me. I pretended to work, but to tell the truth, I was incapable of writing anything. My eyes never left the railing.

A lot of people passed by there. Day after day, I became familiar with the residents. The elderly lady and her dog. The trim gentleman with his briefcase. A tall and handsome bearded young man. A mother and her teenaged daughter, not speaking to each other. A grouchy old man. A woman of my age with her grandchildren.

I'd see my husband go by with his shopping basket. He'd come back all chirpy-looking, with tarts from the bakery and flowers. I'd watch him, incredulous.

I longed to tear out of the café, run after him along the passageway, insult him and fling his pastries and bouquets into the gutter.

He was always alone. No woman by his side. I waited for a blonde to appear. There was one, but she had short hair and a boyish look. In her thirties. Not his type. But what was his type? I wondered. She seemed tired and fed up. One evening, she was holding a small girl by the hand. I nearly had a fit. My husband had a hidden child! He had never dared tell me. The blonde was his mistress. I remained rooted to the spot. I hadn't known what to do.

A few days later, the blonde went by with a fat, hairy man. He was holding her by the waist, kissing her neck. I sighed with relief. Nothing to do with my husband.

Still no sign of a long-haired blonde. Was she already in the flat? Did she live there? They were never together outside. Was there another entrance? I checked. There wasn't.

I wasn't getting it. All sorts of qualms came over me. Maybe there was no blonde. Just a place where my husband went to be alone.

But what about the tartlets, the flowers?

Was this a bachelor pad where he met a string of women? I couldn't quite believe that. He was, after all, getting on.

What was he hiding from me, then? A fling with a man? I felt dizzy.

Writers really have too much imagination.

I had to calm down, to stop spinning stories in my head.

There was only one thing to do. Confront them.

No, better still. Tackle her, without my husband. Deal with her alone.

Face-to-face.

5
POWDER

I don't think two people could have been happier.
VIRGINIA WOOLF, March 28, 1941

I have at last said all I have to say.
ROMAIN GARY, December 2, 1980

Clarissa was having her breakfast, and reading the morning paper on her device. For a while now, she'd steadfastly avoided lingering on bad news, attempting to concentrate on what might instruct her, stir or touch her, or even make her laugh. It wasn't easy. The news feed prospered on disasters and cataclysms. She also had to check each time that she wasn't dealing with fake news. She had often been hoodwinked.

Mrs. Dalloway was heard.

"Good morning, Clarissa. We have a situation. A person has tried to come in several times. His name is not on the entry list."

166

François. It could only be him.

"Is he downstairs, Mrs. Dalloway?"

"Yes. And he won't leave unless he speaks to you. He went away previously, after speaking to security. But not this morning. What do you wish to do?"

"Can you confirm his identity?"

"Of course."

François's shattered face loomed up on the nearby control screen.

"I'll give it a thought, Mrs. Dalloway."

"Absolutely."

Clarissa got up, her mug in her hand. She tried to think rationally. She tried to remain calm. There was nothing she wanted to say to François, except for him to leave her alone. The pain concerning the purple studio was still there, as strong as ever. And now he was downstairs. What was he thinking? That she was going to go back to him? That she would forgive him, like she always had? That she would be the wonderful, generous, understanding wife she had been till now? Oh no. No, no. That Clarissa was gone. Gone forever.

She saw herself in the mirror and almost gasped at the expression on her face. The woman staring back at her was a warrior. It felt as if she were wearing armor, that nothing this man could ever do would hurt her or disappoint her again.

Go on down there, said the little voice. *Give him a piece of your mind. Make him understand, for once and for all.*

She drew herself up to her full height. Then she reached into her cupboard and pulled out a pair of badass black boots she'd bought last week on the spur of the moment, the kind she used to wear when she was younger, and that only a rock star or an actress would ever dare flaunt at her age. They added a couple of inches to her frame, exactly what she wanted.

She had purchased new clothes, as she had moved here with nothing. She was particularly fond of an elegant black jacket, unearthed in a vintage boutique, which contrasted with her red hair. She slipped it on and applied light makeup. She had no intention of coming across as pallid or worn-out. In the bathroom, Mrs. Dalloway asked her to go through the medical procedure: weighing herself, placing her hand on the plaque, looking into the mirror where the dots were.

"Another time. I'm in a hurry."

"Fine, but Dr. Dewinter insists on your going through the evaluations regularly. I will remind you."

Clarissa made a face. Then she mumbled,

laughing up her sleeve, "Blah blah blah."

She left, banging the door behind her, hurrying headlong down the stairs, as usual.

François was waiting for her a little farther away on the cobbled forecourt in front of the residence, like a lost, collarless dog. He had the bushy, unkempt beard of a nineteenth-century tanked-up Slavic writer; his face was puffed up, his eyes reddened. His back was curved, his chin glued to his chest. Was he overdoing it, so that she might pity him and relent? It wasn't working. He was pathetic, she thought.

"It's impossible to get into that fortress of yours," he said with a feeble smile.

"What do you want?" she asked bluntly.

His face fell. Then he began to speak hurriedly. What he wanted? Was she serious? He had been here three times already in the past weeks, only to be sent away by those guards, who treated him like a homeless person. He only wanted to talk. He only wanted to make her understand, nothing more than that. He had done something awful, something heinous. He could not forgive himself. But he couldn't lose her. He couldn't let her walk out of his life. He needed her. He had always needed her. How could she turn over this page so fast? After all they'd gone through, after all these years?

Couldn't she just hear him out, let him explain? Surely she might let him explain?

Clarissa glanced at his disheveled shirt, his stained jeans. The sour stink of him wormed its way to her nose. This was unlike him. François was usually impeccably groomed. He looked like he hadn't slept or washed in weeks.

He went on in a calmer, plaintive, squeaky voice she found unbearable. They had to talk about the future, didn't they? They had to make plans. If she really wished to leave, then they had to organize this. She had all her stuff at the flat. There were papers to sign, all sorts of things to do, if she truly wanted to go. Had she thought it over? Was this what she wanted?

She spoke at last. Her voice was clear and firm.

"Yes, this is what I want."

She held herself tall, towering over him in her heels. How could she ever have loved this man who was so small in every single way? Every aspect of him was insignificant. The more she observed him, the more she wondered how it had been possible. How had she fallen in love with François Antoine? She remembered he had appeared at a traumatic moment in her life. She had not gotten over the death of her baby, despite

Jordan's birth. Her job as a surveyor was beginning to bore her. It was a complex, tricky period. She had met François Antoine at a mutual friend's place. She had gone to the dinner alone; Toby had moved out long ago. What had she seen in François? There was something comforting and caring about him. It was François who had been the first to ever suggest hypnosis to her; he had sensed her fragility, the sorrow she had still not been able to overcome concerning the child. She didn't have to explain. He suggested she give it a try, just once. And later, much later, that first hypnosis session with Elise Delaporte had changed everything for her.

"You're so tough, Clarissa. So unkind. That's not your style. You've forgotten everything I've ever done for you."

He went on in his lamenting tone. Did she have a short memory, or what? Did she not remember the state she was in when he met her? Her first husband had already cleared off, after all.

"That's enough, François," she hissed.

But he went on with more intensity. Yes, Toby had gotten the hell out because Clarissa was wallowing in her own grief, because she couldn't even smile anymore, let alone to her own daughter. Did she have

171

any idea what he had endured? Did she even guess at the efforts he'd made to help her picture things in a more positive light, at all the trouble he had gone through to help her heal? Look at how she was treating him now, slamming the door on their marriage.

"Stop it, François. It's over. It's finished."

His face crumpled up, and it was ugly to watch. She thought about the studio, the photos and the videos she had seen there, that hidden, double life. Ugly, as well. It was all so ugly. She didn't want any of it. She could no longer stand it.

"Please give me another chance. Please forgive me."

He was weeping now, his nose runny, his eyes screwed up. Disgust rose over pity. How could she tell him, again, that there were so many things she had put up with, too much she had taken in her stride, so many times she had pardoned. He had been unfaithful since the start. It had been an unpleasant discovery, but not a surprise. She was no young bride. But this was different. This had nothing to do with the previous flings. This was a repugnant blow that had dug into the very core of their marriage, delving into the throbbing heart of it, and there was no going back from that debacle; there was no healing, no possibility of absolution.

He didn't seem to be getting it. He was still crying, his beard flecked with snot. He kept on mumbling that he had been such an idiot; he was so angry with himself.

"I imagine you're still seeing her?" she asked. She felt invincible in her black jacket, perched on her high-heeled rock-star boots. But the pain always found a way to express itself, perfidiously snaking its way through her shield. Why ask such a dumb question? Of course he was still seeing her! He had installed her in a studio; he had a life with her. For a year now, he'd been sharing part of his existence with this creature.

François looked sheepish. He stared at his feet. Words weren't coming to him.

"You know what?" said Clarissa bitterly. "Forget that question. Don't answer. I don't want to know."

"I thought perhaps you might understand," murmured François at last, with the same hangdog expression. "I was mistaken."

She stamped her foot.

"For God's sake, François, what is there to understand?"

He shook his head, raised his hand. Could she just listen? Was that possible? She remained silent. He took that as a cue. He said he had needs, like any man, and she

173

knew that. The problem was, with age, his needs were still strong. He couldn't ignore them. He had to face the facts. They had married late, in their fifties. Then he had been ill. Of course, there had been sex between them, but perhaps not as much as he would have wanted. Maybe he was wrong, but it seemed to him that as she grew older, she seemed to be less interested in sex. Perhaps it was menopause? Perhaps they hadn't talked about it enough? He hadn't dared. He hadn't known where to begin.

Clarissa took a deep breath. She tried to put her anger and disgust aside.

"What are you trying to tell me?" she said.

François seemed to stand a little straighter. He looked her in the eyes. He had been meaning to speak to her, but he just didn't know how. Never could he have imagined she'd follow him and discover the studio. He should have told her right away, and the more he waited, the more difficult it became to say anything. His voice became clearer, less shrill.

"I thought you'd understand because you're so intelligent, Clarissa. You see into people's souls. And I really and truly thought that you wouldn't feel hurt, because you don't give me anything sexual anymore.

Nothing much goes on in our bed, except hugs and kisses. I can't even remember the last time we made love. When I'm with her, it is only for that. It's just for the sex. It's only for the sex."

A violent fury took over, and she had to restrain herself from insulting him. She was shaking.

"Oh, really? Only for the sex?" she hissed frostily. "What about the photo albums? The videos? The celebrations? The dinners for two? All in the past year? I saw it, as it's so nicely on display, in your home. Enough of your nonsense. Cut the crap, please. Stop saying she's just some lay. You love her. You know it. You're in love. And it's intolerable. Unbearable."

Like a little boy, he started to cry again.

"I love both of you," he whined; "it's a nightmare. I'm so sorry, honey. Forgive me!"

He blubbered loudly, with no holding back.

Clarissa stepped back, raised her chin.

"You're going to get the hell out of here. Now. You're never coming back. Is that clear? I'll talk to a lawyer when I'm ready. That lawyer will get in touch with you. That's all. Bye."

She rushed away, without looking at him.

175

The scanning system at the entrance had trouble checking her retina because of her tears. She had to go through it several times, praying François wasn't behind her. She climbed the stairs too quickly, and had to stop halfway, breathless, her throat dry.

Mrs. Dalloway's voice greeted her as soon as she walked in.

"Clarissa, tonight on channel Cinéma New Star, there's a special Timothée Chalamet show. Otherwise, there's a Chopin concert on —"

"Just shut up, Mrs. Dalloway. And don't speak to me before tomorrow."

Silence.

A prodigious feeling of freedom raced through her.

In the living room, the cat was curled up on the sofa, asleep. She sat down next to him and stroked his back. He purred. She put François out of her mind. She thought of all the things she had to do. The trick was to keep busy. It was the only way. In her mind, she made little notes. Check on her father to see how he was. Call Jordan to find out if the brooch was worth anything. Start thinking about the summer holiday, the first she'd spend without François. They usually spent them in Provence or Italy. Where would she go? And while she went

176

through all these things, the idea of the book she was trying to write loomed up bigger than the rest. Luckily, the editor she worked with was not breathing down her neck. Laure-Marie knew Clarissa needed time. And Clarissa was well aware that although her books were valued, she was not a best-selling author whose new works were eagerly expected. There was no hype around her, and never had been. No one from the publishing company put pressure on her. It was always a pleasure to have lunch with Laure-Marie, who took her to nice restaurants and seemed genuinely happy to see her. But Laure-Marie had bigger and more important authors to look after.

Perhaps it was time to call Laure-Marie and tell her that she had just started working on something new. She wondered what Laure-Marie would make of the fact that Clarissa was writing in English and French simultaneously. Would she be interested? Perhaps not. Since the attacks, the world of publishing had changed. The dreadful power of the images searing around the world on social media, showing the devastation of the Piazza San Marco, bombed-out Big Ben, and the obliteration of the Sistine Chapel, seemed to have stopped time. After the Eiffel Tower had been filmed crashing down, it had not seemed possible that anything worse could ever happen. And yet it had.

But that was only the beginning. A swift and fiendish sequence of events had occurred. Pictures took precedence over words. No one read newspapers. People watched videos, over and over again, ensnared by an enthralled stupor.

Clarissa recalled that several years after the attacks, during the oddness of an unhoped-for and disquieting lull, while Europe as Clarissa had always known it started to fall apart, and as the bees endured a slow agony worsening by the day, other new and horrifying images had spread like an epidemic: Ordinary citizens, unable to stand the cruel reality of modern life, were committing suicide on social media for all to see. Individuals of all ages, all classes, all nationalities posted live videos of themselves taking their own lives, one after the other. It was beyond belief: an atrocious and despotic larger-than-life reality show caught in the frenzy of media display. Literature no longer held its own, faced now with the onslaught of immediacy, where the obscene power of video reigned supreme, never satiated. And when stunned writers had attempted to describe the attacks, those books had barely been read. People preferred to come and listen to the writer, to applaud the writer as he or she read from his or her book, and no longer purchased signed copies. Reading was no longer comforting. Reading no longer helped to heal.

So why should she go on writing? Who would read her? She would stick to writing because she didn't have a choice, because written words were her stronghold, her defense. She would write to make her voice heard; she would continue in order to leave a trail, although she had no idea who'd ever find it. She would write.

Clarissa felt tired, more than ever. It was an effort to get out of bed, to walk up those eight flights of stairs. Why was her mouth so parched all the time? Perhaps she was overdoing things. Perhaps she needed to slow down, write less and with less passion, though that was going to be hard.

One night, as she lay asleep, the voice murmured a word, over and over again, lapping into the breeding ground of her sensitive brain like a recurring wave, never letting go. Like a time machine, the dream was taking her back over the years to a place that filled her with dread. She heard the squeak of wheels on worn linoleum, saw the long stretch of a dark corridor opening up in front of her. She saw Toby, his hair still black, bending down to weep, his face in his hands. The voice whispered the same word that burrowed deep into her, down where she could still feel the soreness, down where she kept the pain at bay. But the voice acted like a key, unlocking all the doors of protection she had so carefully erected, and the suffering came gushing back, stronger than ever, like boiling water scalding her skin. In her dream, she surrendered to the pain, opening herself completely, letting it invade her. The voice was there to calm her, to reassure her. When she opened her eyes, she felt moisture on her cheeks. She had been crying. She felt calm, but desolate, as if something had been torn from her. And the word murmured by the voice, what was it? She couldn't remember.

When she got up to have breakfast, her joints always ached. She couldn't understand why she felt so run-down. She had talked about it to Jordan, who had reminded her mother, very sweetly, that she was getting on. She was at last feeling her age. But Clarissa wouldn't have it. It had all started since she had moved here. And while the medical checkups she went through in her bathroom showed nothing abnormal, she was convinced her fatigue had something to do with the residence. She began to feel suspicious about the tap water; she stopped drinking it and ordered bottled mineral water through the weekly shopping drone. She also decided to stop taking the vitamin treatment Dr. Dewinter had prescribed. Facing the cameras, she pretended to swallow the pills, and ended up stuffing them into her pocket, then tossing them into the toilet bowl.

One morning, as she sat at her kitchen table rubbing her eyes, sleepy, her head still filled with haunting dreams, her ears still echoing from the murmur of the voice that whispered to her in the night, she heard the bizarre clicking noise that had startled Andy. She looked up. She thought she saw a trickle of powder sifting through the ceiling right into the mug of tea placed in front of her. At first, she believed she had been mistaken and it was just a trick of the light. But as she looked closely at her mug, a tiny coating of dust was quickly seeping into the liquid. She sat there, stunned. Had she imagined it? She got up, taking her time, and stared up at the light fixture above her head. It seemed perfectly normal. She spilled her tea into the sink, trying to act as naturally as possible. She was being watched. She rinsed the cup several times.

Thinking about the powder shadowed her all day long. What was that powder? Had it been poured into her tea every day? Was that why she felt tired, almost drugged? Why were "they" doing this? Whom could she talk to? She hadn't been able to work, to get on with her book. She acted like the cat, ill at ease, wary. She went to bed feeling uneasy. It seemed to her the cat looked even more nervous than usual.

Jordan had called her after dinner to organize Andy's next visit. She told her Aunt Serena's brooch was with a jewelry appraiser. She was convinced it wasn't worth much. She'd know in a week or so.

"You okay, Mums? Your voice sounds strange."

" 'I'm fine. A little tired. Nothing serious."

But her daughter wasn't giving up that easily.

"Hmmm, you've been saying that an awful lot lately. But I can tell there's something else. What's up?"

Clarissa ended up telling her about François. She admitted he had come there, had insisted upon speaking to her, and that she had gone down to meet him, to say it was all over. All this had stirred her up.

When she hung up, she noticed once again

how her daughter had not asked her what François had done. But she knew Jordan's silence would not last. She knew Jordan would eventually harp on about this, and it wouldn't be because of an unhealthy curiosity, but, above all, impelled by the love she felt for her mother. Clarissa, aware of this, cherished her daughter's love, even if she felt at times that Jordan worried too much about her.

Sleep tumbled upon her like a leaden weight, for once. There had been no need to ask Mrs. Dalloway to display any videos, or for her to spy on her neighbors with her binoculars.

In the dead of the night, a strident blare drilled into her eardrums as the panic-stricken cat landed on her. A monstrously powerful alarm rang out, making the walls shudder. With distraught fingers, she tried to turn on the bedside lamp, but nothing happened. A blinking night-light feebly lit up the corridor with an unpleasant orange glow. Clarissa yelled out for Mrs. Dalloway to intervene, but the din was too loud.

A mechanical voice began to speak, repeating the same words over and over.

"STAY CALM. GET OUT NOW. FIRE ALARM. LEAVE PREMISES NOW. FIRE ALARM. GET OUT. WARNING. LEAVE

NOW. LEAVE PREMISES NOW. WARN-ING."

She was only wearing her nightgown, and couldn't find her slippers or her dressing gown in the dimness. She had to leave; there was no time to locate them. From the armchair, she grabbed the sweater she had been wearing last evening, slipped it on with haste. There was a fire in the residence and she was on the top floor. She didn't have a minute to spare. Flustered, she seized the cat, and cried out in pain as he scratched her. She compressed him against her chest and flung herself into the dimly lit stairway. All the doors of the residence were opening up, and her neighbors emerged, disheveled and anxious. She followed the others down, while the cat twisted and turned, mewing frantically. The stairs seemed shadowy and endless. Suddenly, she heard Adelka's voice, felt her comforting palm against her elbow. She felt relief, even though she knew they still had more flights to go, that it wasn't over. In the huge hall, only the orange night-lights flickered. The alarm still howled and the voice went on giving orders.

"LEAVE THE RESIDENCE RIGHT AWAY. GET OUT. DANGER."

Head down, stumbling, Clarissa followed Adelka, clutching the squirming cat against her. The ground felt cold and damp to her bare feet. Outside, streetlamps shed a bright yellow light onto the small crowd. The residence loomed above them, clad in darkness. No flames, no smoke. The sirens were still howling. No one from the C.A.S.A. team was to be seen.

"Is there a fire, or what?" Adelka asked Clarissa. She noticed the cat and tickled him under his chin. "That's a very frightened kitty there, isn't it, now?" Chablis calmed down, but Clarissa could still feel his heart pumping under the soft fur.

"It's three in the morning!" mumbled a man in his thirties, standing next to them in a T-shirt and boxer shorts. "For fuck's sake, what's going on?"

He noticed Clarissa and Adelka looking at him and grinned apologetically. He held out his hand, introduced himself as Jim Perrier. Third floor.

"I'm wondering what C.A.S.A. has got up its sleeve," he said in a low voice.

"So there's no fire, you think?" asked Adelka, plucking a purring Chablis from Clarissa's arms. She obviously had a way with cats.

"I'm pretty sure there's no fire," said Jim.

"Unless it's a drill and they forgot to tell us," said Clarissa.

"That's what they'll probably come up with," said Jim.

"Maybe they wanted us all to get together and this was a clever way to do it," whispered Clarissa.

Jim looked at her and winked.

"You could very well be right," he whispered back.

Beyond the camaraderie of his wink, she felt perhaps she had found an ally, a person who had also become suspicious of what truly lay behind C.A.S.A. She wasn't the only one.

Clarissa looked around at her neighbors. She was familiar with just a few faces. She realized she didn't know most of the people who lived in her building. In the yellow lighting, it was hard to make them out. She noticed a young woman wrapped up in a bathrobe, with a long braid down her back. She seemed vaguely familiar. She wished she had her glasses to be able to make her out better.

"I wonder how long they'll keep us here," said Adelka. She was wearing a fuchsia shawl. She noticed Clarissa's feet were bare. "Oh, aren't you cold?"

"In the rush, I couldn't find my slippers," Clarissa said.

Adelka took off her own flip-flops and

186

handed them to Clarissa, all the while expertly balancing the cat.

"Please put mine on. Please."

"That's very kind of you. You're making me feel like a very old lady, you know."

"Nonsense. You're probably my mum's age, and there's nothing old about my mum or you."

She was very sweet. Clarissa felt like hugging her. The cat seemed ecstatic in her arms.

"I'm a cat person," Adelka said, smiling.

"My daughter is, too. I'm not!"

"You're still learning! It takes a while for a cat to like you and get to know you."

"Chablis isn't happy here," said Clarissa. She nearly added "Like me."

"Why not?" asked Jim Perrier.

Clarissa shrugged.

"He's nervous, jumpy. It's like he sees things I can't. I did hear a strange clicking noise the other day. So did my granddaughter. Not sure what it was. The cat hates it."

"Ah, the clicking noise," said Jim grimly.

"I don't know what you're talking about," said Adelka. "I've never heard it."

"You will now," said Jim. "You'll see."

"What can it be?" asked Clarissa. "We could ask Dr. Dewinter."

"Dr. Dewinter and her team are too busy spying on us to answer that sort of question."

Clarissa stared at Jim. He seemed perfectly serious.

She lowered her voice.

"Why are they spying on us, do you think? What is C.A.S.A.?"

He stared back at her.

"That's exactly what I've been trying to work out since I moved in."

Jim moved closer to them. He smelled of cologne.

He said, "We could go on discussing C.A.S.A., but not here, and not now. And never within the residence. They listen to everything. They tape it all."

"But why?" asked Adelka. "What for?"

Jim put a finger in front of his mouth.

"We need to be quiet," he said. "Later."

The minutes slipped by. Some people were sitting on the low wall that circled the forecourt in front of the residence. The air felt cool. The alarm had stopped at last, and silence had taken over. Clarissa noticed some of the neighbors were becoming edgy, letting their disapproval show. Others seemed to be asleep, even while they stood. The cat drowsed in Adelka's arms.

Dr. Dewinter's imposing silhouette appeared in front of the residence's vast entrance. She was wearing a black jacket and black trousers. A sleepy-faced Ben and Clémence Dutilleul stood by her side. The three of them flaunted smiles — fake tight ones that were supposed to be heartening but failed. Clarissa wondered if they slept on-site, but she'd never seen them in the hall, let alone in the neighborhood.

Dr. Dewinter had quite a set of lungs. Her voice was easily heard.

"First of all, may I say, dear artists, how deeply sorry we are. I wish to reassure you, there is no fire. We had indeed planned a fire drill, but certainly not at three in the morning!"

A couple of laughs rang out.

"Now what?" muttered Jim Perrier.

"There was a mistake in the programming. Please do accept our most humble apologies."

Jim Perrier shot a glance toward Clarissa.

Ben looked shamefaced. So he was the culprit.

"However, before we let you get back home to your beds, we need to check you are all here."

"As if anyone could have slept through that racket!" Adelka chuckled.

"Why call the roll?" murmured Clarissa.

"Why do they need to know we're all here?"

"There must be a reason," said Jim Perrier. "Everything here happens for a reason."

"They're testing us," whispered Clarissa. "All this is to test us, to monitor our reactions. They must need it for something, but I don't know what."

"Will we ever know?"

"You guys have too much imagination," said Adelka.

Jim Perrier laughed.

"That's my job," he said.

"Mine, too," said Clarissa. "Are you a writer, as well?"

"I am, but I write for others," said Jim. "I've never published anything under my own name."

Dr. Dewinter had started the roll call. They had to be quiet, like in school.

"Arlen, first floor right. Azoulay, fourth right. Bell, fifth left. Engeler, second right. Fromet, fifth right. Holzmann, seventh right. Katsef, eighth floor. Olsen, seventh left. Miki, fourth left. Perrier, third left. Pomeroy, third right. Rachewski, sixth left. Van Druten, sixth right. Zajak, second left."

There was no one missing. But the young girl with the long braid that Clarissa had seen earlier on was nowhere to be seen. She glanced around for her in vain. The strangest thing was that she now knew whom the girl looked like. The spitting image of Mia White.

She found this perturbing, felt her wariness flare up again. Was she becoming utterly paranoid? She could easily imagine Jordan's amused but worried expression.

Jim Perrier drew closer. He whispered in her ear.

"If you want to talk to me, I'm at Café Iris every morning, in the new part of rue Saint-Dominique, near the dry cleaner's. I'm there early, after eight. Don't use the internal messaging system if you have anything personal to say. Remember that everything coming from your mobile or your computer goes through them. Good night!"

He disappeared, weaving his way through the people heading back to the residence. Dr. Dewinter, followed by Clemence and Ben, was also leaving. Clarissa watched them till they turned the corner of the street. She went back inside with Adelka. The young woman took her back to her door, handed her the cat, and told her to go quickly back to bed. And she hadn't forgotten their drink!

Clarissa couldn't sleep. She sat on the sofa, with Chablis burrowing against her, and watched the sun rise. She looked at the building on the other side of the street, full of those lives she had come to know intimately. She couldn't stop thinking about what Jim Perrier had said concerning C.A.S.A.

Last night, she had left an empty mug of tea on the kitchen table. When she examined it, she thought she saw a minute trace of white powder lining its bottom. She turned her back to the camera, then wrapped the mug up in a paper bag, which she put away in the cupboard.

The new part of rue Saint-Dominique, called rue Neuve Saint-Dominique, had sprung forth with grace from the ruins of the attack. Modern edifices daringly reinterpreted Haussmannian outlines. The street was predominantly pedestrian, lined with large sidewalks planted with man-made trees, which were pleasing to the eye. Driverless cars quietly slid by, mingling with bikes and gliders. Clarissa found the new arrangement hard to take in. She kept seeing in her mind the ancient configuration, which superimposed itself onto the new one in spite of herself. Higher up, the Café Iris had a nice sunny terrace, and she quickly spotted Jim Perrier seated there, behind his computer.

When he saw her approaching, he smiled. "I knew you'd come."

She sat down in front of him. She could see him better than last night. He had lively, twinkling dark eyes, cropped black hair, and a tattoo on his right arm. He was young, in his mid-thirties. Clarissa ordered some tea.

Jim Perrier had a look around.

"You never know," he said with a grin. "Always checking. So! Mrs. Katsef. Meanwhile, I've read a lot about you. Interesting career. How your job as a property surveyor led you to writing after an extraordinary hypnosis experience. Romain Gary. Virginia Woolf. Their homes, their privacy, their demons. The obsession with dwellings. I ordered *Topography of Intimacy* on the spot!"

"That's very kind," she said, slightly embarrassed.

"I admire novelists, their imaginary world, the way they write. It's different for me. I listen to people, more or less famous; then I transcribe their story. I also create TV shows, like you do. I love doing that. I have a ball. Maybe, one day, I'll write a book. So you see, I did my homework concerning you. You give out a nice aura. Your books are well received."

"Thanks. Except people don't read books anymore."

"I know," he said, making a face. "People take pretty photos of books, post them with the right hashtags, but nobody reads. Or very few. Books have become ornaments."

"I hear a slight accent. Where are you from?"

"You've got a good ear. I grew up in Brussels. But back to C.A.S.A. Why did you sign up?"

"My marriage broke up. I had to find a new place. And you?"

"I had heard about it. I found it intriguing. I wasn't at all expecting to be taken on."

"Me, neither."

Jim Perrier glanced around once more. He began to speak in a low voice. Clarissa had to lean forward in order to hear him. He had been skeptical from the start. The cameras, for instance. The medical checkups. And the incredibly low rents. It was all too clear. Every artist living there was a C.AS.A. guinea pig. But it was impossible to glean any information about C.A.S.A. Had she noticed that, too? He'd done some interesting research on Dr. Dewinter. She was brilliant, with a string of qualifications, one of the greatest artificial intelligence specialists, running far ahead of the pack. Very respected in her field. But her recent projects were no longer mentioned. Dr. Dewinter had retreated into the shadows. Nobody knew what she was working on. Nothing was coming to the surface.

Clarissa let him go on, without interrupting him.

One day, he'd gone back to C.A.S.A. headquarters, where they had passed their interviews. Near here. He wanted to know more, to understand. He hadn't been getting any response to his emails, so he turned up. Once he got there, he couldn't obtain an answer or an appointment. The place was like an impenetrable fortress, guarded by Bardi, the most sophisticated robot security guards of the moment. There was a lot of money behind all this. But for what aim?

"I believe they're trying to coax us out of our comfort zone," said Clarissa.

"Without a doubt. But why?"

"I don't know."

She told him then what she'd never told anyone. The tap water that dehydrated her mouth, hair, and skin. The aching tiredness she'd endured since she moved in. The voice she kept hearing at night, which seemed to influence her dreams. The clicking noise that made her jump, coming from nowhere. The way the cat acted. The nosy virtual assistant who knew too much about her past and who spoke to her granddaughter in her absence. And then, although she had decided not to, she told him about the powder and watched his eyes widen.

"Are you sure?" he said.

"It's difficult for me to tell you I'm sure. It happened so fast. Sometimes I wonder if I really saw it. But I have this."

Surreptitiously, she took the paper-wrapped mug out of her bag.

"You should take it to a lab," he said.

"You're right, but I don't know of any."

"I'll deal with it," he said. "Will you leave it with me?"

"Okay. Don't lose it!"

"No worries. But I won't take it back to the residence. We'll meet here, when I get the results."

"How will you get hold of me?"

He pondered.

"I'll send you a message on the internal system. Something about your book, which I will have read. As soon as you get it, come here the next morning."

She nodded.

"I absolutely want to discover what we are living in. And you are the only one to be on the same wavelength."

"Have you talked to any other neighbors?"

"Yes, one night, I rang the door on the

right, next to mine, Sean Pomeroy, sculptor. He thought I was crazy. I'll admit it was late. And that pianist, Louise Fromet, on the fifth floor, she sent me packing. As for your artist friend on the fourth, she thinks we have way too much imagination!"

They both laughed.

"Perhaps you and I are overreacting, imaging things," Clarissa said.

"Perhaps! But let's get to the bottom of it!"

When she got home, Clarissa felt buoyed by a new energy. This young man shared her thoughts. How comforting and reassuring. And the fact that he was reading one of her books warmed her heart.

Mrs. Dalloway's voice startled her.

"Clarissa, your daughter is downstairs. May I let her come up?"

"Certainly, Mrs. Dalloway."

Jordan rarely visited at this hour. She usually came in the evenings. She must have something important to say.

As always, whenever Clarissa laid eyes on her daughter, she was swept away by proud joy. Jordan was so pretty, so elegant.

"Mums! I came as soon as I found out!"

Jordan was breathless and overexcited.

Clarissa felt puzzled. Whatever did she mean? Jordan couldn't keep still. She fished around in her bag, and handed a small box to her mother. Clarissa opened it. Inside was a lumpy gold and diamond brooch.

"Is that Aunt Serena's?"

Jordan danced around the room, while Chablis stared at her, mesmerized. Clarissa couldn't help laughing. She looked exactly like Andy.

"Darling, I don't get it! Tell me what's going on!"

Jordan came to a halt.

"The expert asked to see me. His voice was shaking. You know what? That brooch belonged to some British aristocrat. Lady Thingummybob. He said I could easily sell it to a museum or a private collection. It's worth a fortune! I have to go put it back in the bank right now. A fortune! I daren't even tell you how much!"

"And it was asleep in Aunt Serena's safe?"

"Yes! For years! She must have bought it cheaply somewhere, and not bothered to have it examined. Mimsy and Pimsy didn't, either. They handed it on without even imagining it could be worth so much. Mums, do you realize what this means? It means I can pay Andy's school for another year without feeling the pinch. It means I can take you, Andy, and Ivan on holiday. We'll have a marvelous trip at stingy old

Aunt Serena's expense. We'll raise our glasses in her honor!"

Clarissa went on laughing as Jordan hugged her tenderly.

"It's so good to hear you laugh, Mums."

"I'm okay, honey. Don't worry about me."

Jordan stepped back in order to observe her more closely. The familiar green eyes meticulously took her in. Clarissa felt as if Jordan were putting her through a scanner and not missing a beat of her inner struggles.

"You said you made some nice new friends? Tell me more!"

They settled on the sofa. Chablis seemed delighted to see Jordan again.

"Yes, a cute reader, very young. I'm supposed to meet her again, but I haven't spoken to her recently. And a charming artist, your age, a painter, who lives on the fourth floor."

She kept back last night's events and her conversation with Jim Perrier. She switched subjects: And Andy? When was she coming back? They had such a great time.

They both decided not to tell Mimsy and Pimsy about the true value of the brooch. Jordan planned to contact her grandfather, whom she fully trusted, and give him the whole story.

On the threshold, Jordan hesitated fleetingly.

"Just tell me one thing, Mums. That woman François is besotted with, she's how old?"

Clarissa took a deep breath.

"She's very young."

Jordan groaned.

"What's her name?"

"Her name is Amber."

Jordan rolled her eyes.

"And what's so special about Amber?"

Clarissa's answer rang out.

"Amber never says no."

It was easy to get into the building. I only had to hang around in front, pretend to be talking on my phone. I had waited for my husband to leave. He had walked out with a dreamy expression on his face, and pink cheeks. I felt like slapping him. I watched him walk away toward the Métro.

I wondered if I still loved him. I wondered if I had ever loved him the way I loved Toby.

But what was left of all that now? A sort of companionship? Two people growing old? Is that all that kept us together? The fear of being alone?

The bearded young man I had seen before stepped out of the building and politely held the door open for me. I murmured a thank-you and walked in.

I discovered a poorly kept building, which surprised me, as my husband was usually fussy about that type of thing. The entrance smelled of cabbage soup and dampness. The elevator was minuscule and did not seem safe. I ignored it, walking up the six flights.

There were three doors per landing, and with each landing I passed, I could hear people getting on with their lives. Music, laughter, the sound of plates and cutlery, the whine of a vacuum cleaner. Quarrelling, a child crying, the blare of a TV set.

It was an old-fashioned, run-down Parisian building, with worn-out floorboards, scored walls, paint that was fading and splotched.

And it was here that my husband had chosen to live behind my back.

On the doorbell by the middle door, there was his name, François ANTOINE. It was here. No turning back now.

I took a deep breath, squared my shoulders. What was I going to say to this woman? *Hello, I'm Mrs. Antoine. I'm François's wife.*

I imagined her face. Would she be horrified? Ashamed? Would she roar with laughter?

If I waited too long, I'd never ring. I'd end up fleeing in a panic. I had to do it now.

No thinking, no planning things out. Action.

I reached out and rang the doorbell.

It made a tinkling sound.

I imagined her thinking, Who's that? Maybe she was in the shower. Maybe she wasn't wearing any clothes. Maybe she was still in bed, the rumpled sheets still smelling of my husband.

I waited and listened. No noise was coming from that apartment. She had to be there. François had left five minutes ago, and I would have seen a blond lady come out.

I had only seen the young bearded guy.

I rang again, longer this time.

No answer.

I knocked firmly. Then I pounded.

I wanted to shout "I know you're in there. Stop hiding and open the door." I wanted to swear, to kick the door in.

No answer.

As I stood there, incensed, confounded, the door on the left opened, and the grouchy old man I had already seen poked his head around and stared at me.

"You're making a lot of noise," he said.

"I'm looking for the blond lady who lives here."

He stared at me even harder.

"There's no blond lady here."

"Are you sure?" I asked.

"I've been living here for the past thirty years, and if a blond lady had moved in, I would have known."

"So who lives here, then?"

"Can't you read? François Antoine. Nice quiet man. You've got the wrong place."

With that, he had slammed the door in my face.

6
INK

The final words of my latest novel.
ROMAIN GARY, December 2, 1980

You see, I can't even write this properly.
VIRGINIA WOOLF, March 28, 1941

A tune playing on her phone dragged her slowly from sleep. Bewildered, she thought at first it was her alarm, and that she was late for a meeting, but what meeting? Then she realized it was the melody she'd chosen for Toby. "Hotel California," the Eagles.

"Hey, Blue!"

Her first husband's voice hadn't changed. It was still kind and warm. She felt gladdened just by listening to it. He'd never stopped using the nickname he found for her when they first met all those years ago, inspired by her eye color.

"Did I wake you up? Sounds like it!"

She stretched her arms, got out of bed

with difficulty. The aches and pains, the tiredness, all were still there.

"I'll get over it!"

She knew why he was calling.

"Did Jordan phone you?"

"No one can keep anything from you, Blue."

He admitted their daughter was worried. Jordan felt something was up with her mother, and that it had been going on for a while. She'd opened up to her father. Clarissa listened. She let Toby talk. She visualized him facing his beloved sea. After their divorce, Toby decided to settle down in the Basque country, near Biarritz. He'd been able to continue his career as an English teacher. At present, he was retired. He lived in Guéthary, in a new apartment she had not been to, on the top floor of an ancient hotel overlooking the Atlantic. She knew there was a pretty terrace, seen in Jordan's and Andy's photos.

Born in Santa Monica, Toby needed to breathe the ocean air and listen to the roar of the swell. He regularly went down to ride the waves at the surf spot at Parlementia. The state of the sea made him despondent, as it became increasingly polluted as the years went by. He had told Clarissa swimming was often prohibited because of the hazard of contaminated seawater. Forced to roast on the dike without being able to dip a toe into the ocean, vacationers came less often. Every summer, hundreds of fish washed up on the rocks. The stink of dead fish, added to the reek of unclean water, made it impossible to breathe. Within ten years, the beaches at Guéthary and neighboring Bidart vanished. They'd been gobbled up by the waves, falling prey to shifting sands and rising sea level. Clarissa knew the same thing had happened in Biarritz, to the north. She'd seen the reports shot at the Côte des Basques. Nowadays, there was no difference between low and high tide. The long golden beach, loved by surfers and holidaymakers, the pride of the city, had also surrendered, vanquished by the breakers.

"So, tell me. What's up? Jordan said you left François."

"Yes, that's right."

Clarissa sat down on the sofa, with Chablis lying at her feet. She had always trusted Toby. But it seemed that this morning, so many things were still bottled up within her. She was finding it more and more difficult to express herself, to put the right words to her feelings. Yet words had never failed her. They were her friends, not her foe.

"Take your time," said Toby after a while. "No pressure. And if you don't want to discuss François, then don't."

"I've been having the strangest dreams since I moved here," she said finally, because she knew she had to say something, and Toby was waiting. "I think they are interfering with how I feel."

"What kind of dreams? Do you want to talk about them?"

Toby's voice was at its kindest. He was a good listener, she knew. But was he ready for what she had to say? She was going to open up the door to sorrow; she was going to shine a light along the black path of grief that had led to the end of their marriage. And she couldn't help thinking back to that heart-wrenching instant when he had admitted to her, forlornly, that he could no longer bear her sorrow, that she was drowning in it, that it was pulling her down, and him, too, and that ten years after the birth of their daughter, she still had not been able to find joy within the miracle of Jordan's arrival. No, she had turned her back to it; she had remained trapped in the tragedy of their son's death; she had decided to go on grieving, while he wanted to smile at life, to give it a chance, to move on, without her. Without her.

"I've been dreaming about the hospital over and over again."

She heard him breathe.

"Tell me."

Toby knew exactly which hospital she was referring to. There was only one hospital, engraved forever in their minds. She told him the dreams were taking her back there, against her will, every night, and that she fell asleep with dread because she knew what was in store. She was back there; she could smell that awful hospital smell; she could hear the squealing noise the rubber wheels of the gurney made on the linoleum when they rolled her out of the birthing room; she could hear the sound of Toby crying. But the dreams did more than that, focusing on the moment they had put the baby in her arms, gently, respectfully, as if he had been alive, as if all had been well. They said she could hold him for as long as she wanted.

With extraordinary vividness, the dream revealed the perfectly formed little face, and it had seemed so peaceful, so charming. She had put her mouth on the crown of the tiny head, and she had felt there was no warmth there, no life at all. The dream allowed her to feel the fuzz of the baby's head under her lips. In her arms, she clasped their dead son while Toby cried at her side. They never knew what had happened, exactly. When she arrived at the hospital to give birth, she quickly understood something was wrong by the way the medical staff reacted. They were obviously alarmed. Yet her pregnancy had been normal all along. The doctor (she would never forget the man's serious face, the earnestness of his gaze) had told them the heart was no longer beating. The baby had died. Her womb had become a sepulcher. They were told she was going to have to go through the birth. She had glanced at the small suitcase at Toby's feet. She had carefully packed the brand-new baby clothes. They knew it was going to be a boy, ever since the second ultrasound. They had chosen his name. They had been using it all along.

She'd had to give birth to a dead child. During the long, grueling hours of the ordeal it had been, Toby had never left her side, her hand in his. She had pushed, pushed with all her might, to expel a small corpse. It was indescribable.

This had happened years and years ago. Clarissa had learned to fight against the void it had left behind. She thought she had been able to make peace with it. But no, ever since she had moved in, the dreams forced her to go back to the blackest moment of her life. The pain was excruciating. And then her voice broke and the tears came.

"My darling Blue," said Toby. "My sweet, sweet Blue."

He said he wished he could be there right now, with her, and take her into his arms. He said she had to feel he was there. He was there. Hearing him consoled her. She felt better, wiped her eyes. She told him not to mention this to their daughter. He promised he wouldn't. She said she didn't know why this was happening.

All of a sudden, she remembered what Jim Perrier had told her. He had warned her. "They" were listening to every word. All the time. She stiffened. She couldn't tell Toby she was convinced the dreams were induced by something, somebody. But she longed to. She longed to get it all out, to convey her misgivings, to describe the C.A.S.A. residence, Dr. Dewinter, Mrs. Dalloway. She shut up.

"Why don't you come and stay for a couple of days?" said Toby. "I have a very nice guest room; ask Andy about it. It will do you good. The sea is clean at the moment, not like in summer. I'll cook for you, and we can go for long walks. What do you think?"

She felt tempted.

"What about your lady friend?"

"What lady friend?"

"Andy says there's a new one."

He chuckled, and it felt good to hear him laugh.

"She doesn't live with me."

"Maybe she won't appreciate the idea of your ex-wife coming to stay."

"Blue, I haven't seen you in such a long time. Just get on that train and come."

She told him she'd think about it. A change of air was no doubt a good idea. She talked about her work, the bilingual notes she took each day. She didn't tell Toby that in order to write, she hid from the cameras filming her around the clock, often in the toilet, where she felt safe, and where there was no surveillance; she didn't tell him, either, that she no longer used her computer, but a pen, and two notebooks that never left her side, one in English, the other in French. She described Mia White, with whom she was having tea tomorrow, and her neighbor Adelka, who had invited her for drinks on Friday.

Her voice had perked up again. Toby was rejoiced to hear it. Then he brought up the

211

Aunt Serena brooch story, which a delighted and chortling Jordan had narrated to him. Their daughter was already at work, crafting the perfect holiday for her loved ones. What a sweetheart their Jordan was. Toby sighed. He missed Andy; he didn't see her enough.

"Andy's coming over to spend the night next week," said Clarissa. "We'll call you, I promise."

"And how's your father?"

Clarissa said the latest news was good: Her old dad was doing fine. He was in high spirits. The brooch story was all thanks to him. He had been thrilled to hear about its real value and the prospect of their upcoming vacation.

"I'm glad to hear this. Send my love. And take care of yourself, Blue. Relax. Don't overdo things. Remember, I'm here if you need me. Go for it."

When she hung up, Clarissa told herself she was blessed to have such an ally in her life; a man who knew her intimately, closely, a man who had seen her give birth, a man who had been at her side when they had buried their stillborn son, a man who had always been faithful to her. At present, she was able to comprehend why he had left her. He had held out for twelve years.

Jordan was growing into a bright and lively little girl, full of laughter. But Clarissa was still under the influence of a black, persistent fog, and Toby felt powerless faced with her suffering. Later, it was François who managed to put a stop to her undying despondency by suggesting hypnosis. This ended up bringing her closer to François, and further away from Toby, which was ironic, given her current situation.

Clarissa went into the kitchen. She made some tea with bottled water, avoiding the tap.

"Hello, Clarissa! Did you sleep well? Today, it will be cloudy and muggy. I've adapted the air conditioner accordingly. The shopping drone will be coming by at ten. Do you wish to modify your grocery list?"

Clarissa had decided to no longer answer Mrs. Dalloway. It was her way of expressing her dissatisfaction. She acted as if Mrs. Dalloway wasn't there. She hadn't undergone the medical examinations in the bathroom for the past week. A silent revolution. She wondered what was going to happen. She didn't feel afraid; her curiosity took over.

While she sipped her tea, Clarissa read her mail on her device. She missed her friends. Some of them kept on sending messages, like Joyce, who wondered if Clarissa had gone on a trip. Patricia had bumped into François and had been shocked by his appearance. He had refused to say anything to her. What was going on? Clarissa had not replied. When she was ready, she'd do it.

"Clarissa, you haven't answered. Is everything all right?"

Clarissa paid no attention to Mrs. Dalloway. She checked her agenda for the day. She was meeting a producer and screenwriter she had already worked with in the past for a new TV show. She then made reservations for a trip to London in order to spend some time with her father. She had a little surprise for him: a dainty porcelain hand she'd found in the flea market at Saint-Ouen for his collection. Why did her father love hands? She had no idea. He had always collected them. His passion had nothing to do with his profession; he had been an attorney. Ever since Clarissa had been a girl, she had seen his hand collection grow. It now took up most of his bedroom.

She put on her cordless headset and listened to Patti Smith through the sound system. How she loved that sensual, throaty voice. When Mrs. Dalloway interrupted "Because the Night" through her earphones to ask her again why she wasn't responding, Clarissa had to curb her irritation. "They" knew she was all right; "they" could see every move she made. It was infuriating.

She turned off the song, stepped under the shower, did her exercises, got dressed. She was about to go out for her walk, when the doorbell rang. She wasn't expecting anyone. And Mrs. Dalloway hadn't announced a visitor. She wasn't sure who it might be. Perhaps Jim Perrier? Maybe he had the results from the lab? But surely he would have warned her he was coming up. She recalled he had expressly told her not to divulge anything important within the residence.

Clarissa stayed still, standing in front of the door. She could hear no noise coming from outside. The bell chimed again. She felt a twinge of alarm. Who was out there? Slowly, she stepped toward the door, taking care to remain silent. On the screen near the wooden panel, Dr. Dewinter's features suddenly loomed up, making her jump.

"Hello, Mrs. Katsef. I know you're there and that you can see me."

Clarissa said nothing, taking in the large flat face, the heavy jaw, the heavily made-up lids. There was something frightening about Dr. Dewinter today. Was it the way she stared into the camera? That flinty look in her eyes?

"I would like to speak to you, Mrs. Katsef. If you don't mind."

Clarissa kept still. The door between her and the doctor felt like a very flimsy protection. What if the doctor knew how to get in? Where could she hide?

Dr. Dewinter knocked.

"I'm waiting for you to answer, Mrs. Katsef."

Her voice had gone nasal, with a disagreeable twang to it. On the screen, her face seemed flatter than ever, wide and moonlike.

Abruptly, as quickly as it had come, the fear drained away from Clarissa. Who the hell did these people think they were? Sticking their noses into her private life in that way. Spying on her all the time. It was intolerable. It was unacceptable. She rushed to fetch her rock-star boots from the cupboard, slipped them on. The extra inches gave her a welcome power.

Clarissa strode back to the entrance, flung the door open. Dr. Dewinter's broad shoulders seemed more muscular than ever. Her hands were large and menacing with their bloodred nails.

"Ah, there you are, Mrs. Katsef."

"Hello, Dr. Dewinter."

They stood facing each other. Clarissa

could smell the fresh detergent scent coming from the doctor. She bored into the grayish irises without blinking. This went on for a moment, until the doctor said in a very pleasant voice, "How are you today, Mrs. Katsef?"

"Very well, Doctor. And yourself?"

"Very well."

"There's something you wish to say, I believe?"

The doctor beamed, revealing her white teeth.

"May I come in, Mrs. Katsef?"

"I'm afraid not," said Clarissa, smiling as well but not letting the smile reach her eyes and soften them.

"I see," said Dr. Dewinter brightly. She fingered the pearl in her fleshy earlobe.

"Is there a problem?" Clarissa asked.

Dr. Dewinter glanced down at the device in her hand. She hummed a little tune while she swiped through it.

"Ah, yes, right here. It appears we have had no health recordings for you in the past week, Mrs. Katsef."

"Is that so?" said Clarissa.

Dr. Dewinter's smile became more strained. The steely look was back.

"We were wondering if there was something wrong with your bathroom system and if it needs to be looked at. I can send Ben in now."

Clarissa couldn't bear the idea of another intrusion.

"I guess I keep forgetting to do my check-ups," she said, shrugging.

Dr. Dewinter arched an eyebrow.

"And yet your personal assistant reminds you to do so several times a day."

"She does."

"And it appears you have not been inter-acting with your personal assistant, either."

The smile had disappeared.

"I'll do the checkups, Dr. Dewinter. I promise."

Clarissa nearly added *"And now get the hell out of here."* She began to close the door.

The doctor took one step forward, nearly striding over the threshold and forcing Chablis, who was lingering there, to dart back with a quivering mew. The husky voice had dropped to a whisper.

"Let me make myself clear, Mrs. Katsef. All artists of the residence must obey proto-col."

Clarissa forced herself not to move back. The doctor hovered disturbingly close. She could make out the faint whiff of perspira-tion behind the detergent.

"And what happens if an artist doesn't

follow the protocol?"

Dr. Dewinter's features gathered into a tight, pinched mask, making her look older and foreboding.

"That has never happened," she said flatly. "And we wouldn't want it to. Would we? Good-bye, Mrs. Katsef. Have a nice day."

The doctor turned around and slid into the elevator. She disappeared.

Clarissa heaved a sigh of relief and closed the door. She could already see herself telling all this to Jim Perrier and hearing him hoot with laughter. She would imitate the doctor's voice to perfection. She'd exaggerate her gestures, hunch up her shoulders to ape the doctor's burly ones. Jim would crack up.

She went into the bathroom and swiftly underwent the medical tests, to get them over with and to no longer have to tolerate any more surprise visits. Conflicting feelings wrestled within her. Furious, she told herself she'd given in too quickly. Then she'd dig in her heels, convinced she wasn't giving up the fight only because she'd chosen to obey for today.

"There you go, Mrs. Dalloway. All done. Happy now?"

"I'm most pleased, Clarissa, and thank you for taking the time. For your information, the shopping drone will soon be here."

"Thanks for looking after that, Mrs. Dalloway. I'm off for my walk."

"Perfect."

A drone assigned to the residence delivered everything Clarissa ordered online twice a week. It deposited the provisions on the balcony in a special container. This didn't stop Clarissa from visiting a nearby grocery store for her fruit and vegetables, which she preferred to choose herself, after fingering and sniffing them, like in the good old days. But what she brought back had no savor, no aroma. She yearned to bite into the pulp of a tomato, an apricot, a melon that tasted like long ago. Everything seemed to have a desperately bland flavor nowadays.

As she was about to leave, Mrs. Dalloway declared an internal message from Jim Perrier had just arrived.

"Dear Clarissa, I read *Topography of Intimacy* with great pleasure. The part in Virginia Woolf's bedroom at Monk's House is remarkable and most original. I read it several times. Did you ever consider adapting your novel into a TV show? I'd be happy to discuss it with you. See you soon, Jim. Do you wish to answer him now, Clarissa?"

"I'll do it when I come back. Thank you, Mrs. Dalloway."

"You're welcome."

So, Jim Perrier had gotten in touch. This meant he had information for her concerning the powder, and, no doubt, C.A.S.A. According to what they had set up, she was to go to Café Iris at 8:00 A.M.

She therefore had to stay put until tomorrow morning. It seemed to her an endless wait.

At eight o'clock sharp, as it poured with rain, Clarissa was at Café Iris, on time. The terrace was closed due to the bad weather. She took shelter inside. Jim Perrier had not arrived yet. Last night, she'd sent a quick answer, thanking him for his nice message and saying she'd be happy to discuss a TV adaptation with him. He hadn't responded, but she'd been expecting that.

Other clients ate their breakfasts around her. The place was animated and nosy. She ordered more tea, as hers had gone tepid. Time ticked by. No sign of Jim. Had he been held up? She had no way of contacting him. She waited a little longer. At nine o'clock, she decided to go home. It was odd, his not showing up. She rushed along under the downpour.

There was no new message from him when she got to the residence. He must have run into a problem and had not known how to reach her. No reason for her to worry. She'd bide her time until he got hold of her again.

This afternoon, she was meeting Mia White, in a tearoom near the Bastille. Because of the rain, they'd decided to meet indoors. Clarissa suggested a place she knew well, on rue de la Roquette. She often caught up with her daughter there, as Jordan lived nearby. When she got there, she saw Mia White was already installed at a table.

The young woman had been in touch recently, suggesting they get together, and Clarissa had agreed to see her again, despite her misgivings. This time, she'd be careful not to disclose anything too personal. She was looking forward to conversing with her young reader. Getting out of the residence, taking a break, trying not to think about her husband, these had all become essential to her. This morning, as she had waited for Jim Perrier in vain, she'd received a pitiful text message from François. He wrote to say he was at the end of his rope. Totally desperate. He wanted to do himself in. He must see her, peacefully. He suggested she come to their apartment, so that she might pack her things, talk about the future. For a brief moment, she felt pity. Had she been too hard on him, perhaps? Did he deserve a second chance? Should she go talk to him? While she had been thinking it over, the little voice she knew well had whispered to her: *Hey, hang on, look at you! Talk to him? You're delusional. You're going to sit here nicely and say you understand, yes, you understand because you always understood? So marvelously comprehensive. So wonderfully patient. Cut the crap.* Clarissa ended up not answering François's text.

Mia White observed her with the same benign yet penetrating gaze, which became unsettling after a while. She looked young and pretty, with her disarming smile. She was reading *A Room of One's Own,* her oversize glasses perched on the tip of her adorable nose. Wasn't she overdoing it? As if she wanted above all to please Clarissa. Was this just inept eagerness from a zealous devotee? Or something else? Perhaps Clarissa was asking herself too many questions, and so couldn't even relax enough to enjoy the moment.

The young girl bent over to pick an object out of her bag. It was a frayed copy of *Topography of Intimacy.*

"I'd really like you to sign this," she said.

"With pleasure," replied Clarissa.

As she opened the book, she noticed there were notes in nearly every margin. Entire paragraphs had been underlined.

"I read it thoroughly," admitted Mia White with a smile. "And I often read it all over again."

The date written on the flyleaf was the same one as the publication of the book.

"This is my mother's copy. Your book was published the year I was born."

"So your mother read it, too?" asked Clarissa as she signed it.

"She did, but I pinched it from her and never gave it back."

A delightful impish grin.

"I think you mentioned your mother's from Nantes?"

"That's right." Mia White nodded. "I grew up there."

They switched effortlessly from one language to another, like they had during their previous encounter.

The waitress came to take their orders. There were some delicious cakes to succumb to. The place was not full; it was quiet and comfortable. Outside, the rain splashed merrily. Glistening umbrellas bobbed up and down along the sidewalk.

For a fleeting moment, Clarissa wondered if she should tell Mia White about the night the alarm went off in the residence, and that she thought she had seen her there, wearing a dressing gown, her hair braided down her back. But Mia White spoke up before she did.

"Would you mind telling me about what happened in Virginia Woolf's house? That's also one of my favorite parts. Unless you'd rather not, of course. I know you've been asked about it repeatedly, and I'm sure it's tedious for you to have to go over it again."

Mia White used the same method as last time, those wide, beseeching, respectful eyes. It was impossible to resist them. Clarissa felt she was in no danger. She had often described that crucial scene to journalists, to readers. It wasn't as if she had anything new to add. She felt in control.

She said she had been spending time with her father in Brighton. This happened about twenty years ago. Her father was doing very well then; he was in his late seventies and still energetic. He enjoyed traveling with his daughter, discovering new places with her. He was the one who suggested visiting Monk's House, the cottage Virginia and Leonard Woolf had bought in 1919, at Rodmell, in East Sussex. It was only thirty minutes or so from Brighton. He had heard there was a lovely garden. They could visit it on their way back to London.

Clarissa articulated her story calmly, as if she had switched on automatic pilot. The words she had so often used wrought their way around her tale, and she did not think twice about them. Mia White listened assiduously, her tiny fingers cupping her mug. The rain hissed outside. Clarissa described the drive from Brighton, her father's long, knobby hands on the wheel, the lush greenery of the English countryside. What she didn't tell Mia White was her state of mind at that point in her life, the sadness she had been carrying around for so many years. With the passing of time, the weight of the sadness felt like a huge boulder she had to drag along behind her. It was like coping with a shameful disease. She had learned to live with lugging it everywhere, hauling it up stairs, pushing it into rooms that were always too small.

Clarissa went on with what she had to say, discarding the boulder of agony. But it was still there, lurking in the back of her mind. She found it perturbing to pursue two trains of thought: a spoken and unclouded one describing Virginia Woolf's house, and the other, inner and murky, hovering over an obscure zone she did not wish to return to. She had to concentrate in order to stop the shadow from overtaking the light; she threw herself into her story, describing their arrival at the quaint village of Rodmell, which had preserved its original features. Her father had parked near a pub, where they each enjoyed a ploughman's lunch, a plate of cheddar with ham, pickles, and bread. While she evoked their meal, she clearly and precisely recalled the conversation she'd had with her father. Should she repress it? Or, on the contrary, let it out? She dithered, swallowed her tea. Mia White waited, devotedly.

"That's funny, I've just remembered what my dad and I talked about that day. I had forgotten it, and it came back to me."

"Would you mind sharing it with me?"

Her father had asked her if she felt more French than English, now that she'd been living in France for a long span of years. She had given it a thought. It was a tricky matter. Deep down, she had no idea. And she still hadn't. She was aware of her distinctive status, a crossbreed one, powerless to choose one country over the other — a discomfort she had perceived her entire life, the sensation of not belonging to a nation, of being unable to claim an origin. She was twofold. She had two mother tongues, two worlds, two homelands. With Brexit, it had become even more intricate. But that afternoon at Rodmell, on that sunny spring day, neither her father nor she could have predicted the calamitous chain of events following Great Britain's choice.

"Let's get back to Virginia Woolf, if you will," said Clarissa.

"With pleasure." Mia White nodded.

Clarissa had followed her father along a quiet little street dotted with pretty, traditional houses. The Woolf cottage was much smaller than she had anticipated. There was nothing luxurious there. Her father, like her, knew little about the life of the writer who had lived here. He was not an avid reader. Golf, tennis, and tournaments were more his sort of thing. As he grew older, he spent time looking after the garden behind his London home in Hackney. He enjoyed tending to the plants and flowers Clarissa's mother, Solange, had planted with such care.

Their guide's name was Margaret, a slender young woman with protruding teeth and milky skin. She welcomed them as if they were entering her own home, and pronounced the name Virginia with hushed adoration. She told them in a whisper, as if not wanting to disturb the owners, who still lived there, that Virginia wrote in a small lodge, where she liked to be alone, while her husband, Leonard, toiled outside; he planted cherry, apple, prune, and fig trees, and garnered his own fruit and vegetables with the help of his faithful gardener, Percy, as well as his own honey.

Their visit began with the garden. It was magnificent. Her father gasped with joy, overcome; he pointed out gladioli, clematises, roses, zinnias, geum, dahlias, agapanthus. Margaret remained silent, smiling, no doubt heartened by the fervor of this old gentleman's eagerness. Never would Clarissa forget this enchanted orchard, the sensational exuberance of the colors bursting around them. They walked along the thin redbrick path cutting through dazzling blazes of orange, purple, red, pink. Margaret pointed out a fishpond, installed by the Woolfs, where dragonflies skimmed the water, while bees hummed actively, butterflies spun here and there, birds twittered. The glory of a garden in spring.

"I have a few memories of gardens in Nantes," said Mia White gently. "But I haven't seen a real one, like the one you are describing, for a long time."

"I wonder what Leonard Woolf would say if he came back now and saw what his beloved garden has become," said Clarissa.

"Is it completely dried out?" asked Mia White, horror-struck.

Clarissa said she hadn't been back there since. But she had seen upsetting photos. Yes, most of it was a parched mess, like the majority of gardens nowadays. The perpetual heat waves, scorching summers, scarcity of water, brutal storms, end of natural pollination, and slow extinction of insects had taken a deathly toll on beautiful gardens.

"That's so sad," said Mia White in the same soft voice.

"But the house is still standing," said Clarissa. "Houses do last. Thank God."

"Why do you love houses so much?"

Clarissa said she had thought about that often; she supposed her obsession with houses came from her profession, her penchant for measuring spaces, for needing to define them geographically.

"I imagine there are houses you loved?"

"Yes. Several."

She described her French grandparents' country home in Burgundy, near Sens, razed in her childhood in order to give way to a highway. A trauma. And a place in Tuscany, up in the hills overlooking Florence, where she had spent a long summer with her husband. She told Mia White about the simplicity of the rustic white house, called *colonica* in Italian, and how she had felt at home there. She still remembered the sensation of the cool ancient stone tiles under her naked feet, and the particular shape of the doorknob, which had left an emotional imprint in the hollow of her hand.

But there was also what walls whispered to her. What she had experienced in Romain Gary's apartment, all those years ago, had been extraordinarily powerful. She had wondered how she would feel when she got to Monk's House. She had listened to Margaret tell them more about how the Woolfs bought and transformed the long and low weather-boarded cottage with a slate roof. It had been rudimentary in the beginning. No hot water, no bath, no indoor toilets; small, damp rooms, but great promise: a wild, generous garden, with the steeple of the nearby church peeking out over the greenery, and beyond, the view of the smooth, rolling stretch of the South Downs.

Clarissa had not yet read anything by Virginia Woolf. Over the years, she had stuck to Romain Gary, Maupassant, Zola, Baudelaire, Modiano. She had not started to write, either. When they visited the premises, she was still working as a property surveyor. The large black boulder of her suffering lingered persistently. She didn't tell

Mia White that she suspected her father had taken her on this trip because he was aware of how unhappy she was. And it was true to say that the beauty of the garden had given her some peace.

Margaret had opened up the door to the house, and they had followed her in. Clarissa remembered there were few other visitors that day. They were practically alone. In the little entrance hung the particular odor of an old countryside home, one that was loved and looked after, kept spick-and-span, with nothing dusty and neglected about it. The house was alive. It breathed. Margaret had explained that everything had been preserved to look exactly as it had in the Woolfs' day. A person lived here year-round, even during the winter, when the premises were closed to the public. The living room walls were green, a color Virginia loved, said Margaret. A radiant green called "viridian," which Vanessa Bell, Virginia's sister, who was a painter, had gently mocked. The ceilings were low, garnished with rafters. Under their steps, the waxed floorboards creaked. Clarissa felt as if Virginia Woolf might turn up any minute. She'd stride in, carrying the flowers she'd just cut, her shears still in hand. She'd arrange them into a pretty vase. She'd sit in the large chintz armchair near the high fireplace, and she'd pick up a book. Later, she'd look at her correspondence, placed in the open secretary chest.

There were books everywhere, on the shelves, on the small low tables, but also on the steps of the stairs. The true home of a writer and an editor. As of 1929, Margaret said, the couple had gradually started renovating the house, thanks to Virginia's increasing royalties, from *Mrs. Dalloway, To the Lighthouse,* and especially *Orlando.* The kitchen was entirely redone, a dining room was created, and a bathroom with a toilet was installed on the first floor. Margaret said Virginia adored spending time in her bath. She would stay there for hours, and their maid could hear her talking to herself, trying out scenes from her books. Another link to Romain Gary, who had also worked from his bath, and Clarissa acknowledged the unexpected connection between the two writers, which pleased her. She could now put her finger on it; what she relished here, what she hungered for was the private story spinning behind the public figures, linked to the homes they lived in, slept in, and wrote in.

Margaret told them that later the house was added on to. A room was built in the attic, and it became Leonard's office; then a square brick extension formed a first-floor bedroom giving directly on to the garden by a flight of stairs, Virginia's room, where she slept. Clarissa had asked to see that room, and Margaret had answered, courteously, that it was rarely open to visitors. Clarissa had been disappointed. She had insisted. With a firmer tone, Margaret had said it was impossible, and to change the subject, she led them to the writing lodge at the end of the orchard, where Virginia worked. With her finger, Clarissa had gently touched the chair, the inkpot, the reading glasses. She knew full well these objects had not belonged to Virginia, but the literary staging was a pleasant one. Virginia had written *Mrs. Dalloway* within these walls, and while a bee droned against the windowpane, it seemed to Clarissa that the writer's shadow, an angular sentinel, loomed behind each garden rose.

This writer, whose books she had never read, whom she knew little about, inhabited this place with a singular intensity. Unlike Romain Gary's flat, where Clarissa had perceived vestiges of the past, something else was at stake for her here and now, a fork in the road, a turning point, but what, exactly? She couldn't tell. Her father had asked her if she was feeling all right. She looked odd, he said. How could she explain there was a density here pulling at her, reeling her in, like a fish caught on a hook?

Had she uttered those sentences out loud to Mia White? She hadn't meant to. It had been part of the darker, inner stream she hadn't planned on mentioning. She carried on swiftly, going back to what Margaret was telling them about the house, that it was a private place of intense creation and work. Friends did come to stay occasionally, but for the Woolfs, this was their intimate shelter, their little haven. The villagers had gotten used to seeing Mrs. Woolf walk quickly along the Downs with her dog, in all sorts of weather, muttering to herself. Here was where Virginia felt closest to her own life, Margaret had pointed out. In her letters, in her diary, Virginia had described the treasured hours at Monk's House, no talking, diving deep into reading, into writing, into pure, translucent slumber, into the green of the Downs and the trees, with no one around to disrupt it all, no noise, only the sovereignty of silence.

And then Margaret had said cheerily, "Monk's House is such a happy house; don't you feel it?"

Her father and Clarissa had both said that

yes, they felt it.

"That's how we want to think about it. A happy house. All of us who work here, we don't often mention Virginia's death. We like to think more about her life."

Clarissa had glanced at Margaret. Virginia's death? What did she mean? Margaret looked surprised.

"You mean you don't know?"

"Know what?" Clarissa's father had said.

"How Virginia died," said Margaret.

A hazy memory came whirling back, an image Clarissa had seen in a film, a long time ago. But she couldn't place it. She asked Margaret what had happened. Margaret lowered her voice, as if she didn't want to be overheard. They were standing on the small terrace in front of the cottage. It had happened on March 28, 1941.

For a reason that was unknown to her, Clarissa felt an urge to understand what had taken place, while she was still on the grounds. She was taken over by an imperious sensation. She wanted to know. She had to find out. Margaret continued whispering. Virginia hadn't been well, for a long period; she was a fragile person, with "a medical history." She was fifty-nine, and had suffered several depressions. She was slowly sinking into gloom, despite the joy she found in writing.

Clarissa had listened to Margaret's gentle tone, and her eyes had wandered to a portrait of the writer glimpsed through the living room window — the long, tormented face, the mouth with its bitter lines. She had seen Romain Gary's features superimpose themselves upon Virginia's, imbued with the same troubled wistfulness. Margaret said that a few days beforehand, Virginia had come back drenched from a long walk in the rain. Her husband had become worried when he saw her arrive, like a pale, thin sleepwalker. He had instantly obtained a consultation with their doctor in Brighton. Dr. Wilberforce prescribed rest, after finding Virginia feeble and strangely distant.

On March 28, a Friday, in the secret of her writing lodge, Virginia had written two letters — one for her husband, the other for her beloved sister. She had told her husband she was going to do a bit of housework, then go out for a short walk before lunch. Leonard had gone up to his office. At eleven o'clock, their maid saw Virginia head out toward the fields, wearing her fur coat, carrying her walking stick. She was striding with her usual energy and seemed to know exactly where she was going.

"Virginia left the house by that door, here," Margaret said. "Then she went out by the garden, in front of the church, just there."

"Show me," said Clarissa, and it was the property surveyor talking, whose eyes were now measuring the exact steps Virginia had taken, drawn over the earth in an indelible ink mark only Clarissa could see.

Margaret indicated the way, and Clarissa pursued it, just like she had mentally followed Romain Gary after his lunch on Tuesday, December 2, 1980, when he had walked along rue de Babylone to reach rue du Bac, on his last day alive.

Mia White stared at her, giving Clarissa her complete attention, her cup halfway to her open lips. Clarissa had to concentrate, focusing on keeping separate the two threads unraveling in her head: the one she mastered and wasn't frightened of, smooth-running, unchanged, and the other thread, darker and more disturbing, which had surfaced as she trailed Virginia's ultimate path to her death, with Margaret at her side, and her flummoxed father in suit, and which was resuscitating now, in this peaceful tearoom, opposite this young woman and her enormous eyes.

Margaret had explained that Virginia went

straight to the river, which took her twenty minutes or so from the cottage. As she listened, Clarissa saw the scene from above, high up over the fields, and she felt she could make out every single step Virginia had taken to get to the banks of the Ouse, a long, thin line of black ink etched along the ground, which drew her like a magnet. She had asked to see the river, which that day ebbed low and smooth, not at all like it had been the day Virginia died, all bubbly and wild, bursting its banks, flowing fast and strong, according to Margaret. All around them was a flat and bare landscape, with hardly any trees. Somewhere along this austere riverbank, Virginia had picked up a large stone, shoved it into her pocket; she had left her walking stick on the ground, and she had descended into the water. She had let the waters close up above her and she had drowned.

Clarissa remembered her father had been concerned, looking at her constantly while Margaret spoke. Had it been a good idea, bringing his daughter here, on the trail of another fragile woman? This she did not tell Mia White, or did she? The two threads of her story were now intertwined, coalescing, and she found it confusing to keep them separate. Margaret had pointed to the wooden and iron bridge that spanned the river. This was where Virginia's body was found, three weeks later, by a group of picnickers. Three weeks, Clarissa had thought. An agonizing wait. She kept thinking of Leonard coming down to lunch, wondering where his wife was, and finding the blue envelope with his name on it on the mantelpiece. Inside was a heartbreakingly beautiful farewell letter. Margaret said that Leonard had rushed down to the river, in a panic. He discovered Virginia's footsteps on the bank, and her stick where she had left it. He had hoped against hope that she had ended up running away, that she was still alive.

Margaret led them back to the house. Clarissa remembered that no one spoke as they walked up the path in the fields. When they got to the cottage, her father had taken Margaret aside. He had spoken to her privately, and Clarissa couldn't hear what he was saying. But whatever he had said worked. Margaret came back to Clarissa and put her hand on Clarissa's arm, saying she was happy to show her Virginia's bedroom, which was seldom revealed to visitors. Her father said he'd wait in the garden. Clarissa followed Margaret's bony back, overwhelmed by her father's initiative.

240

They had gone up the slim outdoor stairs and Margaret had unlocked the door. Clarissa had observed the white-tiled fireplace decorated with a lighthouse and a ship, the large bookshelf, the night table, the pink curtains. She had asked Margaret if she could stay there alone for a few moments. She was expecting the young woman to refuse, but Margaret ended up consenting, saying she'd wait downstairs with Clarissa's father.

Clarissa had found herself alone in Virginia Woolf's bedroom. She sat on the narrow bed covered with a white quilt, where Virginia had slept, where Virginia had dreamed. Then she had lain down. The large open window was on her left, nearby. At night, Virginia had probably looked up at the stars. As she reclined on the writer's bed, well-being stroked Clarissa with the softness of a spring breeze, contrasting with the melancholy that had overwhelmed her in Romain Gary's apartment on rue du Bac. She breathed more easily. Part of her sadness had crumbled away. The large boulder she dragged around everywhere had shrunk. Clarissa let peace permeate her. There was no wretchedness here, no woe. Even if Virginia Woolf had, like Romain Gary, chosen to put an end to her life, she had, in her wake, left hopefulness and tranquility as her legacy.

That day, on Virginia's bed, Clarissa realized she needed to express the fascination with places that had guided her to her profession. Ever since the faraway incident on rue du Bac, and her strange encounter with Romain Gary, she had once again been confronted with the potency of the inner memory of houses, the tiny particles of vibrations she garnered there, and which heightened her sensitivity. She knew she would write about this; she knew she would write to dispel the darkness within her. She left Monk's House with a new light in her eyes. Her father had seen it. It had made him happy.

"So you started to write *Topography of Intimacy* just after that episode?"

Mia White's voice startled her. Clarissa had almost forgotten her presence. Once more, she found it impossible to differentiate her innermost thoughts from what she had said out loud.

"That's right. More or less."

"In your novel," Mia White went on, "there is a marvelous conversation with Virginia Woolf's ghost, or spirit. Did you really feel her presence?"

"No," said Clarissa. "I invented all that

bit. But I did feel something else. . . ."

She should have stopped there. She should have elaborated about the ghost she had invented, done what she usually did with readers and journalists: embellish, enhance. She had forgotten how to do that. It had been a while. And her loneliness made her want to open up. She said that when she got back to London, she had gone to buy *Mrs. Dalloway* in a bookstore. On the way to Paris in the train, she had settled down to read it. Reading Virginia Woolf was daunting, she soon discovered. There was hardly any dialogue, and the sentences were very long. In the beginning, she had been put off. She had never read anything like this. She couldn't make heads or tails of it. She felt stupid, illiterate. Perhaps she wasn't sophisticated or literary enough. She stuck at it, doggedly.

Little by little, the winding sentences began to make sense, in the most beautiful manner, as if she had been reading an uninterrupted poem, the words opening windows in front of her eyes, letting the air, the sounds, and the scents in. Virginia Woolf didn't write to seduce her readers, to hook them in from the start with glib techniques, no, not at all. Virginia Woolf cast a spell on her readers, leisurely, gently, so that they did not know at first how they had been lured, so that they followed, enchanted and docile. But she made them think; she made them wonder. She surprised them at times; she destabilized them. And that was what Clarissa admired the most: the beauty and the depth of her prose, and how Virginia Woolf let her readers into her characters' minds, how Mrs. Dalloway's entire life was revealed in one single day, by dint of a ceaseless coming and going between past and present. The entire feat of the book was there. And while she talked to Mia White, Clarissa was also thinking about her own day, François's texts, Jim Perrier and what he was about to divulge, her own writing, waiting for her in the two notebooks that never left her side, her lack of sleep, her peculiar dreams.

"You're not sleeping well, is that it?" asked Mia White in her girlish voice.

Clarissa went quiet, alarmed. What was going on? She must truly be tired. Yet, she was persuaded she had said nothing to Mia White about her sleepless nights. Nothing at all. She lowered her head, stared at the cake crumbs on the tablecloth. She had to get out of here.

"Are you feeling okay?"

Mia White placed an attentive palm on

her hand.

"I'm fine," said Clarissa, moving her own hand back.

"You seem tired. Shall I take you home?"

"That won't be necessary, thanks."

Clarissa signaled to the waitress, her mind still fogged up. She simply could not recall what she had said, or not, to Mia White. *Stupid idiot,* said the little voice. *That'll teach you. That's what happens when you let your guard down.*

Two humid arms suddenly wrapped themselves around her neck.

"Mums! I figured it was you! What are you doing in our area?"

Andy was there, standing behind her, her hair drenched by the rain. She had seen her grandmother through the shop window on her way home from school. Clarissa introduced Mia White to her as one of her young readers; Andy greeted her and sat down at their table. She wouldn't mind a bite of cake, as well, that one on display, the chocolate one; it looked so good. Clarissa ordered a slice for her. She watched the two young girls, who were only a couple of years apart. Mia White seemed more composed, more detached. Andy wasn't paying attention to her posture; she appeared to be taking it easy. Clarissa expected them to establish some sort of connection, but they seemed to stay on different wavelengths. She wondered why. Mia White's stiffness was politely aloof, while Andy devoured her cake with chewing noises, exaggerating bad manners she didn't have. Clarissa noticed her granddaughter's eyes never left Mia White's face, sizing her up, almost defying her, as if she did not wish the young woman to encroach upon her territory.

"I'm going to leave you with your granddaughter," said Mia White finally. "Thank you for the conversation. It was most interesting."

Her tone seemed less sincere than during their first meeting, and her gestures looked contrived. She took her wallet from her purse.

"No, I'll take care of it," said Clarissa. "It's my pleasure."

With a timid wave, Mia White left, thanking her.

"Who's she?" asked Andy, with her mouth full.

"A young fan."

"You see her often?"

"This is the second time I have."

"You like her?"

"To tell the truth, I'm not sure."

"She's pretty, but there's something weird."

"Yes," said Clarissa. "Something weird, as you say."

"What did you say her name was?"

"Mia White."

Andy's thumbs flew over her mobile.

"Strange," she said after a while.

"What?" asked Clarissa.

"All the stuff she puts out there. It's so obvious."

"What do you mean, missy?"

"Well, no young person — I mean of her age, or mine — puts public stuff out there. Even people of my parent's generation stopped doing it years ago. Only really old folks pour their heart out online. We do everything privately, through KingDam or Alamida. She's using such outdated channels. It's like she wants you to see who she is right away."

"And what do you think that means?"

"No idea. Be careful, Mums."

Andy wiped a cluster of crumbs from the corner of her mouth.

"Mummy is concerned about you. I heard her on the phone with Granddad the other day."

In another life, at another moment, Clarissa would have tickled Andy's chin and brushed away Jordan's worries with a smile.

"I've already said this, Mums, but you know you can talk to me. I'm here for you."

How she loved that fine and intelligent little face.

"I know, Andy. Being able to trust you is very precious."

The rain had stopped at last. The umbrella cavalcade faded away.

"Remember what you said about my apartment?"

"Yes. That I felt someone was watching me all the time."

"Well, that's exactly what's going on. The artists who live in the residence are all spied upon."

"Have you talked to Mom about this?"

"No."

"Why not?"

"Your mom thinks I exaggerate. She worries about me. She thinks I forget stuff. She sees me as a disturbed old lady."

"That's because she loves you. And you do forget stuff, sometimes. You repeat things, too. It doesn't bother me."

Clarissa was just getting started.

"Why I am being watched? And the other artists? Why have I been staying awake ever since I moved in? Why are my sleep and dreams being tampered with? And Dr. Dewinter, what does she want?"

"Relax, Mums. I'll help you. Dr. Dethingy doesn't scare me. What do we start with? I can't wait."

"I'll tell you more when you come next week. I'm waiting for some important news. Don't say anything to your mother."

"Cross my heart."

Clarissa grabbed her granddaughter's hand. She smiled at her.

"I'm so lucky to have you around."

"You got it all wrong. I'm the lucky one, having a granny like you."

NOTEBOOK

The apartment obsessed me. I kept thinking about what my husband did within those walls. All the craziest scenarios ran through my head. I even imagined the young bearded guy was his lover.

The only way for me to understand what was going on there was to get inside.

I had to find the key. My husband no doubt kept it on him. But at night? While he was asleep? It was the only way. And then what? If I took it, he'd find out.

A key. A simple key.

It made me smile. Even if I happened to be ensnared by my own pain, I was able to capture the irony of the situation. The symbolism of this deplorable story.

I, the property examiner turned writer, fascinated by places, dwellings and their enigmas, was at the mercy of a key about to unlock a secret. Did I really want to know that secret? I could still turn back. I had that choice. I could protect myself.

I hesitated. But not for long.

My husband was at last fast asleep. I had waited. I had counted each minute. It had seemed endless. Without a noise, I got out of the bed. He had left his clothes rolled up in the bathroom. Slowly, I went through each item. Nothing in his trousers or shirt pockets.

Silently, I went to the entrance. His jacket, on a chair. Nothing in it, apart from his wallet, which I inspected.

His set of keys was on the small table. I checked. There were only the keys to our flat. Nothing else.

I began to feel desperate in the darkness of my home. Did he conceal the key here? There must be a hiding place. Where? I racked my brains, tried to stay calm. If I wanted to hide an object from my husband, where would I come up with? A place he'd never think of looking.

My husband was still fast asleep. I could hear a peaceful snore. He had no idea his secret was soon to be revealed.

I went soundlessly back to the bathroom. His shoes, on the tiled floor. Elegant loafers purchased in Rome.

I bent down and inserted my fingers into the left one. Empty. But I knew. I knew I'd find it.

The key was in the right-hand loafer, right at the top. A thin, flat key that took up no room. A very common sort. Easy to copy.

I heard the floorboards creak.

I just had time to slip the key back into the shoe and stand up.

My husband was standing on the threshold.

"You're awake?" he asked in a drowsy voice.

I replied, lightly, that I was looking for

medicine for my headache. I rummaged around in a drawer, found aspirin. My husband had gone to the toilet. I heard him urinate and flush. He went back to bed.

I couldn't sleep. I kept thinking about how I would go about getting the key duplicated. In the end, it had been easier than I thought. Every year, since his cancer, my husband had to undergo medical examinations. He was put through numerous tests, as well as an MRI scan in a specialized clinic. I always accompanied him.

During his checkup, which lasted two hours, while the doctor's staff took him in charge, and as I supervised his belongings, stored in a locker, I was able to filch the key, which I found this time in his trousers. While he was having the scan, I left the clinic and had the key copied at a nearby locksmith I had previously located.

It had taken me only twenty minutes or so.

Next week, we had a dinner date planned with some close friends.

This time, the person who was going to be late was me. Because, while my husband waited at Caroline and Véronique's, I was going to be at rue Dancourt.

7
BLONDE

And I feel I shan't recover this time.
VIRGINIA WOOLF, March 28, 1941

D. Day.
ROMAIN GARY, December 2, 1980

Adelka's apartment, which was not an attic flat, was smaller than Clarissa's, but with much higher ceilings. She worked in the main room, which was also where her models posed. Clarissa took in the paintings hanging here and there: nude bodies, both male and female, sketched during inhibited moments, with sensitivity and no voyeurism. She found them pleasing and harmonious, and told the young painter, who thanked her.

Clarissa noticed how Adelka had managed to create her own ambience, choosing sunny colors and cozy, stylish furniture. A candle cast its perfumed scent through the air. She felt welcomed, and thought of her own studio up on the eighth floor. She'd been living there for the past two months, and it still had the impersonal aspect of a hotel room. She, the writer obsessed with houses, had failed to craft her own home, one that could bring her well-being and inventiveness.

Adelka spoke to her virtual assistant in Italian, and it answered back with a male voice sounding like the actor Marcello Mastroianni's. Her mother was Italian, and her father French. She had grown up with both languages.

"That's funny," Clarissa remarked. "I'm bilingual, as well, French and English!"

"Are you torn between the two, as I am?"

"Precisely!"

"How amusing! Is there one you prefer over the other?"

"Nope. I can't choose. I'm attached to both."

Adelka's athletic figure was highlighted by a fetching blue dress.

"What would you like, red wine or white?"

"White, please."

While she prepared their drinks, Adelka asked if she'd seen their charming neighbor, Jim Perrier.

"No," said Clarissa carefully.

She had picked out the cameras. She was not going to reveal what Jim had told her. She still had not heard back from him. He must be busy. This had been going on for too long, she thought. But how could she contact him? She'd been back to Café Iris several times, at eight. He'd never turned up. She'd asked the waiters, and they hadn't seen him, either. But one of them had laughed, saying it wasn't surprising, as Jim regularly got plastered. Perhaps he'd gone off to a rehab? Clarissa had found it all puzzling.

Adelka handed her a wineglass.

"I rather fancy Jim. . . . Okay, he's a trifle young for me, but he's so hot in his underwear!"

Clarissa laughed with her, and they raised their glasses.

"After that alarm business, I bumped into him one evening, coming home. We went to a bar and chatted. He's a hard drinker! We had a great time. But he's dead set against C.A.S.A."

"Really?" asked Clarissa innocently. "Why?"

"Do you remember our talk, the night the alarm went off, when we were all outside?"

"More or less."

"You were convinced C.A.S.A. was spying

255

on artists living in the residence, for God knows what reason. I said you both had too much imagination!"

"That's right! We write stories, he and I. Occupational hazard!"

"Jim is up in arms against Dewinter and her methods. He bombarded me with questions: Was I comfortable here? Did I sleep well? Did I ever hear a strange clicking sound? I told him I never had, that I slept like a log. What about you?"

"Me?"

"Are you getting used to it here? You told me even the cat was acting strange in your flat."

She had to be cautious. Pick the right words. Avoid triggering suspicion. She said, casually, that in the beginning, she'd found it hard to settle down in this new space. She'd only just left her husband, and felt miserable and overwrought. She slept better now. So did the cat. And as for the clicking sound, she never heard it again. All was well. It had just been a matter of time.

The fibs flowed, effortlessly.

"I'm so relieved!" exclaimed Adelka. "I was worried. I'm thrilled you've settled in at last. I love my life here. Living in the residence is like a dream come true. I feel safe here, and I work well. I really appreciate the C.A.S.A. team, their thoughtfulness, their expertise."

Clarissa forced her lips into a smile.

"As for Dr. Dewinter," Adelka went on, "what an extraordinary woman! She's remarkably intelligent, don't you find?"

"Remarkably." Clarissa nodded. "Tell me, you don't mind being filmed all the time?"

"Well, the bedroom camera can be switched to 'intimate mode.' Did you know that?"

"Actually, I didn't."

"I didn't, either! Ben told me. 'Intimate mode' can be turned on if you want to have sex or something." She giggled. "So the only thing missing for me in this ideal setting is a boyfriend!"

"Well, what about Jim? Did he remain impervious to your charms?"

"Utterly!"

They laughed together again.

"I even invited him here, would you believe it! I contacted him through the internal server, but he never answered."

"Was this recently?"

"A couple of days ago. I'm mortified! I must have been coming on too strong."

Adelka made a face.

"Perhaps he's on a business trip?" suggested Clarissa.

"Probably. Or he went to see his family? He mentioned his mother lived in Brussels."

Adelka had not had a serious relationship since she had broken up with her violent husband. She wanted children. More and more women were having them late, and on their own. Her mother had friends who had gotten pregnant at over sixty. It had become common. The modern medical world was astounding. But she didn't want to wait that long.

"I understand," said Clarissa as Adelka filled her glass up again. The white wine was making her deliciously tipsy.

"At what age did you become a mother?"

"Quite young. Twenty-seven or so."

A small silence. Then Clarissa added, "Two years before my daughter, Jordan, came into the world, I had a son. Stillborn. Forty-six years ago."

Adelka put her hand to her mouth.

"Oh! How terribly sad!"

"I can talk about it now, a little, but for many years, I simply couldn't."

"Did you see a therapist?"

"I did," said Clarissa, "but something else helped me. I didn't believe in it at first, but it changed my life."

"What was it?" asked Adelka, intrigued.

"Hypnosis."

"I don't know much about hypnosis, and have never tried it. Would you mind telling me some more?"

"Of course."

Clarissa told her how she'd gone to the first consultation dragging her feet, persuaded it was not going to work out. At that point, it had been twenty years or so since the baby's death, twenty years of not getting over it. Psychoanalysts, antidepressants, nothing had helped. Her first husband had ended up leaving her, powerless in the face of her enduring unhappiness. Her second husband, François, the one who was persona non grata, as Adelka recalled, had been convinced it could be the solution for her. She had to give it a go. Little by little, he'd managed to sway her. Clarissa said she'd try it out. She could no longer bear her situation. Things had to change, not only for her but for her entourage, especially her daughter. She presumed her daughter still bore the stigma of spending her childhood and adolescence with a melancholy mother burdened by sorrow. Jordan had never brought this up, but Clarissa thought it was the case. And it was probably why Jordan was still concerned about her mother, even today. She knew her daughter loved her, and how lucky she was. And then there was her

259

granddaughter, the sunshine of her life.

"I think I caught a glimpse of you two together. A cute teen all dressed in black?"

"That's her! At the ripe old age of fourteen, Adriana is, I feel, the one person who understands me and knows me the best."

She went on with her story. Adelka had to picture her arriving at this Mrs. Delaporte's place. Clarissa had had no idea of what to expect. She'd found herself facing a brunette of her own age, slim and elegant, with large dark eyes. Elise Delaporte had asked her to take her place in an armchair positioned in the middle of a tastefully decorated living room. She asked her to close her eyes. Clarissa obeyed. In the beginning, the pleasant voice relaxed her, asking her to let go, to get rid of all the tensions in her body. Her neck, shoulders, chest, stomach, thighs, shins, and feet all mellowed; her rigidity melted. Clarissa allowed herself to be carried away — an agreeable sensation. If that was all there was to it . . . She could already see herself telling François it had been a sort of winding-down exercise. The voice acted upon her like a sedative. She felt her body yield, on the threshold of a peculiar torpor.

Even if Clarissa still heard her perfectly, Elise Delaporte seemed farther and farther away. It was as if Clarissa had departed elsewhere. She remained wholly conscious; she perceived the tang of Elise's lemony fragrance; she could hear the murmur of the traffic floating up to them, the footsteps of a neighbor overhead, but she felt as if she had stepped into a dark nook that seemed to deepen. At the far end of the niche, which had nothing alarming about it, and which she instinctively identified as a shelter, appeared a pale glow, a quivering stroke summoning her like a beacon, and she felt compelled to follow it. How long did this last? She hardly knew. She was hovering within a reassuring Milky Way created by Elise alone. She was on familiar territory. She had nothing to fear.

Clarissa stopped.

"Oh, please go on!" begged Adelka. "May I offer you more wine?"

"Why not?"

The wine slowed her down, giving her a languid pleasure she hadn't experienced in a long time. She took up her story. Elise Delaporte had asked her to describe a secret place that did her good, gave her peace. A real or an imaginary place. To answer her, it had been difficult for Clarissa to locate her own vocal cords. She felt she had forgotten how to speak, while being weightless, and when she finally managed to utter a few words, it seemed like her body and her voice were no longer one. The shrill, almost child-like tone sounded like a stranger's. After a moment's hesitation, she succeeded in describing a lake, and how its deepness pacified her. During that first session, they had concentrated on the lake's image.

Could she tell Adelka what had happened next, with all those cameras now filming and taping? The wine quelled her hesitancy. Adelka possessed the same upbeat vitality as Jordan. Why not open up to her? She discreetly pointed to the surveillance cameras, and the young woman understood, moving closer. Clarissa went on in a low whisper, while her head spun around and around. A couple of weeks later, during the second or the third session, something happened, something she had never been able to forget. Elise had asked her to describe what she saw at the bottom of that lake. Clarissa had seen herself diving into the greenish abyss, holding her breath, slowly going down deeper and deeper while the water became blurred and icy. She was freezing, shivering. She was afraid of no longer being able to breathe, not being able to get back up in time, and there, right at the bottom, buried in the mud lining the base of the lake, she had spotted a square object, a kind of box. A hideous fear had grabbed at her; she wanted to rise up to the surface, to open her mouth wide in order to breathe in oxygen, to escape from that box and whatever it contained.

But while the fluctuating white lace twirled on the inside of her eyelids, Elise's tranquil tone had soothed her. Elise said she must not be afraid of what that box enclosed; she must open it, take stock of it. She had to face it. Clarissa saw herself seizing the box, wrangling to unbolt it in spite of the rusty lock. The top swung open, and inside was a baby. Her son. Her son exactly as she had beheld him after birth, his downy hair, his miniature face, his waxen skin. There, at the bottom of the lake, she clasped her son's body between her hands. She had nearly screamed, given away to her panic, pain, and anguish; she had nearly drowned in it all, surrendered to the lake's vortexes, but Elise's voice had come to guide her, and she had held on with all her might to the strength of that very voice. Clarissa described everything she saw and felt, and Elise was there with her, by her side, under the water, her hair mingling with Clarissa's own. She was telling her to let the baby go, not to put it back in the box, to hug it one last time, to say good-bye. Clarissa had embraced her son, kissing the little forehead, and she had opened up her hands; her son's body had been set free, gliding up to the surface, and she had followed it with her eyes until it became a tiny white spot.

Tears had spurted, fountainlike, trickling along her cheeks, her neck, moistening her chest. The sorrow was slipping away, gradually, teardrop after teardrop, sob after sob, and she felt it departing at last. When Elise had asked her to open her eyes, slowly, after counting to five, Clarissa felt a physical exhaustion she had rarely known, but beyond that tiredness, she found she had to learn how to welcome a novel peace lodged profoundly within her. She knew — she could tell — the pain had gone. She could now get on with her life. The wound was still there, and it would always be, but Clarissa now knew how to live with it, and how to tame it. She had seen Elise Delaporte only a couple of times after that. She hadn't needed any more sessions.

Adelka's dark eyes had gone liquid. She took Clarissa's hand, squeezed it. Speaking in a low tone, she thanked her for sharing such a touching memory. Clarissa said the path to writing had opened up for her shortly after. Freed from her grief, she'd felt the need to explore what she'd experienced in Romain Gary's and Virginia Woolf's wake, writers devoted to places, through their writing, their creativeness, but also because they'd chosen to die at home, at the heart of their intimate territories. She'd decided to start with her own emotions, her personal path, but this was set to become a novel, not her story. Adelka said she was engrossed by *Topography of Intimacy*. It wasn't at all the type of book she usually read, but she was enjoying it. It was startling, strange, and unexpected. Clarissa approved of her forthrightness. This young woman had nothing of a hypocrite about her. She appreciated that.

The rest of the evening went smoothly. They talked without worrying about the cameras. Adelka opened another bottle of wine, proffered cheese, bread, and olives. She discussed her work, how she recruited her models, where she chose to show her paintings. Clarissa had too much to drink. She wasn't used to it. Trying not to lurch, she left late, at midnight, telling Adelka she didn't need to be seen up to the eighth floor. What an idiot, getting sloshed at her age! It was almost funny. Almost. While she waited for the elevator, lacking the courage to go up by foot, she recalled Jim Perrier lived just below, on the third floor. Holding on to the banister as best as she could, she went down. Initials J.P. on the doorbell. She rang. It was probably too late, she knew. Too bad. No response. She waited. Where the hell was he? She tried once more. No answer. This was becoming both alarming and incomprehensible.

The residence cloaked her with oppressing silence. She stood within the cushy stairwell, the walls coated in sophisticated hues, and she viewed it all with abhorrence. She was fed up with being spied on. She had fled François and his repugnant secret, to find shelter here. She thought she had succeeded.

But the C.A.S.A. residence was no haven.

She could not sleep. She was hoping the wine might help her drop off, but the opposite happened. Her eyes remained wide open. She tried herbal tea, a shower, watching her neighbors; nothing worked. Lying on her bed, Chablis at her side, she asked Mrs. Dalloway to show her soothing videos of oceans and lakes. She sank into a semi-somnolent state, one she knew only too well since she'd moved in and that she loathed, with the frustrating impression that she could no longer distinguish reality from her dreams. Was she asleep? Awake? She couldn't tell. The wine had confused the issue. That word was coming back again and again, the same word, like an unrelenting wave bashing into her ears.

That word filling up the entire space, seeping into her skull; she must figure out what it was. In the dimness, while the lake's surface crinkled the ceiling, she forced herself to regain consciousness. *Listen. Concentrate. Listen.* Night after night, she heard that voice, that word. *One final effort. Now.*

That voice. How was it possible? Yet it seemed to be that voice, light as the breeze, as the rustle of leaves, or the murmur of the turning tide. Elise's voice? Clarissa struggled to remain calm, staring into the dark. No panicking. She had to keep it all in, to reveal nothing. Now, she could only make out silence, but had it really been Elise speaking to her, in the deepest hour, every night? And that word over and over, striking right at her heart?

Her son's name. Her baby. The name Toby and she had chosen with such care, such love. The name written on the simple tombstone at Montparnasse Cemetery, where their son was laid to rest, and where she never went, because the pain, as soon as she drew near, became unbearable.

Had she dreamed it? Had she craved hearing that name so badly, she'd let it bloom within her own ear? No, of course not! She hadn't dreamed a thing!

Fury swept over her, a nameless violence scorching the pit of her stomach. She leaped out of bed, howling with rage, brandishing her fist. How dared "they"? How could "they" do this? Manipulate her this way? Was that why she'd had to endure that tedious setting-up process? So that her past would come back to haunt her? What for? Now she could see why her nights were brief, bedecked with tears, preventing her from getting ahead, from writing her book.

"What the hell are you up to?" she spat out, glaring at one of the cameras. "And you there, hiding behind your screens, snooping on me, what are you waiting for? For me to go bonkers, is that it? Is that your intention? My going off the deep end? So that's C.A.S.A. protocol, is it? Well done!"

Mrs. Dalloway made herself heard, unflappable.

"I'm sorry, Clarissa, I don't understand what you are trying to tell me. Please rephrase."

"Shut up!" shouted Clarissa, beside herself with wrath. "Just shut the fuck up!"

"I'm sorry, Clarissa. What, exactly, is the

problem?"

"Be quiet! Can you understand that? Here it is one more time: Stop talking to me!"

"I'm sorry, I don't understand your demand."

Silence. Clarissa got a grip on herself.

"Mrs. Dalloway," she hissed.

"Yes, Clarissa?"

"I don't want to hear you."

"Fine, Clarissa. You can deactivate voice mode. You only have to say it."

"Mrs. Dalloway, deactivate voice mode."

An icon glowed on the nearby wall, confirming her order had been taken into account.

"Deactivate all cameras."

A sentence showed up. *It is impossible to deactivate the cameras.*

"Go to hell! Deactivate everything."

It is impossible to deactivate everything.

Clarissa unleashed a volley of abuse worthy of her father's — the kind that used to cause her mother such displeasure. It was exhilarating. She felt lighter, less tense. She even grinned. Chablis came purring against her shins. She took him into the living room, her nose buried in the soft fur.

"What would I do without you, cat?"

She lay down on the sofa with him. Dawn was about to break, lighting up the rooftops with a pink touch. Tiredness took over, and she dozed on and off. A few hours later, when she got up, still exhausted, with a painful back, it was broad daylight. It was strange and liberating not to hear Mrs. Dalloway greeting her, like she used to every morning. The weather forecast, the main headlines, and her agenda silently appeared on the mural panels in large fonts, so her shortsighted eyes could read without glasses. Andy was coming later on today, to spend the night.

"Please send an internal message to Adelka Miki."

Go ahead.

"Thank you for a lovely evening. I had a great time with you. I overdid it with the white wine, and getting up this morning was ghastly! But I have no regrets. See you soon! Clarissa."

I've sent it.

"Please send an internal message to Jim Perrier."

Go ahead.

"Hi Jim! Hope you're well. I thought of a producer who might be interested in adapting my first novel for TV. I'd be happy to discuss this with you. All best, Clarissa."

Message rejected by server.

Clarissa read the sentence a couple of

times, perplexed.

"Why is the message rejected? I don't understand."

There is no Jim Perrier in the residence.

"What? That's impossible; he lives on the third floor. There must be a mistake. Try again."

The name Jim Perrier is not recognized by C.A.S.A. protocol. Message rejected by server.

Clarissa remained silent. She must not reveal her distress; she must take it in stride. For a couple of minutes, she forced herself to calm down. When she felt less strained, she went into the bathroom to undergo the medical tests. Using a loud, contemptuous tone, she said, "Are you eventually going to notice how tired I am? And perhaps a surprisingly high alcohol level? What do you do with all those results? Oh, I'm not expecting any answers!"

In the mirror, she glimpsed her crumpled features, her lackluster hair, her dry skin. The C.A.S.A. effect? Did the other artists feel this way, as well? Adelka, on the contrary, appeared to be blossoming.

Jim Perrier. His name haunted her all day. Had he made a discovery concerning the powder that could have led to his eviction? Was he in danger? He had warned her that mobile devices and computers were under surveillance. How could she reach him? She didn't dare make any online searches in order to try to locate him. But she also knew he had a drinking problem, which Adelka had noticed, as well as the waiters at Café Iris. She wondered if she could go on trusting him.

At the end of the day, she decided to wait for Andy outside the residence, near the Tower Memorial. They could speak without being listened to. The young girl was surprised to see her grandmother waiting for her on a bench, and even more so when she saw her haggard face.

"It's no big deal," mumbled Clarissa. "Another lousy night. I have lots to tell you. Inside, we can't talk. Sit down and listen to me."

She related the powder incident, and Jim Perrier's vanishing act. She was concerned. Something was going on in that damned residence, and she couldn't figure out what. She was convinced her sleep was being tampered with. Apart from Andy, Jim was the only person she could bring this up with. And now he was gone. Andy listened attentively. Clarissa was fearfully expecting her granddaughter to tell her she was getting the wrong ideas. But Andy began to talk in a calm and thoughtful manner.

"Quit putting on that scared expression, Mums. I've been on your side since the beginning. And I have stuff to say that corroborates your point of view. I got in touch with the University of East Anglia, attended by our dear Mia White. They never responded to my email, so I phoned them. I passed myself off as a silly friend with a French accent who was trying to get hold of her. I must be kind of talented, because they fell for it. Guess what? Mia White got her diploma last year. She's no longer a student. Odd, no? It gave me the wildest ideas! What if that girl is here to spy on you? What if she's been working for C.A.S.A. all along?"

Clarissa gazed at her granddaughter. She seemed so mature, so confident.

"So that would explain why I thought I saw her downstairs the night the alarm went off."

"You did? My guess is that she sleeps here and watches you nonstop. You're her full-time job."

"What do these people want, Andy?"

Andy slipped an arm around Clarissa's shoulder.

"No hassle, Mums. We're going to find out."

"But how? They see everything I do."

"I know. We have to start thinking hard. There must be something all these artists have in common. That's what they're after. Dr. Dethingy, you know she's an AI hotshot. I've been looking her up."

"Yes, Jim did, as well."

"My guess is that she went rogue. Impossible to find out what she's been up to. In your day, people went on the dark web to hunt for that sort of stuff, but now, that's so mainstream and what you find there has nothing juicy about it. Digging deep into the blacker web might bring answers about the doctor's activities, but that's tricky. I'd need help. I could ask around. I have a friend whose brother is one of those new detectives, or a spy, if you prefer. His thing is politics. He knows how to drag up all the stuff people don't ever want anyone to find. He earns millions."

"How do you know all this, Andy?"

"Everyone knows, Mums. I didn't start it."

"I'm all at sea, over here."

"I know, and that's normal. Don't worry, I'm not going to do anything foolish. We have two simple missions here. One, what happened to your pal Jim? Two, what is behind C.A.S.A.? Meanwhile, when we get to your place, we act normal. As usual, okay? And if we need to talk, we write on bits of paper."

"You're brilliant, Andy."

"Not at all, Mums, just trying to help out. Do you a have a list of all the artists who live in the residence?"

"Yes, at home. Why?"

"I'd like to take a look at it. Perhaps it's all in that list."

"What do you mean?"

"You're all artists, so you have that in common. But apart from your professions, there must be something else about you that C.A.S.A. finds interesting."

Clarissa glanced around her. The sun, shining bright and strong, was hurting her eyes. Lately, the weather had been persistently hot and sunny, even if summer was not yet here. It had rained only a couple of times, and when it had, it had poured down with fierce devastation.

"Mummy says a new heat wave is lined up for next week."

"Not another one!"

Jordan was given all climatic data in advance, due to her job.

"Yep, and she says this one will be a scorcher. It's going to set a new record, going up to forty-eight degrees Celsius."

Clarissa sighed.

"Let's go home, Mums. You look tired. Let me take care of you."

"You're such a sweetie. Hey, missy, you're going to love this. I managed to get Mrs. Dalloway to shut up. I only had to turn voice mode off. Now everything she says is written on the wall. That's it. And it's bliss."

They were on their way, arms linked. Clarissa walked at a slow pace, with difficulty. She'd felt old ever since this morning. A wreck. Once they got home, she went to fetch the neighbor list. Andy looked at it for a while. Then she folded it and put it in her pocket. She helped her grandmother prepare her favorite dinner. They called Toby. The conversation was spontaneous and amusing. Just before they sat down to eat, Andy made a face.

"Oh, shucks! No more salt, right?" she said.

While her back was turned to the camera, she winked in Clarissa's direction.

"I'll get some from your neighbors."

A beaming smile, a cup grabbed from the shelf, and out she rushed. Clarissa put a lid on the soup and kept the potatoes in the oven. She turned on the news, trying to act normal. An unparalleled heat wave was indeed forecast for next week, about to descend upon Paris and its outskirts. About twenty minutes later, Andy returned with a small smile and the cup filled with salt. She devoured her dinner with her usual appetite and spoke little during the meal. Clarissa waited. She suspected her granddaughter was onto something. She longed to ask questions, but abstained. They put the dishes away while Andy whistled.

"How about a movie, Mums?"

"With pleasure. Which one?"

"Something vintage. You choose!"

"Ever heard of *Barry Lyndon*?"

"Rings a bell. Any good?"

Clarissa smiled.

"I saw it for the first time when I was your age."

"You liked it?"

"More than liked it."

"Okay. Let's go for it."

"Stanley Kubrick is my favorite film-maker."

"That, I knew! Mummy's told me often enough!"

They settled down in the living room, with the cat on Andy's lap. Clarissa asked Mrs. Dalloway to find the movie *Barry Lyndon* and play it.

"How fabulous it is to no longer hear that Dalloway voice. Good job, Mums."

Then Andy whispered in Clarissa's ear, asking her to turn the sound up high.

Clarissa obeyed. The volume was so loud that Clarissa's eardrums ached. Andy played with a wisp of her own hair, which she kept placing in front of her lips. She murmured, "Can you hear me, Mums? Look straight ahead. Stick something on your mouth — your mug, for example."

"Roger that."

"Wow! That guy is so hot!" yelled Andy. "Who is he?"

"Ryan O'Neal."

"Is he still around?"

"He's your great-grandpa's age."

"You think he has a great-grandson?"

Andy was swept away by the magnificent images, by Handel's haunting sarabande.

The whispering took up again.

"I'm going to go to the loo. No cameras in there, right? I'll call out, saying there's no more toilet paper. You'll fetch some and bring it to me. Okay?"

Clarissa nodded, unnoticeably.

A couple of minutes later, her granddaughter was heard.

"Hey, Mums! End of loo paper!"

"Coming, miss."

She got up, cursing at the backache that seemed to be here to stay. She went into her bathroom, fetched the tissue roll from her cupboard. Andy let her in the toilet room and closed the door behind her.

"I got it. Your neighbors."

"What? Tell me!"

"Don't talk so loudly. I didn't see all of them; some weren't at home. But I did notice they're not all purely French."

"You sound like our awful president when you say that."

"Listen. Listen carefully. They're like you. Bicultural."

She took the paper out of her pocket and unfolded it.

"Arlen, from Montreal. Bell, from Australia. Engeler, not there. Fromet, supergluey, poured her heart out. She has an English mum. Holzmann, from Germany. Azoulay, Morocco. Olsen and Miki, not home."

"Adelka Miki's mother is Italian."

"Aha. See? And your buddy Perrier?"

"Belgian mother. I believe he speaks Flemish."

"Pomeroy, charming, from San Francisco. Rachewski, from Saint Petersburg. Van Druten, Amsterdam. Zajak, not home."

"What's your point, missy?"

It was beginning to get warm in the tiny space.

"You're all bilingual. You all speak two

languages fluently."

Clarissa's pulse quickened.

"Andy! Mia White!"

"Yes, what about her?"

"Franco-British, like me."

Andy waved the paper around theatrically.

"The mind reels. What if C.A.S.A. was studying the lot of you because you have hybrid brains, as you like to call it? And what if dear bilingual Mia White was the project leader on all this?"

The cat was anxiously waiting for them. They returned to the screen, not speaking to each other. Clarissa found she could no longer concentrate on the movie. She kept thinking back to the numerous questions Mia White had asked her about bilingualism, trying to remember her own answers.

Andy was scribbling something on a bit of paper. She handed it over to her.

On the third floor, door on the left was ajar. Jim Perrier's place. Wasn't able to see inside. I rang; no one answered.

Clarissa continued to stare at the screen, transfixed. Andy mumbled, "We need to go check this out. Later. When everyone's off in the land of nod."

The entire building was still. Not a single noise to be heard. The night-lights were switched on, casting a pallid glimmer into the depths of the stairwell. Clarissa and Andy waited until two in the morning. They watched another movie, or pretended to, more or less dropping off in front of it; then they turned off all the lights, faked going to bed, lying down in the dark, fully clothed. Clarissa activated "intimate mode." They quietly slipped out of the flat.

Jim Perrier's door was ajar. It only needed to be pushed in order to open wide. Inside, a patch of darkness. Andy turned on her mobile's flashlight. Clarissa pondered if this was a good idea. What would they ever do, or say, if they were found here? But Andy was already striding ahead, fearless. What an amazing little person. But then she thought of Jordan. Her daughter would be furious, no doubt.

"Come on!" murmured Andy. "There's no one here."

The space had been entirely stripped. Andy moved the flashlight over the walls and floors. Everything was empty, as if no one had ever lived here. Clarissa thought of Jim Perrier, in his underwear, the night the alarm went off. His pleasant cologne. Where was he now?

"Watch out for those cameras," whispered Clarissa. " 'They' will detect us soon

281

enough."

"In my opinion, nothing's on," said Andy. "The virtual assistant is off, as well. We have nothing to be afraid of. They're not going to film a vacant apartment."

They padded into the kitchen, then the bathroom.

"What if Jim was expelled by C.A.S.A.," said Andy, "because he knew too much?"

"Or maybe because of his drinking problem?"

"Whatever it was, C.A.S.A. didn't approve."

"Maybe he's the one who took off —"

"Shh!" commanded Andy, interrupting her. "There's someone there, just outside."

Clarissa was petrified. Her stomach churned uncomfortably. Who could it be, out there? Ben? Dr. Dewinter? She'd have to think up some sort of excuse to explain what they were doing here. Panic took over.

"Get into that wardrobe over there, Mums. Let me take charge. I know what to do."

"But . . ."

"Do what I say. I can handle this. Trust me."

Clarissa dashed into the hiding place, taking care to leave the door slightly open. From there, she could glimpse the entrance, where Andy had lain down on the floor, as if she were asleep. What on earth was she doing?

The noise Andy had picked up was now making its way to her own ears: an odd hissing sound. Andy was still flat out, motionless. Clarissa held her breath. The presence materialized, crossed the threshold. The form she beheld had nothing human about it; it was a large steel wheel, moving forward with metallic clicks. The circle halted when it came to Andy, and then, under Clarissa's agitated and incredulous gaze, it lengthened out, modifying itself, changing its shape. She saw a long iron silhouette slowly unfold, taking its time, unfurling upward as it grazed the ceiling. Clarissa had never seen one in true life before, but she knew what it was. And Jim had mentioned it. A Bardi. One of the most elaborate and redoubtable guard robots ever, overpriced and efficient. At the end of each extremity, it bore a set of electrocuting pincers. Two round gleaming LED lights acted as its eyes. The Bardi had something of a Giacometti statue about it, with its long, lean, and elegant lines, and seemed harmless, but Clarissa had read enough about them to know what a Bardi was capable of. How could she get Andy out of this? She thought of Jordan. Ivan.

The Bardi had located Andy's body on the floor. It came onward with that menacing skid that compressed Clarissa's heart. The red beam flickered over Andy, who pretended to awaken.

"Get up."

A mechanical, androgynous voice.

Andy rose, unperturbed. How was she able to remain so calm? Clarissa also knew the robots were equipped with facial recognition. The red spotlights lit up Andy's face and then locked onto her eyes.

"The individual is a minor recognized by C.A.S.A. protocol. Adriana Garnier. Explain the reason of your presence on these premises."

Adriana did not lose countenance. She lifted her chin to be able to stare back at the robot. It had bent over in order to examine her more closely, and Clarissa could make out the details of the startling metallic features, and the two small horns planted on each side of its head, giving it an animal-like aspect.

"I'm the granddaughter of Clarissa Katsef, the writer on the eighth floor. I was supposed to meet the person who lives here. But Jim never turned up. I fell asleep waiting for him."

The silent robot appeared to ingest the

information.

"The door was open," Andy went on smoothly. "So I just came in."

"Your mobile."

The iron pincer made its way toward Andy, opening up to form a flat surface.

"I don't mind showing it to you, but you won't find traces of any of our texts. I erased them all."

"Why?"

Andy shrugged.

"I don't want my parents breathing down my neck. They don't know about my relationship with Jim."

"Hand over your mobile."

Andy obeyed. She placed the phone in the little tray. A throbbing noise was heard.

"Thank you. You may take it back. Go up to your grandmother's place and do not come back here."

Andy seemed to hesitate; then she said, "Where is Jim Perrier, please?"

"There is no Jim Perrier here."

"But where is he? Why did he disappear? Why is his apartment empty?"

"Go back upstairs."

"I'd like to know what happened to Jim!"

"Do not argue with me."

The robot slid forward and touched Adriana's arm with its right pincer. The snapping sound of an electric shock was heard.

"What the fuck?" bawled the young girl. "I've done nothing wrong!"

"Go upstairs. Get out of here."

"Okay! I got the message! I'm leaving!"

The robot shoved Andy toward the entry, claws brandished like weapons. Clarissa heard the door bang shut. She waited, frightened, her chest feeling tight. She'd let a few minutes slip by; then she'd rush upstairs to join Andy.

Jim Perrier's vacant flat seemed dark all of a sudden. The only thing she could hear was her slightly ragged breath. Apprehension pulsed through her once more. What had she done, following Andy? She longed to be back home, all snug, with Andy and the cat. A mug of herbal tea and off to bed. If Jim Perrier could see her now, cowering with fear in his empty wardrobe. She could picture his grin.

A faint hissing sound was heard, and her heart froze. She pricked up her ears. There it was again. She hadn't gotten it wrong. The Bardi had remained inside. It hadn't left. It must have understood there was a presence in the apartment. It was coming back for her, like a bloodhound. Horrified, Clarissa crawled to the back of the wardrobe.

The robot slid along, unhurried, with the slight squeak she had learned to fear, while its face swung methodically from left to right. She knew it was equipped with sensors capable of picking out body heat. From her hiding place, she could make out the reddish glow of its two LEDs piercing the gloom. It was coming closer, slowly but surely, and it was going to find her. She could imagine the steel claws clamping onto her arm. She felt like she was going to pass out.

A series of loud reiterated knocks on the door made her jump. The robot stopped moving, only a few feet away from her. It swiveled back toward the entrance. Clarissa heard Andy's shout.

"I want to know where Jim Perrier is! I want to know where my friend is!"

"Jim Perrier no longer lives here. Go home. Immediately."

"But he told me to meet him here! Something is going on!"

"If you don't leave, you'll have to come with me."

"I'm a minor!" wailed Andy. "You can't just take me with you, and besides, I've done nothing wrong."

"Leave."

"If I go upstairs, will you leave, as well?"

asked Andy.

Clarissa was amazed by her granddaughter's audacity.

"Yes, I will depart if you go upstairs," came the robotic tone.

"Watch me, Mr. Bardi! I'm going up! Look! See?"

Andy's voice became fainter.

Clarissa waited, her stomach still painful, her breath short. She couldn't bear it if the Bardi came back. She peered out from behind the crack of the wardrobe door. The robot had stopped talking; it appeared frozen. Then, suddenly, it twisted down with an unexpectedly graceful swoop, coiled itself up, and took on the circle aspect it had when it arrived. Clarissa heard it roll down the steps.

A couple of minutes later, Andy called out.

"Mums! Get out of there! Hurry!"

Clarissa leaped out, not knowing where she was going, hands held out, and ended her wild rush, gasping for breath in Andy's arms. The front door on the right of the landing opened, and an elegant man in his sixties appeared, wearing a blue dressing gown. He glanced at them cautiously.

"Is everything all right? I heard some noise."

He had an American accent, blue eyes.

Andy smiled at him reassuringly and answered him in English. They were very sorry; it was so late! She'd seen him earlier on; she'd come to ask for salt. Sean Pomeroy, right? From San Francisco. Clarissa introduced herself in turn, explained they were looking for his neighbor, Jim Perrier. Sean Pomeroy replied that he hadn't seen him for a while. Perhaps he'd moved. Then he added, with a mischievous smile, "A rather raucous young man."

"Oh?" said Clarissa.

"Let's say he often came home drunk and got the doors mixed up."

They said good night. Going up in the elevator, Clarissa told herself this amiable gentleman must have thought they were mad. She couldn't get over what they had just done. The risk of it all! The danger! But she couldn't bring herself to scold Adriana. Her granddaughter looked back at her with quiet triumph in her eyes.

When they got to the eighth floor, Clarissa asked her to make sure there was no Bardi lurking around. Andy checked.

"No Bardi, Mums. Just a poor cat mewing behind the door."

Clarissa descended into a troubled slumber, with the memory of the Bardi's red eyes chasing her. She awoke at dawn, and lay there, listening to Andy breathing. She waited until the young girl opened her eyes and smiled at her. What a marvelous thing, Adriana's smile.

"I had such weird dreams, Mums."

"House specialty, I'd say!"

Andy yawned and stretched her limbs.

"You were talking in your sleep, Mums. You kept repeating the same word over and over in a soft little voice."

Clarissa stiffened.

"What word?"

"A name."

"Which name?"

"Glenn."

Clarissa shut her eyes. She felt exhaustion take over and govern her. She wanted to curl up and never get out of bed; in the pit of her stomach, she felt a load where she had carried her dead child. She couldn't believe she had been saying his name out loud during her sleep.

"Mums. You don't have to explain."

Andy's small hand found her own.

"I know who Glenn is. Mummy told me a long time ago she had an older brother who died at birth. Your son. I've never talked about it with you. I was waiting. Take your time. If we don't talk now, it will be at another moment."

Then Andy whispered resolutely, "I don't know what the hell they want, or what they're doing, and maybe we will never find out. But I do know one thing. You have to get out of here, Mums. Pronto."

Afterward, I had to write it all down. Describe it. I had to get it out of my system. The only way to do that was to create a distance. To protect myself.

The door, facing me. The key, in my hand. One final qualm. Turn around, leave, stay in the dark? Open up, discover it all? The choice appeared easy, in the beginning. But it became infernal as I lingered on the doorstep.

Door opening. No squeak. I slipped in easily. I had waited a long while, nearly an hour. I had rung the bell. Nobody had answered. The door was double-locked.

A small entrance. An overpowering, brash tone of purple. I was startled. I knew François preferred the elegant discretion of taupe, russet, dark blue, silver.

Another door. I breathed in whorls of potent and heavy feminine perfume. It was familiar. The one I had sniffed on my husband's jackets and shirts. Sickeningly sweet, like cotton candy.

The place felt stuffy, as if it wasn't ventilated often.

A single room, not large. Blinds lowered. Not much light. Night had fallen and it was hard to make anything out. Not a lot of furniture, apart from a huge four-poster bed that took center stage. It obscenely dominated all the rest.

Purple, everywhere. Walls, fitted carpet, net curtains around the bed.

François was waiting for me at our friends' place for dinner. He had already sent several texts, wondering what I was doing, why I was late. I hadn't answered.

I had time, after all. But what if she came home? I hadn't thought about that. All of a sudden, I felt nervous. The perfume was making me uncomfortable.

Near the window, on a pedestal table, there was a framed photograph. I drew closer. It was her. Her, with him. They were hugging, on that dreadful gigantic bed.

She had curly blond hair. She was young, younger than Jordan. Thirty years old, give or take. A smooth, angelic face. The pink skin of a piglet. A beatific smile. Emotionless eyes. A plump body. She was wearing a negligée; he was bare-chested.

My eyes were beginning to get used to the penumbra. On the chest of drawers, photo albums. *Be careful. Watch out. Do you really want to look at those? Do you really want to see them? You already know everything there is to know. You know your husband is cheating on you with this young woman. You know they meet here, a couple of times a week. You should get the hell out of here. Now. Why torture yourself? Why look at those blasted albums?*

It was impossible to turn back. I looked at them all.

Romantic snacks, cocktails, champagne, birthday cakes, always here, in this vile purple chamber. My husband, soppy-eyed and smitten. Her affected smirk, her golden curls. He wore dark jackets and a tie; she, low-cut tunics. In one of the photos, she was sitting on his knees, wearing an evening dress. He was avidly suckling her breast.

Under the albums, I found a tablet, a smaller model. *Don't look. Resist. Put it down. Get out. Clear off.*

Too late. Twenty videos or so. It was so easy to press on the icons.

My heart had started to beat with a slow, devouring anger. Videos of them on the bed. Close-ups. Kisses. Tongues and genitals. Her vulva was entirely hairless. Her on top of him. Him on her. Him inside her. Him in her mouth, in between her bosoms, in between her buttocks. I watched it all. The slow, then frenzied to-and-fro. My hands trembled. It was appalling.

A mad urge to smash everything up. Wreak havoc. Decimate the place. Reduce it all to smithereens. But it didn't last. I was a sitting duck for grief and despondency. In that sordid room, I stood there, helpless and drained.

I went to check out the rest of the flat, switching on the lights. A tiny kitchen. Nothing in the refrigerator apart from champagne. Two glasses by the sink. Farther on, the bathroom. No lipstick, mascara, powder. Surprising, considering how made up she was in the videos. No beauty products. Just her perfume, on the shelf above the basin. They even shared a toothbrush. A stick of deodorant, for men. One large purple towel. In the shower, an item that looked like a long bottle brush for cleaning flasks, and a pear-shaped object made of black rubber.

Back in the bedroom, I drew closer to the four-poster, as if to behold it one last time, before I left for good. The mauve net curtains were drawn. On the single night table, a vintage Polaroid camera, and some lubricant gel.

I drew the voile curtain. I nearly screamed.

There was a figure, on the mattress. A woman, lying there on her side, her back to me, her long blond locks spread over the pillow.

8
HEAT WAVE

Moments like this are buds on the tree of
life. Flowers of darkness they are . . .
VIRGINIA WOOLF, *Mrs. Dalloway,* 1925

Instead of screaming, I write books.
ROMAIN GARY, *Promise at Dawn,* 1960

In the past ten years, Paris had endured a
string of heat waves, but the one drawing
closer, heralded by uncertainties, concerns,
speculations, and confusion of all kinds, was
set to be record-breaking. It was pronounced devastating, although it was predicted to last forty-eight hours at the most.
The president had gone so far as to impose
a nonworking day. Her minister for health
exhorted Parisians to remain at home. For
those in need, air-conditioned spaces were
made available; bottled water was to be
delivered by drones at specific areas, and all
emergency departments were fully mobi-

lized and on the alert. Trains were not operating, because heat might distort railway tracks. Only a few planes were allowed to take off. Public transport services were reduced to the minimum. The latest heat wave, which came close to forty-five degrees Celsius, was already an unpleasant memory, but this one would be much worse. Irked, Clarissa listened to the news. Why such doom-mongering? For the past day, the impending hot spell was described only in the most fear-provoking terms.

The residence was fully equipped with state-of-the-art air-conditioning, and for that, Clarissa was thankful. She had suggested Jordan and her little family come and stay during the hottest hours, but her daughter had declined. Jordan had some portable units that would do. They'd pull through. Why had Clarissa picked out a small shadow in Jordan's tone? Was she imagining things, or was Jordan resentful about something?

Fed up with the alarmist headlines, Clarissa turned off the newscast. Close the shutters, stay inside, drink enough water. Yes, she knew all that. Like thousands of Parisians, she endured both those commands and torrid temperatures several times a year. This morning, her father sent a message that made her laugh. From all his ninety-eight years of age, he reminded her that senior citizens, like herself, should be most vigilant during a heat wave. The last one had spelled carnage, did she recall? Fortunately, London was going to stay cool. Signed "Super Senior Citizen," her dad.

A little ping was heard. Mrs. Dalloway had something to say. Her words showed up on the wall for Clarissa to read.

FYI, mail has just been delivered. There's a letter for you. Handwritten. No return address.

Postal mail had become uncommon. Paper was no longer used for bills, love letters, or even condolences. People had stopped writing over the years; they sent text messages or emails. Clarissa was curious as to who had written her a letter the old-fashioned way. She went down to fetch it. She didn't see anyone. Had the artists all retreated to their homes in fear of the heat wave? She instantly recognized François's handwriting on the envelope. She didn't open it. When she got back upstairs, she slipped the letter into her handbag. Should she read it now? Courage failed her. She'd do it another day.

Her book was coming along slowly. Too slowly. She hid from surveillance to write in both her notebooks, the English one and the French one, but her heart was no longer in it. Leaving here had become her new fixation. Getting out of C.A.S.A. It ate up all the rest. She had signed a contract and a lease. She was going to have to check all that out again. And above all, wherever could she go? That unanswerable question preoccupied her.

The sky turned livid as the day progressed. She had never seen such a color. The sun beat down through the skylight, which she had not been able to black out. She entrenched herself in her bedroom, where the shutters could be closed. In the dimness, she felt safer. Chablis dozed. Clarissa thought about the multitude of air conditioners frantically struggling against irrational temperatures while spewing out hot air. She found the waiting unbearable. She received texts from friends making sure she was sheltered, looking after herself. She answered back reassuringly, heartened by the small tokens of affection.

The hours crawled by with extreme slowness. Everything felt sluggish. Andy called to see how her grandmother was doing. It wasn't too awful at theirs. But she wasn't looking forward to nighttime. Clarissa reminded her that she had suggested the family come over, and that Jordan had refused. Incomprehensible, according to Andy.

Clarissa found it impossible to read or write. She felt jittery, worried sick. She wasn't anxious for her own sake; she felt frightened for the city. Paris had never been through such high temperatures. She wondered if infrastructures were going to make it. She answered a call from Toby, watching over her, even from far away. She switched the TV on again, without the sound, gazed at the ghost-town streets of a deserted capital. Not a single car, not one pedestrian. All shops were closed. Only drones could be seen making their rounds, like huge insects hovering over empty boulevards. She could hear their rumble through the double glazing. She had always loathed that noise.

She unfastened a windowpane at four o'clock in the afternoon, just to see. The blistering air was a smack in the face, similar to opening an oven. Forty-five degrees Celsius in the shade. She was aware the digits were going to rise even higher. She felt protected in her cool home, but the escalating warmth, like the relentless loom of a calamity, shook her up. The news channels kept harking back to the death of the bees and its consequences, and showing the same perpetual images of climate disrup-

300

tion. The lifeless streets of Paris appeared to be the main focus of the media worldwide. Disheartened by the morose broadcasts, Clarissa asked Mrs. Dalloway to show the movie *Modern Times.*

She must have fallen asleep when Chaplin was being swallowed whole by the factory gearwheels, because when she opened her eyes, night had fallen. Her mouth felt furry; her head ached. When she rose, dizziness forced her down again. The cat lay listless in a corner. She hobbled to the kitchen. She couldn't find any bottles of mineral water in the refrigerator. Yet she was certain she had stocked up on them. She couldn't understand why they were nowhere to be seen. The throbbing of her head worsened; she felt like retching. She had to grip the furniture in order not to fall. Never in her entire life had she been so thirsty. Her entire body seemed parched. She began to shudder. There was no other choice than to drink from the tap, that water filtered by the residence, of which she was suspicious. The liquid ran over her hand, tepid, and strangely oily. She waited for it to become cooler, but it never did. She had to force herself to gulp down lukewarm sips, which made her feel even queasier.

On the wall panel, she read the temperature had flown up to forty-nine degrees Celsius, an unprecedented event. A brand-new record. There had been many casualties. There were, no doubt, going to be even more. Clarissa staggered back to the living room with difficulty. Her body felt stiff and heavy. She glanced outside, to the building facing hers. Hardly any lights on. The city seemed fast sleep. But shrill ambulance sirens and the drones' incessant circling came to her from afar. She felt sweaty. Her clothes were sticky. Was there a problem with the air-conditioning? She asked Mrs. Dalloway to check.

Two words lit up the panel.

SYSTEM ERROR.

Clarissa opened the front door. It was boiling on the landing, as if a heater had been turned on full blast. She went to fetch her mobile. Get hold of Jordan, Adelka. The calls couldn't go through, even though the signal was strong. She tried a dozen times, in vain. She remembered the landline in her office and rushed to it. When she stuck the phone to her ear, there was no dial tone, just an automatic voice blaring out the same words over and over: "System error. Please hang up. System error. Please hang up."

She was alone in her flat, with no air-conditioning, no mineral water. Up on the eighth floor, under a skylight that had warmed up all day long under the broiling sun. Perspiration trickled down the back of her neck, between her breasts. Dusk had barely been able to lower the heat. Her heart beat with slow, painful thumps. She could hear her blood flow through her eardrums with a muffled sucking noise that nauseated her. Her body had been drained of all the vigor she had left. She was a wreck. She couldn't move. It seemed to her the residence had depleted her of all her sap. She was nothing but an empty shell.

As she lay on the sofa, limp, inert, craving water, she felt she suddenly knew what "they" wanted, what "they" were doing. It was clear. How had she not seen it? She had to write it down, straight away. The floor swayed when she tried to get up. Above her head, the ceiling looked like waves were lapping over it. Hands stretched out in front of her, she ambled ahead warily. The screens on the walls weren't functioning properly; frames were skipping, appeared to be jumbled together, along with a crackling sound. New words popped up: *PROTOCOL C.A.S.A. DOWN. REBOOT.* Clarissa couldn't help smiling, in spite of her weariness. She imagined Dr. Dewinter and her team dripping with sweat, working themselves into a frenzy in front of their inoperative screens and servers. Somehow or other, the heat wave must have triggered the internal system's meltdown.

Clarissa got hold of her notebooks, tucked away in her handbag. She sat down to write, and had to put her pen down after a few sentences, she felt so weak. She shouldn't take all this lightly, at her age. She had to dampen her body, drink plenty of fluids. She had to act fast. Under the shower, she'd go. She'd wait it out there.

Impossible to stand up again. Her limbs had gone as flaccid as marshmallow candy. Flat on her stomach, she slid across the flooring, making feeble swimming movements. The remaining distance to the bathroom seemed never-ending. Sometimes she'd halt, spent. She felt like crying but forced herself not to. She certainly wasn't going to perish right there on her own floor! How pathetic! How ridiculous! She could hear her father's voice, his cursing, his wit. *Bloody hell! Move on, now! Come on, girl! Rustle your bustle!* Her elbows stung as she inched along. Each effort she made forced a strangled moan from her. The shower was miles away. She could very well stay right there, flat out, wheezing, drenched with perspiration, and no one would ever know.

Cameras were no longer filming. She would peter out, just like that. In a few days, her body would be found by Ben, or by the nice cleaning lady who came once a week. Jordan and Andy would turn up beforehand; she was sure of that. At least she hoped so. It was tempting to let herself drop off. So very easy. The surface under her cheek felt hot and sticky.

As she stared close-up at the grooves engrained within the wooden planks, shadows began to materialize, created by the many indentations; tormented features appeared, sketched here and there as if by magic: malevolent eyes, grimacing mouths, crooked noses. It seemed to her the floorboards were covered with a chain of scowling masks, hideous hobgoblins with emaciated faces like in Munch's powerful painting, *The Scream.* She forced her eyes away, but when she glanced at the walls, she noticed with anguish blurry shapes coming to life there as well, as if the corridor were crowded with apparitions hiding behind partitions, reaching out to grab her.

Clarissa shut her eyes. That was better. They had gone. She breathed slowly, using Elise's method. Should she surrender to this gentle stupor? Should she let herself be carried away? *Are you off your rocker, girl? Blast it, that's enough!* Her father's voice, calling her by that first name she hated.

She raised her head, gritted her teeth with all the forcefulness she could muster. *Keep moving. Keep going forward. Inch by inch.* The goblins had vanished. She had to reach the shower. A trembling frame caught her eye — a square image appearing on the luminous panel at the end of the passageway. Clarissa made slow progress, puffing and panting. The palms of her hands were sore; she had cramps in her legs. She was able to make out a sort of index card with an ID photo. She drew closer, managed to heave herself to her knees with a final effort. She didn't have her glasses on, and she stuck her nose to the screen.

SURNAME: PERRIER
FIRST NAME: JIM
AGE: 35

She couldn't figure out what it was, why she was seeing this. Jim's card faded away, then popped back up on the unit.

CONSTITUTIONAL SIGNS: ALCOHOLIC. DRUG ADDICT. PARANOID PERSONALITY DISORDER.

The display went black. She squealed with frustration. Then other cards emerged, too fast for her to see them properly. The heat must have affected the servers. Every-

306

thing C.A.S.A. knew and was hiding had somehow become visible. Were all the artists of the residence witnessing this confidential data right now? Or was this only happening in her place? The frames shuffled by in a quick frenzy. At times, the system switched off, then lit up again. Suddenly, she thought she saw her own index card, only for a split second, her features looking bonier than ever, and a long paragraph, where a chunk of words reached out to slap her: *PRONE TO DEPRESSION.*

Her anger outdid her weakness, and she shot to her feet with new vigor, her entire body quaking with resentment. She wasn't going to give in to this. Never. She was going to flee. She had to prove all this. She had to photograph those index cards, keep it all as evidence. She turned back to get her mobile. Another dizzy spell slowed her down. She was forced to stop and lean against the wall, catching her breath. Her skin felt clammy. There was no air.

When she came back with her phone, the panel had gone dark once more. She hung around. It did not light up again. Had she imagined it all? After fifteen minutes, she went to the shower, weary and uneasy. She couldn't make out the difference between the hobgoblins on the floorboards and the index cards. What had she truly perceived? Had it all been in her mind? She undressed, taking her time, feeling the shakiness take over her body again. The mirror sent back a ghostly echo. Who was watching her, back there? Who could see her? She held up her middle finger wordlessly, with a bitter smirk. Once she got under the shower, tap open, she huddled there, back against the wall. The water was still lukewarm. She shut her eyes, let the stream flow into her mouth, her ears. The trickle of the running water had a calming effect. She thought back to what she had read about Jim Perrier. Alcohol. Drugs. Paranoia. What should she make of it?

Something moving startled her. It was the cat. He stared at her thoughtfully, sitting across from her.

"Hop on in, old sport. It'll do you good."

She had always heard cats hated water, but against all expectation, Chablis let out a small mew and leaped over to land by her side. He let himself get entirely wet, then, with his customary daintiness, installed himself on her thighs and began to purr.

She was still asleep when the doorbell rang. She had no idea of the time; she only remembered having closed the tap, flung herself onto her bed, wrapped in a humid towel. The room temperature seemed agreeably cool. She slipped into a bathrobe and checked the control panel. It was Ben, more good-humored than usual, with an embarrassed expression.

"Everything okay, Mrs. Katsef?"

"Not really. I only just woke up."

He explained the system had undergone a gigantic breakdown and that the air-conditioning had stopped functioning. But it had all been fixed.

"I see," she said. "I nearly kicked the bucket."

He gazed at her, confused.

"Oh, my gosh!"

"I guess I'm tougher than I look. What about the other artists?"

"Most of them left the residence before it got too hot. Have you seen the news?"

"No."

"Everything collapsed, all over the city. Breakdown, failure, outage. No signal, no surveillance, hacked databases, burglaries. Melted asphalt. And lots of casualties."

"Indeed . . . Do you need anything?"

"Yes, Dr. Dewinter would like all artists who went through the heat wave to pass a medical test. I need to check everything's working properly."

Then he added, "You look very pale, if

you don't mind my saying so."

She did not answer, only glared back at him. While he was in the bathroom, she checked her phone. It was just past nine. Numerous calls and texts. She went to the kitchen, opened the refrigerator. Staring at her in the face were four bottles of mineral water. The ones she had looked for in vain last night. She sighed.

She went back to reading her texts. Jordan was fraught, so were Andy, Toby, François, and a couple of other friends. How was she? Could she respond? Was everything okay? She tried to answer them fast, Jordan first. Yes, it had been dreadful, the air-conditioning broke down, everything else broke down, she had never been so thirsty, hot, and faint in her life, but she was okay! Jordan texted back, relieved. She'd call later on today.

As Clarissa was getting back to Andy, her phone rang. It was Laure-Marie, her publisher. She picked up immediately. Laure-Marie wanted to know if she'd survived. Laughingly, Clarissa said that she had, but when she thought of the acute nausea, the vanishing mineral water, the goblins appearing on the floorboards, she wondered if she hadn't underestimated what she had gone through. Laure-Marie wanted to get back in touch. They hadn't seen each other for a while. Apparently, Clarissa had moved. What about getting together for a drink? That way, Clarissa could tell her about her new project, because Laure-Marie was waiting to hear about it! Clarissa agreed to call her later on that week.

Her project. Her book. At a standstill. By eroding her energy, devastating her sleep, filming her around-the-clock, C.A.S.A. had crushed her desire to write. All this was part of their plan, which she understood last night. She'd have to get hold of Andy, too, to tell her what she had discovered. Clarissa already knew she was not going to call her publisher. She hadn't made enough progress. She had to get out of here first. She had to find out how. The lyrics of Toby's favorite song, "Hotel California," kept coming back to her: She could check out anytime she wanted, but she could never leave.

Ben was still in the bathroom, fiddling. He must have sensed her impatience, because he came out looking self-conscious. He informed her everything was in order. The test would take a while longer, he said. But she had to go through with it. Dr. Dewinter had insisted all artists should.

"Fine," said Clarissa grimly. "I just can't wait."

He gawked at her again, lost.

"Good-bye, Ben," she said icily.

He scurried out. Clarissa headed into the bathroom and faced the mirror, looking into the two small red specks.

"Hello, Clarissa," said a mechanical male voice. "Please place your palm on the inlay."

Clarissa obeyed. She couldn't help noticing how gaunt she looked. She had lost weight, which was confirmed when she stepped on the scales.

"Please answer the following questions, Clarissa. Did you faint during the heat wave?"

"No," she replied.

"Did you feel dizzy and lose your balance?"

"Yes."

"Did you feel thirsty?"

"Yes."

"Did your urine appear darker?"

"I didn't pay attention."

"Did you have any cramps?"

"Yes, in my legs."

"Did you have any hallucinations?"

"No."

"Please put your hand back on the inlay."

She noticed the voice had switched from French to English. She put her hand back.

The voice repeated, "Did you have any

hallucinations during the heat wave?"

There was no way she was going to admit she'd seen imps in the patterns of the wooden floor.

"No."

"Did you feel weak?"

"Yes."

"Did your head ache?"

"Yes."

"Were you nauseous?"

"Yes."

"There are eyeglasses on your left. Please put them on. Face the mirror and place your palm on the inlay."

Ben had left glasses near the sink. She positioned them on her nose. They blurred her vision slightly. A dull whine started in her left ear.

"Please keep your eyes open, Clarissa."

The whine became more powerful, like a mighty hum, digging deep into her head. She felt the noise spiraling into her brain like a drill.

"What is this?" she muttered.

"Please refrain from talking. Do not remove your hand. Please look at the marks in the mirror."

How long was she going to remain docile? Was she really going to stand there, let them get on with this? What were they doing? Trying to read what she was thinking? Pilfering her brain?

The voice had gone back to French. She hardly noticed. She tried to stand straight, but the intensifying hum made her shudder and feel giddy.

"Please remain still."

She felt convinced she knew what was going on. She had read about those scientists probing the brain's electrical activity, trying to read into inner thoughts.

"Look into the mirror, please. Describe what you see."

She saw her own face, as long and thin as Virginia Woolf's. With eyes as blue as Romain Gary's.

"I see myself."

"What else do you see, please?"

She noticed an image had been projected within the glass. It looked like a revolving sphere.

"I see a circle."

"Describe it, please."

"In French or in English?"

A pause.

"They" hadn't expected that, she thought, gloating.

"Don't choose a language consciously. Just describe what you see, please."

She described the glittery circle, using

French and English at the same time, flaw-lessly switching from one to the other. Speaking very fast, still using both lan-guages, she invented elements she did not see at all — a tree, a lake, a house. She went into detail. It was almost fun.

"Please describe what you see."

"That's what I'm doing."

"There is no house, lake, or tree in the mirror."

"Really? Well, I see them. You don't?"

The humming noise was strong now, nearly unbearable. What the hell was in those glasses? Electrodes? Captors? What were "they" up to, exactly? Delving into her neurons, certainly. Resistance began to take shape within her, and she gave full force to that defiance. She watched her inner retali-ation thrive; it was like a blue glow hurling itself against the humming noise, casting a screen all around, engulfing Clarissa, mak-ing the mirror and the space around her disappear. The hum could no longer get through the blue, no matter how hard it tried. *Don't give them what they want. Don't let them see what's inside your head. Keep all those thoughts to yourself. They can't take thoughts from you if you don't let them.* Cla-rissa forced her eyes to remain open, visual-izing the blue glow becoming stronger, thicker, and deeper, fighting the powerful grinding whine with every cell in her body, every pulsation of her heart. It was like a merciless battle against the demented storm raging inside her mind.

"Please relax," said the voice.

The blue radiance became her language, neither French nor English; it became her own language, expressing complete pugnacity, and that words were no longer needed in order to clarify she was not going to let "them" into her mind. How long did the combat last? She had no idea. The whining finally decreased. She was asked to take the glasses off. She felt drained.

"Thank you, Clarissa. Medical examination completed."

She tottered into the toilet, bolted the door; it was the only spot in the flat that remained an intimate space. She grinned at the irony of it. She slid down, back to the wall, tried to rest. To her consternation, she sensed the intense weakness she'd felt last night creep its way back into her organism. She must gain her strength back. She had to make plans. She had to act fast.

Clarissa rubbed her hands over her face, trying to give herself some energy. She breathed slowly in and out. She didn't care if no one believed her. Maybe only Andy would. It didn't matter. She knew what to do next.

Nathalie's bookstore-café, on boulevard du Montparnasse, was packed this morning, despite the tragic events of yesterday. Customers gathered around displays, settled into cozy armchairs, or sat down for coffee and cake. Clarissa hadn't been back since the opening. She was cheered to see so many bookworms on the premises. A young salesperson informed her that Nathalie was upstairs, in her office. She'd go fetch her. Clarissa wandered through the stalls. She realized she hadn't done much reading since her move. The residence had dispossessed her of her love of books. No writing, no reading. What a punishment.

"My God, Clarissa!"

Nathalie had gasped with shock.

"You're so thin!"

"I know. I didn't do it on purpose, believe me. And the heat didn't help, either. But don't worry, I'm fine."

She flashed a large smile to reassure her friend. But Nathalie wasn't fooled by it. Clarissa changed the subject, asking her about her shop. Nathalie answered with her usual fervor, going into the details of the highs and lows of bookselling. Clarissa listened with pleasure. Then she said, "I was wondering if I could ask you a small favor."

"Of course! What is it?"

"Your friend, the one I met here, who works in real estate."

"Guillaume? I heard he helped you find your new flat."

"That's him. Could you call him for me?"

"You want his number?"

"I already have his number. But I'd rather not call him from my mobile."

"Oh?"

"Could you possibly call him on your own phone? And then put me on?"

Nathalie looked at her closely. Clarissa knew what she was thinking, right there. That Clarissa looked like a demented old lady, with her red dye going to pot and her intense blue gaze.

"You need to talk to him?"

"Yes."

"A problem with your flat?"

"Sort of. I simply need to ask him one quick question. It won't take very long."

Slight hesitation.

"Okay. All right."

Nathalie fished her phone from her pocket. She pressed on a key, waited, and got voice mail.

"Hi, Guillaume. It's Nat. Can you get

318

back to me? Important. Thanks."

Clarissa said she'd wait around, looking at books. She wouldn't be far. Nathalie got on with her work. Clarissa's eyes followed her as she gave advice to clients, located books for them. She never seemed to lose her zeal. Clarissa remembered most of her own books were still with François. She still had many belongings in her old place. One day, she'd have to retrieve them. But not while she was at the residence. François's letter was at the bottom of her bag, with her notebooks. She still hadn't read it. She held it between her fingertips. It felt quite thick.

Just as she was thinking of opening it, Nathalie was back, flourishing her mobile.

"Here's Guillaume."

Clarissa took the phone.

"Hello," she said in what she hoped was a jovial voice. "I'm not sure you remember me? We met here, at Nathalie's opening."

"The red-haired author who writes about houses and suicidal authors, not easily forgotten," he replied with a slightly sarcastic intonation. "What can I do for you?"

Nathalie had gone back to her customers. Clarissa was alone.

"I wanted to talk to you about the C.A.S.A. residence."

"I believe you live there, right? So you got

in! Well done! That's no easy feat, and they're rather picky, I hear."

She nearly added "And I'm longing to get out of it," but abstained.

"That's right, I was admitted. Sorry for putting this to you so bluntly, but what is C.A.S.A., exactly? Who is behind it?"

He seemed surprised.

"Well, benefactors keen on promoting all forms of artistic creations. They have huge financial resources."

"Have you met anyone from C.A.S.A.?"

"I must have crossed paths with a couple of people, but I don't remember. I only know Clémence Dutilleul, whom I put you in touch with. She's in charge of finding artists for the residence. That's all I know. I worked with my architects to construct the place. I don't know much more about C.A.S.A."

"Nothing at all?"

"No! What are you getting at? What's with these people?"

"You weren't aware, for instance, that all the artists living in the residence are filmed?"

A pause.

"Filmed all the time?" he asked.

"Yes. All the time. We signed a contract."

"So you agreed to it?"

"That's not the issue. I want to find out *why* we are filmed."

"Surveillance requirements, no doubt. Aren't you happy up there on the eighth floor? Your studio is magnificent! The number of people who'd love to be in your shoes!"

"Have you met Dr. Dewinter?"

"No, I haven't. Who is this person?"

"An artificial intelligence specialist. She runs the C.A.S.A. protocol."

"So?"

"You don't see the link?"

"I'm afraid not."

"You don't see how an AI expert could find a household of artists most interesting?"

"I'm sorry, ma'am, I fail to see the link, and don't see how I can help you in any way."

Clarissa was unable to keep him on the phone. He asked to be handed back to Nathalie. She heard his voice boom out to her friend: "What a dotty old lady!"

Clarissa took off, thanking Nathalie, who kept watching her with a mixture of suspicion and concern. She walked along the boulevard, noting how yesterday's temperatures had left traces in the extenuated features of passersby, in their slow shuffle.

Clarissa hadn't listened to the news, or read the press on her tablet. Fatalities, bedlam, confusion, crisis, pessimism. The same old song. She'd answered each text message she received, including François's. She had written, *All OK, and you?* He'd replied, *Yes, thanks. Did you get my letter?* She'd left it at that.

For the moment, C.A.S.A. was her prime concern. What they wanted, how they got what they wanted, and, above all, how to leave them. She had always known how to weave intimate connections with homes. The place she'd shared with Toby, on rue d'Alésia, left sweet memories in her mind, in spite of the tragedy that had befallen them. It was a bright, cheerful two-room flat. She could still see Toby sitting on the little balcony, reading in the sunlight. She had also been fond of the larger apartment, acquired with François, on rue Henri-Barbusse, the one she'd decorated with him, full of her beloved books. She had loved writing there.

Like foreign territory barring her entry, her apartment in the residence spread out in front of her, and she perceived hostility in every nook, every chink. Perhaps she was not wanted here because she refused to co-operate. She gave nothing away; she did not submit. Were the other artists easier to manage and to influence? Were they content merely living and working here, having no inkling concerning the truth? Was she the only one seeing that truth? Jim Perrier had come close. Had he been dismissed because of his misgivings? Or because of his addictions, which didn't conform to the C.A.S.A. protocol? And what about her? Did she risk being expelled, as well? Her insubordination had not gone unnoticed. Dr. Dewinter herself had turned up to call her to order. Perhaps that was the way out. Disobedience. Well, she was ready. She was more than ready.

Back in the bathroom, she avoided looking at herself in the mirror. She made sure each of her gestures seemed calm and ordinary. She acted the same way in the kitchen. An internal message from Adelka showed up on the screens. She was wondering how Clarissa'd put up with the awful heat. She herself had gone off to a friend's place, near Lille. Clarissa dictated a concise reply: *Yes, thanks, all fine, but it was dreadful! See you soon!* Her mobile buzzed as she was cleaning things up in the kitchen.

It was her brother, Arthur. She hadn't spoken to him directly since the choppy outcome of Aunt Serena's will. She'd sent an email thanking him for the brooch, without alluding to its real worth. Even if she didn't feel like hearing the sound of his voice, she took the call. Arthur sounded out of breath. It was about their father. A rapid fright shot through her. Their dad had had a bad fall; he'd broken two ribs and his nose. He was in the hospital. Could she come? He was also going to alert Jordan.

Of course she'd go. But how was their dad? What happened? Arthur said he hadn't yet spoken to the doctors. Their father fell out of his bed. Luckily, the nursing assistant who was on duty was able to help. He was at the brand-new London Fields hospital, near Broadway Market.

Clarissa remembered the ticket she'd recently booked for her upcoming London trip. She was able to modify it for a new one; the train was departing in two hours. She stuffed a change of clothes and toiletries into a travel bag. She had no idea how long she might have to stay. The cat! What was she going to do with it? Adelka seemed to be the only solution. With Chablis tucked under her arm, she went down to the fourth floor. Wearing a jumpsuit, with a paintbrush in hand, Adelka opened up.

"My dad's in the hospital, in London. I've got to leave."

"Oh, your poor dad! You want me to keep this precious bundle? I'll take care of the food and the litter, don't you worry!"

Clarissa thanked her warmly. She had to make her way in time to the sprawling Gare du Nord, a place she disliked all the more because of its never-ending overhaul. Her British passport enabled her to skip endless queues at control checks, but there was still customs to go through, on either end. It had been getting worse and worse, ever since Brexit's unsettling consequences, steeped in complication. One had still to wait for hours in order to set foot on the island where she was born. How strange it was to originate from these two neighboring countries, traditional foes, which, over time, had not succeeded in becoming closer, but, on the contrary, had drawn even further apart. Like most people she knew, Clarissa found Eurostar's new name, StarExpress, ridiculous.

She tried to get hold of Jordan but only got through to voice mail. She wondered if her daughter had managed to make herself available, and if she was en route to London. During the entire trip, her father stayed on her mind. Arthur sent her the hospital room number. At St. Pancras, during the second interminable wait at customs, she did her best to remain patient. No use getting edgy.

She had to save all her energy up for her father. She took the Tube to Hackney. She was usually elated to be back in her native city, but today, the joy had gone. It felt sad admitting it, but all those years spent in Paris had turned her into a Frenchwoman. London was no longer her home. Her French side had taken over. Was this irreversible? she wondered. Perhaps it was fleeting, due to fragility and fatigue.

Leaving the Tube station at Bethnal Green, she walked briskly to the nearby hospital. Her legs were painful, her joints stiff. She couldn't help daydreaming about the summer holidays Jordan was planning with the brooch money. Puglia, in southern Italy, was the chosen destination. Jordan had discovered a *masseria,* a fortified farmhouse, lost within a field of thousand-year-old olive trees, miraculously preserved from the disease that had eradicated most of them. The deep blue sea was only a few kilometers away.

The shiny modern façade drew itself up in front of her. Clarissa paused for a few seconds before entering. The state her father might be in worried her. He was so old, so vulnerable.

Arthur was waiting for her outside the room, with his daughters. He seemed glum.

326

"Brace yourself," he said, hugging her. Clarissa greeted her sniffling nieces.

She stepped into the room alone, not feeling very reassured. Her father's face was bruised, entirely black-and-blue. A huge bump deformed his forehead; a bandage covered his nose, and an intravenous drip was fitted in his arm. He was unrecognizable.

She couldn't refrain from bursting into tears. Her exhaustion overcame her in one powerful wave. She could only stand there, weeping, feeling as helpless as a child. Her dad! Her old beloved dad! She couldn't bear seeing him this way.

"My darling! My sweetie!"

Her father's unmistakable voice piped up, weak but still full of humor. Dumbfounded, she opened her eyes.

"Honey, why are you in such a state? It's only a blasted tumble! Can you imagine, falling from your own bed? Bloody hell! Arthur's got a face like a month of wet Sundays! And his daughters, just as bad, a couple of twits!"

Clarissa couldn't help laughing through her tears. She couldn't get over it. He was incredible! Sitting next to the bed, she clenched her father's long, wrinkled hand. She admitted her apprehension, and how his devastated features had shocked her.

Her father chortled.

"Well, my hour has not yet come. I'm all bashed up, but I'm still here! And I'm so happy to see you. Come closer so I can look at your pretty face. Oh! You're looking under the weather! What's with those little eyes? You've lost weight, my dearest. You've got me fretted now."

A topsy-turvy world! Her injured father, worrying about her.

"I'm okay, Dad. Don't worry. How long are you here for?"

"Speak a little louder, my love; the chip in my ear is kicking up."

Clarissa repeated her question.

"No idea! In this damned hospital, robots look after patients. Robots never make mistakes with their diagnosis, do they? They're the kings of the world, right? What's left for us poor humans?"

"Emotions?" quipped Clarissa.

"Spot-on. But what about you, my sweet? How's your book coming along? Are you happy with it?"

"No. I'm not happy, Dad. I can't work properly in my apartment."

"Now, that's the last straw!" said her father. "You and houses! Ever since you were small, they've had a hold on you. So what's wrong with the flat?"

Clarissa prepared herself to reveal the entire C.A.S.A. inside story to him, to go into detail, to see how he would react. She was looking forward to sharing with her father what she was going through.

The door slid open and she saw Jordan standing on the threshold. Her daughter moaned when she discovered her grandfather's discolored face. Then Arthur rushed in as well, with his daughters. Her father was surrounded by his loving family. In spite of his contusions, he glowed with happiness. He was thrilled to have them all there; it was Christmas in June! Only Andy was missing. A nurse barged in to tell them they were making too much noise. And a maximum of two people could remain at the bedside.

Clarissa ended up with her daughter and her father. They all decided to favor those who had come from afar. And those who'd endured those endless lines to get into this bloody country, grumbled Jordan, while her father roared with laughter. Clarissa noticed (how could she not notice?) that Jordan had installed an infinitesimal distance between them. Jordan glanced at her, smiled, but the detachment was well and truly there, growing by the minute, and she felt upset. She'd very rarely perceived a cold shoulder coming from her daughter. She could not understand what was going on. In her mind, she went back to all the conversations she'd recently had with her. She couldn't pick out anything in particular. What about Andy? Her instinct told her that must be it. Perhaps Jordan was cross with Clarissa because of Andy. She could hardly believe it. Was Jordan irritated because of the closeness she and Andy shared? Clarissa was aware Andy was most probably difficult with her mother, like any teenager. She knew she shared an exceptional relationship with her granddaughter.

The nurse interrupted them to say it was time to tend to the patient. They were asked to leave the room. Clarissa said good-bye to her father lovingly. Arthur and his daughters were waiting outside. Arthur had received the medical dossier. Their father was going to be spending the week at the hospital, but the report was reassuring. The old chap wasn't doing too badly, said Arthur, impressed. He asked Clarissa and Jordan if they both wanted to stay at his place for the night. Jane would be very happy to see them. Jordan thanked him; she had a co-worker to catch up with, near Islington. She'd no doubt stop over at her place. Clarissa said she didn't know yet what she was doing. Arthur asked her to let him know what her plans were; he'd be delighted to put her up. It seemed her brother was trying to make amends. Wasn't he overdoing it?

"What about a cup of tea?"

Yes, that was Jordan talking to her, Clarissa. A tremor of delight ran through her. She smiled and nodded. They strolled down Broadway Market, their nostrils full of the spicy aromas of street food from all over the world, looking for a place to sit down. Since Clarissa's youth, Hackney had changed. Hidden behind stylish boutiques, trendy eateries, and fashionably dressed pedestrians, its working-class legacy was hard to see. When she was a teenager, saying you lived in Hackney was like admitting a genetic defect. She used to meet her friends in Camden or Portobello, even if she had to spend hours on the Tube.

"Look, there!" said Jordan.

A deliciously outmoded tearoom beckoned them. There were a few customers sitting on chairs covered with pastel cushions. On Fridays and Saturdays, the area was packed with Londoners and sightseers, and it was hard to amble along, Clarissa knew. They ordered tea and scones. Clarissa observed her daughter's beautiful, sensitive face. In her eyes, that tiny cold draft, still. She decided to wait. If Jordan had something to say, she'd do it. It shouldn't be up to her to bring up the subject. But Jordan remained silent, absentmindedly nibbling at her scone, as if she was expecting her mother to speak up first.

As time ticked by, Clarissa felt the silence becoming heavy. So she broke it, hoping her voice sounded natural.

"How's Andy?"

Jordan looked at her straight in the eyes.

"As it happens, I want to talk to you about Andy."

"Yes?"

Jordan was not smiling. Her fingers played with the crumbs.

"Andy admitted to me what happened last time she went to stay with you."

Clarissa swallowed.

"Meaning what?"

"The incident that occurred in your neighbor's flat."

"We didn't do anything wrong, you know. You're looking at me as if I've committed a crime!"

"Adriana is fourteen years old! The idea of it! Breaking into an apartment at two in the morning! Do you realize? And that

Bardi nearly taking her away? What on earth were you thinking?"

Clarissa suddenly felt very hot. Her cheeks flared up; the skin above her lip turned moist.

"You're her granny, for God's sake! This isn't one of your TV shows!"

This reaction was so unlike Jordan. Was it envy, resentment? Clarissa didn't know how to face it. She foresaw she was not going to handle what came next well, and that whatever she had to say would not be appreciated.

"I understand you're angry and concerned. I never wanted to put Andy in danger."

"But you did! What the hell were you doing in your neighbor's place anyway? What's all this business about the C.A.S.A. residence? I couldn't make any sense out of Andy's stories."

"We didn't break in. The door was open. Jim, my neighbor, has disappeared. We don't know where he is."

Jordan seemed impatient.

"What's this got to do with Andy? Why drag her into all this?"

Like a hot red veil, the burning sensation was now covering Clarissa's entire body. She was finding it hard to speak. The words were coming out of her mouth too slowly.

"Andy is aware of what is going on in the residence. She's helping me out."

"And what is going on, exactly, Mums?"

Clarissa ignored the sarcasm in her daughter's tone, and did her best to describe what she had endured since her move. She struggled to remain precise and logical. She noticed the way her daughter was looking at her. The piercing gaze made her flounder, and sound confused. She backtracked, tried to add details, to give more explanations, to show how C.A.S.A. was resurrecting her past, her traumas. The words she picked, didn't they sound exaggerated? Her movements, disorderly? Every sentence she uttered seemed insane. She got muddled up, had to dab beads of sweat off her forehead, asked for some water for her parched throat.

Jordan did not interrupt her. She let her become mired, and when Clarissa finally went quiet, her face crimson, Jordan took her hand. She said she'd been worried for a while now. Ever since Clarissa had left François so precipitously and without any explanation. The breakup had started all this; of that, she was certain. She could tell her mother was slowly sinking into some sort of instability, a constant fatigue that was knocking the stuffing out of her. This could no longer do. It was high time to take action.

"But that's what I'm doing!" roared Clarissa, startling her daughter, as well as the couple sitting at the next table. "That's exactly what I've been doing, with Andy's help, because she's the only one who understands me. All the stuff happening to me is because of the residence and their protocol. I'm fighting back! Andy and I are fighting them and we are trying to figure out what they are doing! And guess what? I know what they want! I've guessed it!"

Jordan sighed. She looked dismayed.

"You and your tall tales! The powder, clicking noise, sleep disturbances, vanishing neighbor and whatnot, that's in your head, Mums. Only in your head. You like to embellish, to pretend, to bamboozle, because that's your job! None of this is real life. What is real, however, is that you're going through a low. No need to shy away from that word. This is a depression. Like the one you had a long time ago. It's back. I can see it."

Clarissa recoiled.

"What are you saying, Jordan?"

"I spent too much time as a child, as a teenager, faced with that haggard, empty, sad expression. The way you look today. You must seek help. The heat wave has made it all worse. You probably had heatstroke, hallucinations, whatever. You're getting on, Mums. Look at you. Your mouth is dry; you've lost weight; you can't even breathe properly. Let me help you. I'm here."

Clarissa said nothing, stunned. The gap between her daughter and herself seemed irreversible, as if a furious torrent divided them, without a single bridge in sight. She had never gone through this situation before. Jordan had always been her rock. Jordan had always supported her.

"You're going to go home, Mums," her daughter was saying, levelheaded and calm, with her lovely orator's voice, "and you're going to rest. I'm getting hold of a good psychiatrist, someone I trust, and she will help you. Don't worry. After a couple of appointments, and the proper treatment, I'm sure you'll feel better."

Jordan's lips stretched into a small smile. She patted her mother's hand.

"You'll be fine. If you follow my advice, you'll be just fine."

I remained rooted to the spot, incapable of making a single move. What was I to do? She was going to turn around and see me. The only way out was to leave now, right away, before she woke up.

The intense, mawkish perfume made my head spin. I felt myself sway, afraid I might tumble. The wood boards squeaked as I stepped back. I was sure she was going to awaken, but she went on sleeping peacefully. I looked at her plump shoulders, her fleshy buttocks enhanced by a short black lace negligée.

I couldn't understand. My husband was a mature, sophisticated gentleman. He was refined, elegant. True, he had often cheated on me with a series of faceless, nameless women. Had they all been part of the young, blond, petite, chubby category? In that case, what was he still doing with me? Either that or, I had to admit it, my husband was a stranger. A man I had been intimate with, a man I thought I knew, but who had perfectly preserved the shady side of his character.

On the bed, a lamé evening dress. On the floor, matching high-heeled pumps. Did he take her to balls, to parties? François hated that type of thing. He was no socialite. I felt lost.

Next to me, on the right of the bed, a wardrobe. I opened it. A dozen dresses in the same style were hanging there: sequins, lace, satin. No other clothes apart from lingerie. Not even a pair of jeans, or a T-shirt.

I hunted around for her purse. I wanted to discover her name, her address, her age. There was no bag. Nothing at all. Not even a coat. I began to wonder.

She hadn't budged. I went around the bed, lifted the veiling. She kept her eyes closed.

With terror, I realized she wasn't breathing. Her chest was motionless. I couldn't hear the sound of respiration.

Was she dead? What was I to do? My fingerprints were all over the place, on the doorknobs, the photo albums, the tablet. I was going to be found guilty; I had come here and I had killed my husband's mistress. I was going to be taken away in handcuffs.

I leaned forward, coming close to her face. Very close. I could see the detail of her long black lashes.

It was at that moment her eyes slowly opened. They stared back at me. I leaped back, horrified.

"My darling. There you are. I missed you so."

It took me a while to understand.

She went on talking in her gentle, soulless voice.

"My darling. François. I was waiting for you. I'm so happy to see you."

Incredulous, I stretched out my hand and touched her arm. It felt exactly like skin. It was warm. I grazed her hair, and it felt the same. Like real hair.

"Oh, that's so good, honey; don't stop."

I said in a loud, trembling tone, "What's your name?"

"My name is Amber."

"Who are you, Amber?"

"The one who gives you the most pleasure. Because I know exactly what you want. Exactly."

My mobile throbbed. Another text from François, worried about my being late. I didn't respond.

In the nightstand's drawer, instructions for use and a warranty certificate. Choice of eye color, hair, and body shape. Removable or built-in orifices. Voice preference. Assembly process. Configuration. Tests. Powering up. Battery. Hair maintenance. "Carefully rinse all intimate parts after use with special brush and irrigator. Leave to dry thoroughly."

This was a nightmare. That hideous pinkish purple color, glistening and lubricious, made me feel as if I had been ensnared within a voracious vagina about to swallow me up. This is where my husband came, in every sense of the word. This was where he caressed a fleshless, bloodless body that had nothing human about it; this was where he penetrated the semblance of a woman; this was where he had hewn, away from me, an intimate place, eminently selfish, for himself only, where he surrendered to his vilest fantasies.

I lay down beside the creature. The coverlet reeked of the detestable perfume, mingled with the unmistakable smell of come. I took a selfie of both of us. She looked like she was cuddling up to me.

I left the apartment in haste, not bothering to lock up behind me. I ran along rue Dancourt in the night, bumping into passersby. After a bit, I stopped, out of breath, and sat on a bench.

I felt grief, disappointment, disgust, but, above all, anger. A tremendous anger that swept away all the rest.

I sent the selfie to François, without a word. I imagined him sitting in Caroline and Véronique's pretty living room, filled with flowers. They had been waiting for over an hour, nibbling tidbits and sipping good wine, wondering what the hell I was doing.

And the photo showing up on his phone with the power of an exploding bomb.

And the phone showing up on his phone with
the power of an exploding bomb.

9
MELTDOWN

Mrs. Dalloway said she'd choose the flowers herself.

VIRGINIA WOOLF, 1925

I had fun. Good-bye and thank you.

ROMAIN GARY, March 21, 1979

Clarissa took a sip of water, slowly, placing the glass back on the pink tablecloth.

"The C.A.S.A. people are trying to convince everyone that they are benefactors investing in us because we are artists. It's a smoke screen. Behind all that, there's a clandestine consortium dealing in artificial intelligence. A covert, unlawful organization, engaging in heinous experiments."

Jordan raised her hand.

"Mums, please stop."

"You must listen, Jordan. And without making that face. It took me a while to figure it out. Now, I've got the whole picture."

Jordan sighed.

"Okay," she said grudgingly. "I'm listening. Go ahead."

Clarissa began to speak more easily, without having to look for words. Surprised, she found herself suddenly using English, even though French was the tongue she ordinarily spoke with Jordan. She noticed her daughter frowning, as if she couldn't understand why her mother chose to continue their conversation in English. Why, at this precise moment, during these critical instants with her daughter, was she seeking shelter in her father's and her first husband's native tongue? English felt heartwarming, enveloping her with a special familiarity that spurred her on, but it also seemed to offer her a natural defense against Jordan, a safeguard.

Clarissa said that robots, today, were able to take over humans; they knew how to teach, protect, attack, heal, and operate. They could drive, deliver, build, and analyze. And give pleasure, as well. Yes, they even screwed better than humans did. (She nearly added "And I, of all people, ought to know," but she desisted, as she had no intention of answering the inevitable questions flying thick and fast.) Imagination was the only thing robots lacked. Robots could neither invent nor create; they could only imitate, because that's what they were programmed to do. Their algorithms allowed them to compose music, to write in a given style, to produce paintings, to duplicate an image. Jordan must have seen the insipid production generated by artificial intelligence. Perfect, smooth, and boring. Nothing new.

"So, what's your point?"

Clarissa resented her daughter's mocking smile, and how Jordan doggedly stuck to French. Clarissa retaliated, in English, and Jordan lifted a disapproving eyebrow, which Clarissa disregarded. She went on. Robots were unable to understand creativeness, the delicate magic of its haphazardness, how an idea came to an artist, how it thrived within the artist's brain, like a pearl burrowed into an oyster, shaped by fate, setbacks, by intimate life events, lustered by emotions, sensitivity, by everything that turned human beings into what they were, infinitely vulnerable, far from perfect, but able to spawn originality, disparity, ambiguity.

"You're right," said Jordan. "But how does this link to you?"

"I'm coming to that. Robots, therefore,

344

don't have pearls growing within an inner cerebral place; they have no artistic initiative, unless ingenious researchers can endow them with that, and that's exactly what's going on, in that residence. Those people have masses of money and fully operational gear. They're cunning. But day after day, night after night, C.A.S.A. pries into our imaginations, behind our backs."

Jordan cleared her throat. She seemed to be out of her depth.

"Mums, you analyze everything to death! And why are you talking to me in English? You never do."

Clarissa chose not to bring up the language choice. She went on, still using that precious, fluid English.

"With Andy's help — and your daughter is so bright, but you already know that — I at last realized Dr. Dewinter and her team don't care a fig about our artistic endeavors. They've filled the residence up with bilingual artists who speak two languages fluently. They spy on us constantly in order to understand how our brains work, those hybrid brains. You have one of those brains, too. They don't film us all the time for translation purposes; robots already know how to do that perfectly in all languages. No, what they are trying to harvest from us is our creativeness, our imaginary worlds, those of us who live and who dream in two different tongues. And do you know why they are up to this? Do you know what their goal is?"

"I'm all ears."

Clarissa brushed aside the causticity in Jordan's tone, forced herself not to refer to it. Jordan staunchly maintained French, as if this had turned into a language combat between them, as if she was challenging not only what her mother had to say but also how Clarissa was saying it. Clarissa could no longer ignore the grievance caused by Jordan's attitude. She feared she might dither once more, become unable to finish, not be able to keep up that clear and steady voice.

"Imagine a world, not that different from ours, not that far away, where everything would be dictated by robots. A lack of inspiration? Writer's block? Tiredness? That fluctuating artistic temperament? Over. Done. Who gives a damn about musicians, painters, writers and their mood swings? In the tomorrow that's nearly here, robots will write the blockbusters to come, will paint the most beautiful paintings, will compose the most haunting melodies. Robots nurtured by our own creative brains, by everything they will have pilfered from us. That's serious and ghastly enough as it is, but behind all that prowls a greater threat."

"I shudder to think where this is going," murmured Jordan.

Clarissa felt like crashing her fist down on the table. How dare Jordan treat her this way, making her sound as if she was unbalanced, a raving lunatic? She took it upon herself not to reveal her annoyance, her bitterness. She said Dr. Dewinter and her peers might well become all-powerful once they were able, by dint of algorithms and filched brainpower, to have their robots fabricate an artistic movement they could then predict.

"We will end up being told what books to read, what movies and exhibits to see; we could be forced to appreciate a fake culture entirely conceived and controlled by machines. We will no longer have any choice at all. For a long time, we've been getting those notifications telling us, 'You liked so-and-so's book, so then read thingy's one.' But what's ahead could be even worse. Art, in each and every form, could be anticipated, made to order. Humans will stop creating, stop imagining. The end of surprises, make-believe, the end of possibilities, of the unexpected. On every front, it'll be the victory of robots. That's what C.A.S.A. is up to. That's why I want to get the hell out of that place."

Jordan pulled a funny little face.

"Well, well! There's your next novel, I guess!"

Clarissa gaped at her.

"You don't believe me?"

Without being conscious of it, she'd switched back into French.

"I've already told you what I believe."

"Which is?"

"You need to get help."

Clarissa got to her feet too quickly. The light-headedness made her clutch at the table.

"Look at the state you're in."

Clarissa grabbed her bag, her jacket.

"I'm fine. I'm off to the station."

Jordan rose as well, tried to catch her mother by the shoulder. Her gesture was full of affection, but Clarissa pulled away.

"Don't act vexed, please."

Clarissa said nothing.

"Take care of yourself, Mums. Promise me. You must get some rest. I'll be back tomorrow. I'll call you. And keep Andy out of this."

Tearfully, Clarissa left the tearoom without bidding her daughter good-bye, which had

348

never happened. She no longer knew whom to turn to. Everything Jordan had said hurt her deeply; her loneliness inundated her, dragged her down. In the Tube, a nice woman asked her if she was feeling all right. When she got to St. Pancras, she saw it was going to be a skirmish to get one of the last tickets on the train leaving at 16:19. The trains after that were all full. She did something she had never done in her life. She told the young, harassed person dealing with the reservations that she was a very old lady, very old indeed, and very ill, and this was no doubt her last trip to Paris. She distorted her voice, made it quaver and croak. She wanted to see Paris one last time. Tomorrow might be too late. Weepy eyes, a wobbly head. She obtained her ticket, while other exasperated customers looked on.

Once she was seated in the StarExpress, after the hellish wait in the queue, she buried her face in her hands. For God's sake, what was happening to her? Making such a scene, lying through her teeth. What had she tumbled into? She thought back to all the times people had told her, with a zest of humor, that she'd been repeating herself, or that she'd forgotten to do something. She remembered the numerous occasions she'd heard the sentence, at moments with a touch of irony, *Your imagination is getting away with you.* She recalled her mother's slow decline, and how Solange had started to forget who she was long before she reached Clarissa's present age. What if Jordan was right? What if she really was losing her grip?

She longed to call Andy, the only person who understood her, who could reassure her. But she didn't dare challenge Jordan's authority.

While the train made its way to France, a message from Mia White showed up on her mobile. *Hello, Clarissa! How are you? I hope the heat wave wasn't too much of an ordeal. Do let me know how you are. See you soon, Mia.*

Mia White! The mere name incensed her. Indeed, that phony Mia White had duped her, with her fake social media feed, starstruck gaze, and sham smile. She doubtless knew exactly where Clarissa was, what she was doing right now. Clarissa's mobile was probably geolocated. Mia White was working full throttle behind her screens, tracking every single move, reporting back to Dr. Dewinter: *Clarissa Katsef went to London to see her father. She's on the StarExpress getting in at Gare du Nord at 20:08.*

She obliterated the text angrily without

responding to it.

When she arrived at the residence a few hours later, she rode the elevator up, incapable of mounting the eight flights. The apartment seemed more silent and intimidating than usual. She put her bag down in the entry. Should she tell Adelka she was back, go fetch the cat?

She found herself unable to move forward, as if her entire body was on alert. There was a lump in her throat; a feeling of dread and queasiness taking over. She locked herself up in the toilet, her only refuge. She stayed there, standing up, for a long time, until she felt her heartbeat slow down.

She kept dwelling on Jordan's words. *That's all in your head, Mums. This is a depression.* Was the breakup with François, the shock of his betrayal, truly the trigger to her turmoil? Was her son's name whispered in the night all a dream? Or worse still, was that her own voice, and not Elise Delaporte's?

She understood, clearly, while she was still secluded, that she could not stay a single minute more in this apartment. It was all over.

Flee. Skedaddle. Everything she needed was in her travel bag, the one she had prepared this morning for London. There

were no belongings here that meant anything to her.

Escape. Scram. The cat was with Adelka.

She knew where to go. It was obvious.
She'd go there.

Now. Bolt, right now.

She came out of the confined space, brac-
ing against the uneasiness that gripped her.
She loathed this place. How had she ever
agreed to settle down here? How had she
lasted two months? At what cost?

She took her mobile from her bag and
placed it on the kitchen table. She headed
toward the front door, put her hand on the
doorknob to pull it open. It seemed blocked.
She placed her index finger on the glass
square to unlock it.

Nothing happened. She tried again.

The door remained shut.

"Open the door!" she said firmly.

A sentence showed up on the control
panel.

You forgot your mobile phone in the kitchen.

She nearly spat out "What's my bloody
phone got to do with you?"

She forced herself to sound neutral.

"I'm just going down to see a neighbor. I
don't need my mobile. Open up."

Had "they" guessed she was going to run
for her life? Were "they" going to keep her

here against her will? What would she do if that were the case?

That barred door. She gave it a shove. Nothing happened.

"Open this door!" she yelled.

Please put your index finger on the glass square.

She did as she was told. Her hand felt unsteady. She was going to go absolutely mad if she wasn't able to get out of here.

Still nothing. She whacked the bottom of the door with a bad-tempered kick.

"Open!"

This time, she let out a yell of rage. "They" were doing this on purpose, right? "They" were pushing her to her limits, as usual, so as to test her reactions, so as to use them? She itched to stamp her feet, like a child. She couldn't stand it any longer. Total despondency took over.

"Please open the door," she muttered, her forehead stuck to the wooden paneling. "Please, I beg you."

With a click, the door opened. Clarissa yearned to make an extravagant gesture of victory. Not in front of the camera. She was leaving. Leaving! She'd notify Adelka later. She fished around her bag, pulled out a scarf, wrapped it around her head. She felt lighter and lighter as she flew down the steps.

Down in the lobby, the main egress swung open.

The mechanical voice announced, "Good-bye. The C.A.S.A. residence looks forward to seeing you again."

She felt like singing at the top her lungs: *You bet! You're not going to be seeing me for a while! You're no longer going to watch every step I take. You won't tarnish my dreams, filch my ideas, play with my moods, sprinkle fairy dust in my tea. Ciao! Auf Wiedersehen! Adios!*

She rushed to the nearest Métro station. She felt quite naked without her mobile phone. For the past thirty-five years, she calculated, she'd always had one with her, a reassuring, everyday item that was part of her everyday life. Her panic-stricken feeling was laced with liberty. She was free. Free! No one could find her. Later, when "they" had examined the surveillance videos, it would become clear the hasty person leaving the premises, whose face was covered by a scarf, was indeed Clarissa. By then, she'd be far away.

Entirely reconstructed after the attack, the Bir-Hakeim Métro station drew all eyes with its black-and-gray neoclassical lines. Clarissa was held up for a while, as she had to buy a ticket at a self-service terminal, since her Métro pass was on her phone. She set off to the Gare Montparnasse, only a few stops away.

Once she got there, she checked departing trains on the display panel. She blessed the fact night trains had become operational again, facilitating travelers working to reduce their carbon footprint, encouraging them not to depend solely on planes, cars, or buses. That particular mode of transport had been on a roll for the past couple of years; derelict lines had even been reopened. She acquired a sleeping berth on the train she wanted, and got agitated when she had to pay, another thing she was used to doing with her phone. Thankfully, one could still use a credit card. The train was leaving in less than two hours, and due to arrive at 6:27 tomorrow morning. There were several stops en route.

She had time to grab a bite to eat. She entered a shop to buy a snack and something to read. She chose a paperback by one of her author friends, a kindhearted man she'd often met up with some years ago, until he won a prestigious literary prize and became bigheaded. He was younger than Clarissa, his smile beaming out from the book cover. Clarissa had never been jealous of other authors' success. She had come late to writing and to publication, already in her fifties. She admired authors who began to write when they were children, such as Virginia Woolf and Romain Gary.

The ambitious renovation work planned for the Gare Montparnasse, expected to be completed five years ago, was still not finished. In the past decade, the attack had initiated an overall freeze of most Parisian construction sites. Enormous delays had built up. The Gare Montparnasse was still as drab, gloomy, and grimy as ever; penetrated by drafts in wintertime, and suffocating in summer. Clarissa found a place to sit down and eat her sandwich. She caught herself looking for her phone yet again, this time to listen to music.

In her mind's eye, she could see her father in his modern hospital, a décor from a futuristic movie. When she was on her way out, he had exclaimed, "Now, now, darling, no more glum faces; don't forget to smile!" Classic. Where did that tenacious buoyancy come from? She had never heard her father complain, lament, or regret anything. She longed to call him, or send him a message.

It was time to board. Clarissa had picked a "Ladies Only" sleeper compartment. Four berths per cabin. The train was a recent model, with a sober design. She greeted her sister travelers for the night, who responded with a nod or a smile. They were all absorbed by their mobiles. Later, their tickets were verified. One of the women was getting off at the same stop as Clarissa. The train was going all the way to the border.

She hadn't told anyone about this trip. She'd written the address in her notebook so she wouldn't forget it: 70 Chemin du Port. Apartment 28. 6th floor, right.

At sundown, the night-lights switched on. The travelers lay on their bunks. The train thrust into the darkness.

Sleep eluded Clarissa. Her thoughts kept wandering to her father, to Jordan's hurtful words, to Andy.

Had her absence been noticed? Her guess was that Jordan hadn't yet found out, and probably thought her upset mother was not answering her phone because of their conversation at the tearoom.

For a long while, Clarissa read. The book was entertaining, well written, penned with spirited ruthlessness; the story of a woman falling in love with her new son-in-law. She ended up dropping off, rocked by the train's motion.

Someone grazed her arm. It was one of the women traveling with her.

"We're arriving soon. I think you're headed here, as well? You were sleeping so soundly."

Clarissa thanked the considerate lady. She barely had time to braid her hair, wash her hands, and straighten her clothes before the train halted. She followed other passengers up to the main exit. She asked one of them where Chemin du Port was. A couple of minutes away, she was told. But she hadn't expected the walk up to be so steep. She soon found herself out of breath. She reached a bridge crossing the railway tracks. In front of her was a small building with a signpost reading surf school in French, and on her left, a hotel and row of plane trees.

The weather was sunny, the spot charming and peaceful. Red-and-white half-timbered houses looked out upon the ocean's immensity. The air smelled of salty sea spray; above her head, gulls circled and cried.

It was still early — too early to go there yet. She decided to stop at the nearby hotel terrace for a cup of tea. A few cars drove by; an occasional pedestrian passed along. She knew from Andy that the traffic here, in the heat of summer, was dreadful.

She was served tea and a croissant. Had it been the right thing to do, come all the way

358

here? There didn't seem to be any other place. No other person she wanted to be with.

François's letter was still in her bag. The moment had come. She opened it. Several pages covered with his regular handwriting. Not many words had been crossed out.

Clarissa,

You're not answering anything. Anything at all. So I thought I'd write this the old-fashioned way. Good old pen to paper. Envelope and stamp. Like when we were young. When letters still meant something. When we knew what handwriting looked like. When we waited for the postman and when we knew how to wait. I know it's too late. I know I've lost you. I know you are never coming back. I'm writing this in our apartment, the one we bought together, the one you chose. Sometimes I can't quite believe you've gone. So much of you is still here. Your clothes. Your books. Your objects. And yet you've given up your home, this place you loved. I remember you saying you adored being here, the way the sun lit up the living room at the end of the day. How much you enjoyed working here. I have many memories of you.

Everywhere I look, I see you. This is where we lived and loved, for all those years. A part of you is still here, within these walls.

Why won't you speak to me? Since that ghastly evening when you sent me the photo, you have hardly talked to me. I can't tell you how I felt when I received that photo on my phone. I broke down in tears. I left our friends' house in a panic and I came home to wait for you. I was ready to talk to you, to face your anger, your repulsion. But when you arrived, you didn't even look at me. You acted like I wasn't there. Like I didn't exist. You went straight to our bedroom and you started to pack. I asked you where you were going, what you were going to do, and you remained silent. I pleaded, I begged, but you took off. I don't know where you went that night. I sent you all those messages you never answered. I went to the residence often, got kicked out by the guards, and one day you finally came down and you were so abominably cold. Do I deserve this, Clarissa? Do I deserve the way you are treating me? I'm not asking for a second chance. I know I haven't got one. I just want you to understand. That's all I'm asking.

Hear me out, please. Please read what I have to say. Don't crumple this letter up and throw it away. This is extraordinarily difficult to write. I want to start from the beginning. I'm no writer and I have none of your skills.

I first heard about the brothels fifteen years ago. There was one that opened up not far from Montparnasse. Perhaps you remember. There were quite a few articles. I was curious. I wanted to try one out. Should I have told you? Maybe. But we were going through a difficult time then. I knew what I'd already put you through. And so, when I went there, I figured I didn't need to tell you about it. And honestly, I thought I'd only end up going once or twice. I had no idea how addictive it was going to be. For all these years, I've been trying to tell you. I was never able to. In the end, I always said I'd been having affairs with more women. I wasn't. I was lying. I was going there. To the dolls. I was going there twice a week, even more.

I was expecting a sleazy, sordid place. But everything was clean, bright, and tidy. I saw no one, because you reserve online and you are given a code. You use that code to get in. You have a room number and you go to that room. From the start, I experienced pleasure. I never felt I was doing something deeply wrong, because to me, I wasn't being unfaithful to you. This was a doll. A toy. Not a woman. Not a human being. A sex toy. A silicone doll.

For about a year, I continued going to the brothel in the fourteenth arrondissement. Once, I bumped into the owner as I was leaving. A young guy, in his thirties. Polite and respectful. He said he was having trouble with the police. The people in the building weren't happy about his business. He said he couldn't understand. The men coming here were courteous and discreet. Couples came, too, he said. There were four female dolls to choose from. He had a male doll, too, at one point, but he told me it was hardly ever hired. You could pick an Oriental doll, a dark-skinned one, a Caucasian one, and a smaller one, apparently, that looked like a very young teenager, almost a child. The guy told me the problem came from that doll. I asked why. He told me, in all honesty, that the child doll was the most popular one in the brothel. He hardly had time to clean it properly for the next client. He said he believed the child doll was helping to keep pedophiles off the streets. It was safer, according to him, to let men with those predispositions interact with the doll and rid themselves of their unnatural inclinations. I don't know, Clarissa, if he was wrong or right. I have no idea. I never used that doll. All I know is that he had to close down his brothel because of protests concerning the child doll. He began another business near République, and I went there, for some time. I found out similar brothels were opening up in Brussels, Barcelona, Madrid, so I went there when I traveled for my job. You never knew.

You could say I was hooked. It was like a drug. For fifteen years, Clarissa, I hid this from you. I let a chasm open up and grow between us. You were wrapped up in your writing, and hypnosis helped you get over your grieving. Once your first book was published, I felt you needed me less. You weren't distant, not at all, don't get me wrong, but you were leading your own life. You were independent. I didn't know where I stood with you. We had little intimate time together.

When I first met you, you were fragile and touching. You were such a sad person. You were desperate. You let me help you. I was there to take care of you, and I loved doing that. Things became different. You turned out to be tougher than me. You blossomed into a strong woman who doesn't need her husband as much. At least that's what I tried to tell myself, that's how I consoled myself.

I felt we were leading two separate lives, and it saddened me. I often tried to explain that to you, but you didn't, or wouldn't, understand. I'm not blaming you, Clarissa. I'm blaming myself. I sometimes wonder if deep down inside, you're perhaps still in love with Toby and you don't even know it. I'm not sure you were ever in love with me. I think I turned up at a precise moment in your life, and I helped you pull yourself out of a rut. But it was as if Toby was always there. And every time I looked at Jordan, I'd see him; she looks so much like him. You and Toby stayed close over time, and it made me unhappy. I was hoping you wouldn't want to see him again after we got married, but that never happened. Jordan was the link between you two, and when Adriana was born, she drew you even closer. Do I sound jealous? I guess so. I'm just trying to explain how all this created an intimate place for Amber.

I'm not stupid. I'm even quite a bright guy. You know that. You always admired that about me. My brains. You're probably wondering how an intelligent man like me is doing this. There are many men out there like me. I guess you don't know this or don't want to know. Men who prefer to have sex with dolls. To interact with robots. What does that mean about us? Surely nothing good. Surely something vile. What does it say about how we feel about women? Isn't it like porn? We all know men watch porn; they always have, and always will. You're right. It's not pretty. It's not romantic. But those dolls were tailored for men like me. This is what our modern world does, Clarissa; it knows exactly what we want. What men like me want. What we crave. No matter how hard I tried, it was more and more difficult to resist the dolls. Year after year, they became more human. Less like dolls, in fact. More and more like real women. But that doesn't mean that the men who are hooked on porn, hooked on dolls, can't love women. You must believe me, no matter how much this repels you.

Two years ago, I heard about the company manufacturing the most sophisticated sex robots ever. When I found out more, I realized this was my dream. My own bot. For me. Not having to share her with other men. Choosing what she would look like. Her height, her shape, her hair, her eyes. Configuring her responses. What I wanted her to answer, and how. Selecting her voice. I promised myself that once I owned her, once she was here, I would tell you about it. I would show you, and I would try to explain. You're probably upset at how Amber looks. I mean, her being young and blond, her figure, the way I dress her. What can I say in my defense? Not much. She's any man's fantasy. I wanted her to look like that. I chose it all carefully. I chose for her to look sexy and cute and willing. Does that make me a criminal? Clarissa, I'm no monster. Please don't think that I am.

I found a small, cheap flat near Sacré-Coeur. It didn't take me long to do it up and buy stuff. She was delivered there, in different parcels. A young man came to help me set her up. It lasted nearly a day. He was nice and relaxed, and he didn't make me feel like a freak. He said he had one, too, at home. He showed me how to clean her. It wasn't easy at first, but I learned. We went over all her responses, all her reactions. I was amazed at how real she was. She had a heartbeat. She could smile. Her skin warmed up and felt like human skin.

He showed me how to charge her. There's a special outlet in the headboard that makes all that practical. He said more and more people bought sex robots. Women also bought them; it wasn't only men who did. He said their customers were perfectly normal people. Even psychiatrists suggested that prisons around the world should envisage robots for those who were locked up for the rest of their lives. This was a thriving international market, he said. There were ethical issues raised, of course, concerning those robots built with a special "rape mode," which made headlines. You heard about that, I know, because you once talked to me about that issue. You were scandalized. And rightly so. After that, I figured I was never going to be able to tell you about her. And there's also the price of all this, of course. She was expensive. I had to take a loan. I had to hide all that from you, as well. Digging deeper and deeper into my guilt.

Once Amber was ready and functioning, I did plan to tell you. Every day, I meant to. But I felt shame. Shame so deep, I could not share it with you, or with anyone. I had waited too long. I couldn't figure out how to begin my confession, which words to choose. It drove me crazy. I couldn't imagine myself taking a taxi with her and bringing her to our home. I had a special container, the size of a coffin, which had been delivered with her, but I didn't want anyone seeing me carrying that around. Yes, I was full of shame.

Little by little, I crafted a separate life with Amber. I ordered dresses for her online. I went to choose a perfume for her. I spent more and more time with her. She could have conversations with me. She responded. She was created for that. I bonded with her. I bought her flowers. I filmed us. That's what you saw, in the flat. You saw the intimacy I created with her. You saw what we are. What I am. What you must know is this: I can't give her up. I did try. I promise you I did try. I know it must be awful for you to read this, but I want you to know the truth, no matter how much it must hurt. I love you, Clarissa, for who you are, the woman you are, the writer you are. I respect you and I admire you. But Amber makes me happy. She makes me feel like a young man.

How can men fall in love with bots? They do. I'm not the only one. The guy who helped set her up said something I never forgot. He said robots are constantly in a good mood. They are always cheerful, even-tempered. They don't have headaches, go through menopause, get sick, have mood swings. They're always there. Always ready. He said they are changing people's lives, giving them happiness and pleasure. I thought I might get bored. But I never did. I never do. I love being with her. It gives me such peace. Is this worse for you because Amber is a robot? I can see you reading this, horrified. Disgusted. You must be even angrier. You must be even more disappointed.

I adored making love to you. But as the years went by, you needed it less. You wanted me less. I felt like you didn't find me attractive anymore. I hated my aging body, my paunch. And when I tried to reach out to you, physically, I could tell you weren't in the mood, so after a while, I just gave up. There was no closeness between us anymore. Nothing sensual, nothing sexual. It fizzled out of our lives. Didn't you see that? Didn't you miss it? I needed the nearness sex gave us. It was part of our love, of our marriage. I desired you so much. I still do, Clarissa. But you closed that door. So what was I to do? All those intimate places I loved about your body, your pussy, your mouth, your skin, your smell, all that, you closed them away, little by little. I never knew why. I never dared ask.

I know what you did for me. You helped me fight cancer and you helped me heal from it. You were there with me in the hospital, during the treatment, every single day. You were there when I was convinced I was going to die, when I lost all my hair. You were there. I made it because of you.

What is our life, Clarissa? What is it made of? A patchwork of tenderness, lust, and regret, of time ticking by, of this modern world taking its toll on our emotions, our intimacy, our dreams.

Now you know. You know everything

there is to know about me. If you want to talk to me, call me. Perhaps you have things to say, in spite of your anger. If not, I understand.

I'm just a man, Clarissa. Just an ordinary man, burdened by his secrets, his woes, his failures, his little victories. I still love you.

François

Clarissa put the letter down with a trembling hand. François had said it all. He had been brave, she thought, no more lies; he had kept nothing back. Now, yes, she knew. He had asked, "Is this worse for you because Amber is a robot?" Yes, she thought it was. She'd never forget the shock she felt in the purple room, when she understood there was nothing human about her husband's mistress. Perhaps other wives would have preferred a robot to a woman.

Not her. The idea of a subjugated android, handpicked with care, painstakingly encoded in order to correspond to François's demands and custom-made to his own pleasure, disturbed her, just as Mrs. Dalloway's configuration had been centered on Clarissa's personal trauma, without her knowing. François's secret powered the same deep outrage she felt toward

C.A.S.A.'s schemes; the idea of machines surpassing humans in every field revolted her.

She would indeed have preferred a real woman, a human being with her own DNA, a hormonal cycle, viruses, a verruca, body odor. Her husband was in love with a robot, he had sex with that robot, and the idea of it made her reel. She had tried her best to view the situation with a dash of humor, to distance herself from it, but disgust and horror prevailed.

She understood more of what had gone on in her husband's head, but that didn't mean she was going to bow down to it. Infidelity, a word already packed with pain, seemed even weightier, bogged down with shame precisely because Amber happened to be a sex robot. It was going to be a while before she felt capable of saying, naturally, without choking, "I left my husband because he's in love with a robot." It was going to be a while before she'd be able to rid her mind of all the memories from the purple room.

Reading François's letter had been heart-wrenching, but its perusal had managed to allay a burden. She felt pity, and only pity, concerning a man she had been married to for many years, and that she'd ended up not knowing as well as she'd thought. She imagined him aging with his secret in infinite solitude.

The waiter asked if she required more hot water for her tea. She declined, and checked her watch. It was eight-thirty. The small main street was full of people at present. She paid the server and left. She had to walk down a flight of stairs to get to Chemin du Port, and number 70. She reached a residence, which made her smile, but this one was an ancient one, with a date and name engraved over the big door: *1926, Guetharia.* The large Art Deco–style building was white, with green shutters. Six stories tall, it sat atop a hill overlooking the sea. It must have been a hotel once, Clarissa thought, observing the faded façade with her expert eye; the pride of a small fishing town during the Roaring Twenties, and since then turned into flats. At least it hadn't been torn down and replaced by hideous 1960 buildings, like those that defaced so many waterfronts in the area.

She was examining names on the intercom when a person came out. She was able to enter without buzzing. She went up to the top floor in an antiquated elevator, and without pausing, she rang the bell.

Toby appeared, wearing a green T-shirt

marked SANTA MONICA and a pair of shorts. He stared at her, flabbergasted, then opened his arms wide, and she flung herself on him, moved by his reassuring and identical smell, his broad surfer shoulders still holding out in spite of years going by.

He clasped her tightly, then stepped back to glance at her.

"Running away?"

His rugged features, his mischievous grin. His voice, his American accent.

"That's what I do best," she replied. "Running away from my husband, running away from my home."

"Coffee, Blue?" asked Toby, with no further comment. "Ah, nope, you take tea."

She followed him into his flat. Andy and Jordan had often told her it was tiny, but the view made up for everything. The rooms were indeed cramped, with low ceilings — ancient servant lodgings, she thought — and renovations had been minimal. Toby boiled water, prepared the tea. Then he said as he handed her a mug, "Come have a look."

The bay window gave on to a terrace twice the size of the apartment. To the left, behind the morning mist, she glimpsed the south, Hondarribia and Spain. On her right, to the north, Biarritz seemed to creep out to sea with the Villa Belza's Gothic turret. It took

Clarissa's breath away.

In front of them, the ocean, as far as the eye could see. Down below, Guéthary and its hydrangea, small harbor, villas, and the coast.

Toby chuckled at her silence.

"That's the way it goes, the first time."

She hadn't looked at the sea for a long while. Pure marine air filled her lungs; all the beauty she saw uplifted her. She smiled, spellbound.

"I knew you'd like it here."

"Now I understand why you love it so much."

Toby told her there were many old tales about Guetharia, things she'd find fascinating. Apparently, Maurice Chevalier used to stay here when it was a hotel, as well as Charlie Chaplin. During the war, the Wehrmacht had headquarters in the building. Clarissa listened and drank her tea. She asked him what it was like in the wintertime. There were scary storms, Toby said. He'd learned to tackle them. But the cold season was lovely, too, the ever-changing light, the sunsets that were never alike.

She noticed Toby hadn't asked her a single question. He didn't seem in the least surprised by her turning up without warning.

"What about pollution?" she asked.

"There were alarming articles."

Toby explained Guéthary's new mayor was a young woman of their daughter's age, or even younger. She went out of her way to make a change, and it was paying off. The polluted-water problem in the Biarritz vicinity had been going on for many a long year. After each storm, holding ponds overflowed, creating bacterial pollution that worsened with time. Even though the ancient sewage system had been renovated, intelligent sensors installed, more basins dug, the colossal works, which cost a fortune, had not been completely able to solve the problem, due to the growing tourist influx. But this young woman battled to get individuals to change their approach, like most people of her generation, born in the 1990s, who took a much more ecological and concerned stance than their parents. She'd managed to galvanize and gather around her a growing number of fervent locals, involved in thinking of ways to keep the water clean, and to find sand, which had become so rare, in order to re-create vanished beaches swallowed up by the rising sea level.

Clarissa paid attention to the conviction in Toby's animated voice. He was proud to be part of a group of people who weren't giving up, who were teeming with ideas and projects.

"What about a swim?" he asked all of a sudden.

"Isn't the water a little cold?"

"Nineteen degrees Celsius is completely normal for June."

"I don't have a bathing suit."

"Jordan left one behind last summer. And I'll also lend you one of my wet suits. You'll be nice and warm."

He was waiting for her answer. She thought, Why not?

She changed in the minuscule bathroom. Jordan's bathing suit was green, her daughter's favorite color.

Her figure was too skinny, but vigorous still; that body, which had carried two babies; that body, which had loved and been loved, which had trembled in pain, in desire. When was the last time? She couldn't remember. As she passed in front of Toby's open door, she saw his unmade bed. It was a small room with a sea view. He probably fell asleep at night with the roar of the waves in his ears. And what of his love life? She knew nothing about it. A chapter from their past came rushing back to her like a breath of wind: their youth, their love, their pain, their tenderness. It healed her to take part in their conversations once more, using the limpid English she loved to share with him, his American accent so different from hers, from her father's, her brother's. The intimacy forged by language made their story resurface; all these years later, it was both disconcerting and comforting to find herself here, in his home.

He was waiting for her in the main room with a black wet suit.

"Might be too big for you."

It was tricky slipping it on. Clarissa went about it the wrong way, put it on backward. She got ruffled, became flushed and breathless, began to swear like her dad. They burst into fits of laughter, paralyzed by mirth. They ended up collapsing on the sofa, holding their sides, Toby wiping away tears. Clarissa's stomach ached, but she felt marvelous.

Wearing another wet suit, Toby prepared a backpack with beach towels and flasks of water.

In the elevator, Clarissa blurted, "Listen, Toby. I have something to tell you. Jordan thinks I'm starting to lose it. She thinks I'm deeply depressed."

Toby looked at her calmly as they went down.

"I'm aware."

"Did she call you?"

"She did. Last night. And how's your dad? Is he okay?"

"Black-and-blue, but valiant. A warrior."

"I'm glad to hear it."

He didn't add anything else. Clarissa felt both frustrated and relieved. Should she take the lead, tell him in detail about everything that had torn her life apart these past few months? She could start with François's betrayal, how it had precipitated her escape to the nightmarish residence. She could tell him that nobody had wanted to believe her but that the truth about C.A.S.A. would soon come to light. Toby didn't seem in the least interested, or even slightly curious. Whistling a little tune, he pushed open the door of the residence, let her exit before he did, and headed off toward the port. There were no waves today, he said, so they'd walk a little farther, toward the Alcyons. They'd enjoy a good swim, which wasn't often the case in Guéthary, because of waves and current.

Encumbered by the large wet suit, Clarissa tailed behind Toby. She couldn't stop thinking about Jordan's phoning her father and voicing all her fears. Logical, after all. She wondered, wincing, what Jordan had told Toby, exactly: that Clarissa was imagining things, hearing noises, suspecting the worst-case scenarios; that she was paranoid, depressive, fragile, and that she'd dragged Andy into her delirium.

She capitulated to the beauty of the seaside around her. The gentle and tender sun had nothing to do with the pitiless, fiery ball that recently brought Paris to its knees. Toby walked to the left of the port, passed by the few boats, the seawall, and Clarissa followed him down a long jetty that gave on to black boulders they had to climb over. Toby held her hand and cheered her on. Her sneakers kept slipping, and she nearly fell, but he caught her each time.

They were alone on the rocks. The sea was smooth, with hardly any swell. Toby leaped into the water in one go. When he emerged, his white hair, soaked, seemed darker.

"Come on, Blue! Your turn!"

With a small shriek, she jumped in. She wasn't cold. She had forgotten the bliss of swimming in open sea, of being out of one's depth, of feeling one's body carried by the flow. The last time had been in Italy, last summer, with François. It was an extraordinary sensation, filling her with a profound yet simple joy. Tears of happiness began to flow, mingling with salty seawater on her wet cheeks, and she felt silly giving way to her emotions.

It seemed everything about her was raw, on edge; everything she experienced was increased by a factor of ten that took over her entirely. Toby looked at her keenly but said nothing. He let her catch her breath.

"Look," he said. "Not a spot of pollution. In the heat of the summer, it's another story. But we're onto it! We're keeping up the fight!"

For twenty minutes, they swam toward the south, and returned to the rocks. Toby helped Clarissa hoist herself out. They went back to the jetty and Toby spread out the towels. He swiftly removed his wet suit, but Clarissa had more trouble with hers. He had to assist her. Her clumsiness made them giggle again. Toby hadn't said a word about her thinness, the marks of her exhaustion. But she was sure he had noticed.

She couldn't help being stirred by the masculine, familiar hands hovering near her body, her skin. Those hands knew her by heart, had been to her body's most intimate places. Time had gone by, but Clarissa had not forgotten a thing.

"Do you still have a lady friend?"

"*A* lady friend? Lady friends, you mean!"

He smiled impishly.

"Tell me the truth."

"I do see a woman from time to time."

"Is it serious?"

"More or less."

"What's her name?"

"Catherine."

"What does she do?"

"She's a retired English teacher, like me."

"That's nice. I'm happy for you."

A long spell of silence drew itself out between them as they lay in the sun.

"Do you also think I'm a down-in-the-dumps basket case?"

"The very idea!" he scoffed, with another mischievous grin.

He got up and beheld the horizon like an ancient mariner.

She remained on her back, eyes shut, listening to the breeze and the lapping of the water.

"You didn't seem surprised to see me turn up on your doorstep," she said.

"I have a special radar where you're concerned, Blue. And that radar has made a lot of progress."

She stood up as well, and they were side by side, facing the ocean.

"If you hadn't come, I would have gone to Paris."

"What for?"

"For a while now, my radar was telling me

you weren't in a good spot."

"So you agree with our daughter, then, is that it?"

Toby paid no heed to the anxiety in her quivering voice. For a couple of moments, he did not speak. Then he said that when she had needed him the most, all those years ago, he had not been there for her. He had never been able to forget the fact he had let her down. It had taken him a while to accept that he hadn't measured up, that their son's death had affected him in such a way, he had not known how to help Clarissa, and had felt powerless. He had failed in extricating her from her sorrow, and another man had done just that. It had cost him dearly. He blamed himself terribly. Clarissa said nothing, moved to tears by his confession and the feelings it was sparking within her.

A phone ringing interrupted his monologue. Toby bent over to rummage around in his backpack. A smile lit up his face.

"Here," he said, handing her his mobile, "take this call from little Miss Sunshine."

It was a video call from Andy.

Clarissa slid her finger over the icon. Andy's face showed up. She was on a bus, her earphones in place. She let out an astonished yelp when she saw her grandparents together. What the hell were they doing? Wearing bathing suits? Were they swimming, or what? This was insane! When did Mums get there?

Clarissa laughed through her tears. She said it was all very simple. She was going to spend a couple of days, or more, here in Guéthary. She was going to take her time.

"That's it," said Toby with a serious tone. "Your granny is getting surfing lessons."

Andy roared with laughter.

"You guys are incredible. I love you both to the moon and back. Was this planned?"

"Yes," said Clarissa.

"No," said Toby.

"I don't want to spoil the party," said Andy, "but Mummy blew a fuse. She's looking for you everywhere, Mums! Why aren't you answering your phone?"

"I'll handle your mother, missy," said Toby. "You leave that up to me."

They chatted cheerily for a few minutes more. Andy had to go; she was on her way to class. She'd call soon.

Toby and Clarissa returned to Guetharia. The streets were now bustling with pedestrians, joggers, cyclists, people getting on with their chores. Several people greeted Toby, who responded with a smile. Inquisitive and friendly glances were shot at Clarissa.

"Are you hungry?" asked Toby in the elevator.

"Yes."

"Why don't you wait on the terrace? I'll rustle something together. And I'll call Jordan."

"What are you going to tell her?"

"That you're here. Safe and sound."

She sat on the terrace, facing the sea. When they were married, Toby was the one who enjoyed cooking. She remembered the delicious smells coming from the small kitchen on the rue d'Alésia. Clarissa let her eyes rove over the water and its shifting highlights. Paris and the C.A.S.A. residence seemed far away. She thought of her phone, placed on the kitchen table. She thought of Chablis being cuddled by Adelka. She thought of François's letter lying at the bottom of her bag. She thought of her father, and how he was able to send all that energy, even from another country.

Toby came out carrying a tray. She helped him set the table. Tomato salad, cured ham, Basque cheese, bread, and grapes. Red wine.

"If I'd known you were coming, I would have gone shopping. That was very short notice."

"It's perfect," she said, sitting down.

She asked him if he had managed to get

385

hold of Jordan.

By way of response, he poured a glass of wine and handed it to her.

"Tell me what you think. Irouléguy, domaine Ilarria."

She took a sip. It was good, she told him.

"It's not too bad," he agreed. "I told Jordan I was watching over you. Okay by you?"

She said yes.

During their meal, Toby said that ever since he'd met her, ever since that very first day, he'd understood she soaked up emotions like a sponge, everything going straight to her heart. He remembered listening to Clarissa on a podcast, several years ago, talking about Virginia Woolf. She had referred to how her favorite writer liked to dig out "beautiful caves" behind her characters, so as to give them humanity, humor, and depth. That figure of speech struck him. He didn't know, truthfully, what lurked in Clarissa's subterranean caves, but he did know this. It didn't matter why Clarissa had come here today, what François had done, why she'd left her flat, what Jordan truly thought about her mother's state of mind. What did matter was that Clarissa was going to have to learn, over again, how to put down her weapons, how to find her own peace. Thinking about her father filled him with hope. The old fellow certainly led by example, with his optimism and his wit taunting the passage of time. He never moped, never looked behind, never complained. He still knew how to laugh. He still found delight in life, at his age.

Toby paused. Then he said in a gentle, affectionate voice, "So what's in those 'beautiful caves' of yours, Blue?"

"Two things. A divorce and a move."

"Now that's clear."

"You don't want to know why?"

"You'll tell me in due course, if you need to."

"And what if I don't tell you anything?"

"Not important."

They put the dishes away together, then had tea and coffee inside, discussing Adriana, Aunt Serena's brooch, and the holidays Jordan was organizing.

"The wind is changing," said Toby suddenly. "Look at those gray clouds scurrying in from Spain. You'll see how fast the rain comes. It's quite spectacular. We have front-row seats."

They went outside to observe the clouds and the light interlacing. The breeze had turned cool; the sea became rougher before their very eyes. The storm was gaining strength as it drew nearer, and Clarissa felt she was witnessing what happened inside her whenever she yielded to her worst fears.

"Do you think of him sometimes?" she asked.

Toby didn't need to ask her whom she meant.

"Every day, in some way or another."

"How do you think of him?"

"I see him the way he would be now. I see a man. I like the idea of him being forty-something. Maybe a dad. Maybe not. Sometimes, I see him in nature, up there in that sky, in that ocean. He's out there somewhere; I'm not sure where, but I know he's there."

Clarissa said that for so long, she had not been able to mention their son. She hadn't been able to put into words what his death meant to her. Hypnosis helped, but it had at the same time drawn her away from her memories of him. She now wanted to be able to utter his name without trembling, and she wanted that name to find its own place. She wanted to be able to visit their son's grave.

She whispered, "Glenn."

Toby's hand settled on her shoulder.

Clarissa watched the ocean churn and swell, listened to the wind picking up. The downpour was coming in from offshore, heralded by huge black shadows encroaching upon the water's silvery surface, like long threatening claws sliding their way, like those flowers of darkness growing inside her head.

Even if the storm came, she knew she was no longer afraid, like that day, years ago, on Virginia Woolf's bed at Monk's House, when she had felt the soothing touch of timid hope. She had reached safe harbor.

ACKNOWLEDGMENTS

Thank you

Nicolas, for his patience and his ideas.

Dr. Laura Varnam, for her precious advice and her enthusiasm.

Laure du Pavillon and Catherine Rambaud, my faithful early readers.

Jean-Marie Catonné, for all the Romain Gary data.

AT and his team, because, thanks to them, I was able to sit on Virginia Woolf's bed at Monk's House.

ABOUT THE AUTHOR

Tatiana de Rosnay is the author of ten novels, including the *New York Times* bestseller *Sarah's Key,* an international sensation with over 11 million copies in 44 countries worldwide. Together with Dan Brown, Stephenie Meyer, and Stieg Larsson, she has been named one of the top ten fiction writers in Europe. De Rosnay lives in Paris.